PRAISE F

"Secret Legacy kept me spellbound from page one to the very last word! The tension and relationships are beautifully written and will keep readers coming back for more. I got chills up my spine more than once. I can't wait to see what happens next."

— JJ KING, USAT BESTSELLING AUTHOR

"A whimsical tale that will transport you from the first page."

— CARLYLE LABUSCHAGNE, USAT BESTSELLING AUTHOR

"This book is packed full of awesomeness! Supernatural academy? Check. A girl who feels like she doesn't belong? Check. Sexy, mysterious boy? Check. And alllll the secrets, twists, and turns to keep you flipping pages. You don't want to miss this one!"

— LIZA STREET, USAT BESTSELLING AUTHOR

Published in 2020 by Carissa Andrews

Paperback ISBN-13: 978-0-9910558-8-3
Hardcover ISBN: 978-1-953304-06-3

To my brother Scott, my dear friend Julie Blanchard, and to all of you who are either fighting or have won your battles against cancer... I dedicate this book to you.

ACKNOWLEDGMENTS

2020 has been a year of expansion and growth in ways I could never have imagined.

To my incredible PA & BFF, Jenny Bodle, I could not imagine my writerly world without you & your beautiful daughters in it. I am blessed beyond words to have such an incredible team supporting and challenging me. Thank you so much for all you do.

To my husband, Colin, I can't begin to express my gratitude for your extreme efforts in bringing ***Secret Legacy's*** idea to life in my first live-action book trailer.

To the entire cast and crew, you are incredible. Thank you for joining us on this crazy journey. <3

Kayla Richey, Pacey Andrews, Katjanna Tauzell, Isaac Sample, Mitch Bodle, Chad Frink, Jenny Bodle, Mackenzie Andrews, Evandyr Elg, Kira Richey, Elianna Elg, Alexie Tauzell, & Natalie Halverson

SPECIAL THANKS

I would like to thank my incredible friends, family, and readers who supported my endeavor to become a bestselling author this year. I set up a GoFundMe campaign to help cover advertising costs toward this epic list-aim and I couldn't have done it without them. They include:

Ranel Capron, Kellie Haehnel, Gaby van Halteren, Christina Forster, Kimberly Clement, Kathleen Stiles, J. Blanchard, D. Liebeg, Richard Callanan, Colleen Adrian, Monika Hamlin, Terry Scribner, Sherry Adrian Dumpprope, Jason Moengen, Tracy Korn, Erin & John Buscher, Katie Cherry, Colin Andrews, Robbin Suzanne O'Connor, Margaret White, Jenny Bodle, Jennifer Eding

SECRET LEGACY

Book 1 of the Windhaven Witches

CARISSA ANDREWS

CHAPTER 1
SHOULD I STAY OR SHOULD I GO?

By the absurd color of my mother's face, it's safe to say I'm royally screwed.

"I asked you a question," Mom says, her hazel eyes trained expectantly on me.

My mouth drops open, and I shake my head. "I don't even know what that is."

"Don't play coy with me, Autumn. This is a big deal—a *behemoth* deal. You don't get a packet like this to the Windhaven Academy unless they've accepted your enrollment," she says, placing a protective hand across the large purple packet with sparkly stars across it.

Instinctively, I grab for the envelope, tugging it from under her palm. I pull it to my chest without even looking closer at it. It's got some heft to it, and I float through the decisions of whether to toss it in the trash or walk off with it.

"Look, Mom, there's gotta be a mistake here. Or maybe someone is playing a practical joke on me. The Windhaven Academy...that's a school for kids with unique abilities—*the supernatural kids*. Why would I apply there, let alone get accepted? It's ludicrous."

"That's what I would like to know. Imagine my shock when the mailman passed it over," she says. "The last I heard you were planning on going to the U next year. I know it's not as early as you would have liked, but trust me, saving for it was a wise investment. Especially with the student loan snafu—"

"You can relax, Mom. There's nothing to this at all. I still plan to get my forensic sciences degree, for crying out loud."

I turn on my heel to vacate the premises before things escalate. Mom and the supernatural world don't have the best of track records, but Mom and money are even worse. The last thing I want is a four-hour discussion about the nature of things and how the system is built to "keep us little folks down."

Mom follows me. "Why are you walking away, Autumn? We're not done here. What aren't you telling me?"

Spinning around, I scrunch my face, trying to hold it steady without drawing out her imagination. "N-nothing."

"Well, that was convincing," she says, placing a hand on her hip. "You know, I always thought we had a pretty good thing going here. I know we've had our ups and downs, and this last year having to work at the craft shop hasn't been ideal, but I never thought lying would be a thing."

"It's not. *I'm* not—" I say, unable to contain the anger building inside me. "Mom, I have no idea what this is or why it arrived. If you can't trust me, *or believe me*, then that says more about you than it does me."

Her mouth pops open, but words don't tumble out at their ordinary pace.

Without wasting another moment, I turn my back on her and stomp upstairs to my bedroom. It's the one space in this tiny house that's off limits for her, and she knows it. After closing the door, I fling the packet onto my bed and lean back against the wood doorframe.

My brain whirls around, trying to make sense of the past few minutes. There is literally no reason for me to apply to the Windhaven Academy and even less reason to be accepted. I have no powers at all. None. Trust me, I'd know after the years of wishful thinking and trying to make something amazing happen. I've seen close friends learn their abilities and go on to do incredible things. But I'm still here—stuck in Mistwood Point until I can afford the state university like a completely ordinary girl. Meh. At least going for my forensic sciences degree would be more interesting than helping out all the old biddies in town with their fabric choices.

"We're not done talking about this, Autumn..." Mom's voice filters from the other side of the door.

"I know," I mutter under my breath as I close my eyes. "I just need a bit of time to decompress. I'll be down soon."

As much as I love my mom, her hovering can be suffocating at times. I'm twenty years old, for crying out loud. If I wanted to go, *and could actually afford it*, there is literally nothing she could do to stop me.

"Please, promise me you'll just toss it in the trash. Because that's what it is," she says.

Refusing to answer her, I look up at the ceiling and breathe in slowly through my nose. I've never understood her extreme reaction to anything supernatural. I know something happened in her past, but she's refused to clue me in. Who's the one keeping things from whom?

Shaking my head, I whisper, "Maybe I should get a place of my own."

It would set me back on my timeline for college, but it might be worth it. I'd gain more autonomy and be able to make my own decisions without a dramatic conversation over every little thing.

My gaze falls to the purple envelope, and I swallow hard.

Could my mom be right? Is it really an acceptance packet? Why would they even send me an acceptance?

Unexpected excitement bubbles inside me, and I can't seem to contain it. However, the inner voice implanted in the back of my head by my mom tells me I'm being crazy. Even if it was, it's not like we could afford the tuition. Windhaven is insanely expensive; without pulling a bank job, I'm pretty sure I'm a couple of hundred thousand shy of meeting their requirements.

I bite my lower lip and take a tentative step forward. Despite myself, morbid curiosity wins out. Taking the final few steps to the bed, I drop down and pull the monolithic envelope onto my lap. The setting sun streams into my room, creating a soft glow that entices me to live in the moment. I run my hand along the outside edge of the packet. The texture is more like soft silk than paper, and the stars across the top twinkle with multifaceted dimension in the sunlight.

However, I'm a tiny bit disappointed there's nothing innately *magical* about it. It doesn't fly, or talk, or do anything unusual at all. Surely a supernatural school has resources to do something like that, right? Or am I just being incredibly naive?

I take a deep breath. "Well, here goes nothing..."

Flipping the packet over, I pull the ripcord from the top edge. I half-anticipate letters to come flying out or a bright light to shine from the heavens. But again, I'm sorely disappointed. Inside is just a packet of paperwork. Ordinary, mundane paperwork.

We haven't even met the digital age, I guess.

On the upside, the paper is the same graceful, soft

texture, and I can't help but wonder what it's made of. Maybe magical spiders wove their silk into the fabric of the paper? At least that would be cool. As I shuffle quickly through the contents, I find, in addition to the papers, a large booklet of information about the courses available, the history of the school, and other details, like off-campus events for supernaturals. There's a map, a few event flyers for the campus social groups, and of course, right on top...*is my acceptance letter*.

I suck in a quick breath and scan through it quickly.

Dear Ms. Blackwood,

Congratulations! It is with great pleasure that I offer you admission to the Windhaven Academy Class of 2024.

Your thoughtful application and magical aptitudes convinced us that you have the intelligence and innate talent to be amongst the best here at Windhaven Academy. Among the over 15,000 applications, yours stood out immediately, and our seers recognized the incredible gift your lineage brings to our ranks. As such, we are thrilled to welcome you and look forward to your unique and extraordinary contributions as you adjust to our academic and campus life.

The exciting next steps can only be taken by you. As I'm sure we are not the only university you're considering in the coming weeks, I encourage you to learn more about us and the legacy we share. We invite you to attend our next orientation weekend called the Witching Stick, coming up on August 25-26. You'll be given guidance on your particular gifts, as well as an introduction to the curriculum crafted especially for you and the dynamic campus we have here.

Should you choose to matriculate, I am also thrilled to inform you that your enrollment has been fully paid for by a donor who wishes to remain anonymous. This is truly a once-in a lifetime opportunity and one I sincerely hope you do not miss out on.

Once again, I congratulate you on your admission to Windhaven

Academy and welcome you to our family. We look forward to seeing you in August.

Sincerely,
Marva Arlo
Director of Admissions

I stand up, practically squealing. "Holy shit."

My brain spins out of control as I read it again, but this time more slowly, paying close attention to certain parts.

I don't know which aspects to focus on first.

Thoughtful application? Lineage? Legacy?

I stand up, clutching the letter in both shaky hands. The rest of the contents from the packet fall to the floor, but my eyes can't move from one small phrase.

Fully paid for.

Confusion and excitement tussle through my mind, fighting for a ruler.

Without thinking, I move to the door, opening it wide, and running down the stairs to find Mom.

Her wide eyes greet me as I rush into the kitchen.

"You opened it," she says softly, disappointment rolling across her features.

I ignore it, walk up to her, and take a seat at the dining room table. "Mom, it says here I have a free ride. As in, *fully paid for*—" I shove the paper at her. "Look, right here."

"I don't need to read it," she says, eyeing me closely.

"But, Mom, it says I don't have to pay for it—*you* don't have to pay for it. I can go for *free*," I repeat, stressing the part that immediately lightened an enormous burden I've been carrying around.

"You can't go," she says slowly.

"What are you talking about? Of course I can. They *want* me there," I sputter, scooting my chair back.

"Everything comes at a price, Autumn. Including this. You might not have to pay for it, but trust me, it will have a cost. Besides, how do you think you'll fare in a school with supernaturals? Have you even given any of this some real thought?"

"It doesn't matter. I'll figure something out. And what about this?" I say, pointing to the line about the gifts my lineage brings. "Any idea what this means?"

The blood drains from her face as she looks up, but she shakes her head a second too late.

"I don't have any idea what they're talking about," she says, her eyelashes fluttering.

I narrow my gaze. An awkward silence stretches out between us. There's more going on here than meets the eye.

"Mom, if you're keeping something..." I warn.

"Young lady, I don't like what you're insinuating. I've put a roof over your head. I've given you everything—"

"That's not what's in question here. Answer me. Do you know something about this? Do you know what they're talking about?" I sputter. My heart threatens to burst out of my chest and I can't believe any of this is happening. Especially now.

Something resembling defeat flashes through her eyes, but she exhales slowly. "I wouldn't blame you for wanting to be closer to your dad. Maybe that's why you applied. Things haven't always been easy here," she says, ignoring the question.

"Mom, I'm not trying to get closer to Dad. I haven't even talked to him for over a year. He barely shows an interest in my life. This is something else entirely. I don't know what happened or why they think I applied...and you're not answering my question," I say, my fingers tapping nervously at the paper.

"It says here that you sent in a *thoughtful application*. So perhaps we both have things we'd like to gloss over," she says, arching her eyebrow high.

"Ugh, you're ridiculous. You know that, right? I'm not a child, and I don't need your sideways answers." Snatching the paper back from her, I fold it up and stand to slide it in my back pocket. "You know what? I just...I'm an adult now and I can make this decision with or without you. I'd just hoped you'd be a little more objective and less...*you*."

I wave a hand dismissively, putting an end to the conversation as I head for the front door.

"Where do you plan on going?" she asks, shooting her chair back as she stands.

"Doesn't matter," I say. "Don't bother waiting up."

I walk out, closing the door harder than I meant to.

Truth is, I don't have a clue where I'm headed. I just know I need to get out of here so I can think for myself. Mom's always tried to steer me toward a reasonable direction, and I can't fault her for it. But when life hands you something this big, you at least have to consider the possibility.

Regardless of the decision I make, there's no doubt my life is about to change in a major way and I'm not sure I'm entirely ready for it.

CHAPTER 2

AND THEN THERE WAS AN ANGEL

As I walk down the darkening streets, I try to shake off the conversation with my mom so I can rely on my own intuition to be my guide. The twilight streets and moonlight have never steered me wrong before, but I don't know if they're strong enough to tell the truth right now. On one hand, I don't want to go to Windhaven as a knee-jerk reaction, but at the same time, everything inside me is screaming that this is the opportunity I've been waiting for. But can I really trust it?

The cool, crisp air assaults my senses, helping me snap out of my funk. I tip my chin upward, gazing at the full moon as I zip my jacket.

Is Windhaven this beautiful? Would I like being there this time around?

It's been thirteen years since the last time I was in Windhaven. I was seven, going on eight, and living at my dad's house in the woody outskirts. He wouldn't even let me leave the gigantic house to play outside in the courtyard. Forget talking to the neighbor kids or interacting with anyone besides him. I don't remember where my mom was—I think it must have been during the separation. What I do know, however, is I was not fond of the experience.

I haven't heard from him once in a year, which is surprising. He's typically made a pretty big deal about my birthday at the very least. Maybe he's just been giving me some space now that I'm an adult? However, he always had an open-door policy. Or so he said. I suppose I could always reach out to him to see what he thinks of this situation. He might have some insights that could enlighten all of this. Communication is a two-way street, and I'm just as much to blame for our lack of contact at this point.

"Are you really considering this, Autumn?" I say, pulling my insanely curly hair into a ponytail as I walk down the sidewalk. "What about Mom?"

My gaze expands out to the space in front of me and I walk on autopilot. Tears of confusion and agitation threaten to spill from the edges of my eyes but I can't let them get to me. Part of me agrees with my mom. Who am I to think I could attend Windhaven Academy? I'm just an ordinary girl. On the other hand, there's a part of me that would have killed to go there when I was younger. And if I'm truthful with myself, there's still a part of me that wishes I had more potential than going to state university to become a forensic scientist; even if the work does sound incredibly interesting.

My feet instinctively carry me to my favorite nighttime place in all of Mistwood Point—*the cemetery*. I don't know what it is about this place that always draws me in. Maybe the silence, or the mystery in the old tombstones and ancient trees. The town is one of the oldest in the state. Younger, in fact, only to Windhaven. Some of the gravestones date all the way back to the early 1700s.

Slipping through the narrow opening on the haphazardly

locked gate, I meander inside. No one will notice—they never do. Besides, I don't deface the stones and always clean up after myself, unlike some of the miscreants who enter at night. I traverse quickly through the center of the round, circular drive that allows those who don't really want to visit, but think they should, the space to slow down in a drive-by silent prayer to their lost loved ones.

As far as I know, I have no one here to visit. Most of my family comes from Windhaven. So I don't feel pulled to visit anyone specific. I can just...*be*. No judgment. I've spent entire evenings, and more than a few early mornings, walking these graves. I love spending time hunting for the oldest one here as I dream up stories about their lives and how they died. Maybe it's morbid, but I can't seem to help it.

Without any real destination in mind, I slip beyond the ugly flattened headstones meant to make it easier for the caretaker to mow, to the space housing the older sites. The ones still vertical, albeit only just, with names and dates all but worn off with age.

The rising moonlight cascades through the trees, lighting my way deeper into the older part of the cemetery. The air is pungent with the scent of turning leaves and those decaying in the ground around me. I inhale it deeply but keep walking. When I feel I've gone far enough, I slow down and flit my gaze to the headstones, but not really taking them in.

Admiring one of the monolithic monuments, I reach for the small bottle of whisky hidden in the inner breast pocket of my coat and take a seat facing it. I keep it there so I don't have to explain to my mother that yes, this twenty-year-old actually drinks on occasion. I know I'm not supposed to, but I have to at least live a little, right? Otherwise, I may as well just be one of these fine folks.

For whatever reason, I've always tried hard to avoid my

mom's judgment whenever possible. Yet, here I am, seriously thinking about directly defying her wishes. I must be outta my damn mind.

"Charlotte, what do you think I should do?" I ask the woman whose grave I sit upon. "Should I take a risk and go to the Windhaven Academy? Or should I just do the sensible thing and go to the university later?"

I take a swig, letting the liquid burn my insides on the way down. It has a kick. A burst of cinnamon, which is good because most booze is pretty disgusting. This one tastes more like liquid Hot Tamale candy.

A part of me wishes she could answer me. Give me the insights I'm seeking the way spirit guides are supposed to. Instead, I know better. Dead is dead. And when you're gone, your body goes back to being part of the elements that brought you here in the first place.

Nearby, an owl hoots loudly, making me jump and spill some of the contents of my drink over my shirt.

"Dammit," I spit, wiping furiously at the mess.

At the same time, my phone starts buzzing in my pocket; a sure sign my mom is wondering when I'll be back. Ignoring it, I take another sip of the potent liquid, cursing myself for not asking my coworker to purchase a larger bottle.

"You look like you could use a friend," a voice calls out of the darkness.

Again, I jump. This time downing the contents and sputtering them back out.

"Christ. What the f—" I say, dropping the bottle and clutching at my chest.

Stepping out into the moonlight, bright silvery-gray eyes watch me intensely. There's a sparkle of mischief hidden in their depths, despite the calm demeanor of their owner. The guy can't be much older than I am, but I've never seen him before. And in this town, everyone knows everyone.

"Hey, didn't mean to freak you out. Just wasn't expecting to find anyone else out here," the guy says softly, holding his hands up. His jet-black hair and black leather jacket would almost blend into the darkness if the moonlight wasn't refracting off them both.

"Yeah, that makes two of us," I mutter, trying to catch my breath.

He grins, raising an eyebrow in a cocky, self-assured kinda way.

"Fair enough," he chuckles. In two giant strides he bounds over to me, plopping down in the grass to my left. "So, wanna talk about it?" he asks.

"Talk about what?" I say, narrowing my eyes.

"Whatever has you drinking teeny-tiny bottles of...what is this?" He picks up the bottle. "Fireball whiskey. Nice choice."

He lifts the bottle to his lips, downs the last drop, and hands it back to me.

I lower my eyebrows. "No offense, dude, but I'm not overly in the *sharing* mood right now," I lament, hoping the double meaning presses itself upon him.

"Well, then, don't share. I'll share," he grins, reaching inside his leather coat and pulling out a silver flask. Spinning the top open, he takes another sip and passes it to me.

I turn up my nose at first and eye it suspiciously. "What is it?"

"My own concoction. Not nearly as fancy as your drink of choice, but it will do in a pinch," he says, a hint of confidence smoldering in his tone.

I contemplate for a moment whether or not it's entirely within my best interests to drink with this strange, obnoxious, albeit kinda hot guy. Especially out here in the cemetery. Alone. Where no one *technically* knows I am.

"Thanks, but I'll pass," I say, suddenly more alert.

"Suit yourself," he says, shrugging and taking another long draw from his flask.

Throwing him a sideways glance, we settle into a semi-awkward silence.

"So, what's your name, anyway?" he asks, tipping his chin toward me.

I chew on my lip a moment, deciding what to say. I finally decide on, "Drusilla."

It's the first name to pop into my head from my mom's favorite TV show. So lame, but in a sorta good, sorta dorky oh-my-god-I'm-not-gonna-ever-tell-my-Mom sorta way. It's literally the only connection I've ever seen my mom have with anything supernatural, so I guess I have to take what I get.

The guy actually snorts.

"Yeah, okay. And my name's Angel," he laughs.

My eyebrows flick upward, surprised.

I mean, c'mon. My name *could* actually be Drusilla. The show is ancient enough. Besides, I think Mom even said she thought about it but decided she didn't want to give me a complex about being named after a deranged vampire.

After a second, I tip my head. "Yep, I can totally see it. As long as it's not Angelus, I think we're five by five."

"Ha—even quoting Faith. See, now I know it's bunk," he says, winking at me. "I knew I'd like you."

I've never seen a wink actually pulled off before where it didn't look like some sort of spasm—but damn, he does it. And it suits him.

"Figures you'd be a fan," I chuckle despite myself and

narrow my eyes. "How about this? I'll tell you mine if you tell me yours."

"I have a better idea. How about we leave things as-is," he says, a big, cheesy grin spreading across his lips.

"Hmmm... Trying to hide, are we?" I say, eyeing him suspiciously.

"Not at all. Just trying to honor the mystery. I mean, this is a small town. We're bound to find out each other's real names eventually. Right?"

I cross my legs and turn to face him.

"Deal. Nice to meet you, Angel," I say, jutting out my hand.

"The pleasure is all mine, Drusilla," he says, taking my hand in his as he kisses the top in an old-fashioned kind of gesture.

I snort under my breath as I pull it back. Despite being a dorky move, something about it breaks the ice between us.

"So, what are you doing here? Planning which graves to tip over?" I ask, lowering my eyebrows playfully.

Shock, with a hint of horror, flash across his features. "Absolutely not. That...you're not planning on doing that. Are you?"

I shake my head. "No."

He exhales slowly, clutching at his chest. "Thank goodness for that."

"So, if not to tip graves, why are you here?" I ask. Not even my friends understand my fixation on this place, so I can't help but want to know his reasoning.

His eyes lock with mine and for the briefest of moments, a wave of sadness consumes him.

I glance down at my hands. "I'm sorry. I didn't mean—"

"No, it's okay. I guess you could say I feel sorta drawn to the spirits here."

When I look up, a faint smile graces his lips.

"Do you have family buried here?" I ask, looking around the space, as if somehow I'd know which ones are tied to him.

"You could say so, I guess," he says, fiddling with the flask lid.

Pressing my lips tight, I divert my gaze to one of the older stones. The words are all but worn off, but there's a certain elegance to the scrollwork and sculpture of the stone itself.

"Do you believe in ghosts?" he asks, his silver eyes watching me closely.

I shrug. "No, not really."

Confusion flashes across his features. "Really? That's surprising, actually."

"Why?" I snicker.

"Well, you clearly like supernatural stuff. Ergo the Buffy references." He looks over his shoulder, eyeing the headstones around us. "You're here, in a graveyard, talking to... who was it? Charlotte?"

Heat creeps up the back of my neck as I glance back at the headstone. He was listening to my conversation with the headstone. Lovely.

"So, if you're not here for the ghosts...why *are* you here?" he asks.

Swallowing hard, I weigh my words. "I guess because it's the only place where silence reigns. I can think here."

He chuckles softly. "Silence, huh?"

"Yeah, silence," I say, smirking. "What else would you call it? It's not exactly loud out here."

"Depends on who you talk to." He smirks, taking another swig from his flask.

I roll my eyes. "Oh boy. Let me guess, you're a ghost hunter?"

"Not exactly," he says with a mischievous twinkle in his

eyes. "But I *was* meant to meet you tonight, Drusilla. I can feel it."

Narrowing my gaze, I hold my hand out, and flick my fingertips. "All right, I changed my mind. Better give me a sip of that."

Without a word, he holds out the flask.

Spinning the lid off, I press the cold metal to my lips and let the cool liquid splash over my tongue. Surprised, I pull back and sputter.

"What in the— Is this...is this *flavored water*?" I laugh, thrusting the flask back at him.

He grins like the Cheshire Cat.

"Maybe? Being a rebel doesn't *always* have to mean rebelling with the bad stuff, right?" he says, shrugging sheepishly.

I shake my head, and a deep, boisterous laugh escapes. It feels good—*really* good. Things have been really heavy lately, and I didn't realize just how much I needed a little bit of humor in my life.

"You're so absurd," I say.

"Look who's talking. Absurd? Who says absurd anymore? What are you? A hundred years old? Did you just watch *Titanic*? That's it isn't it?" He laughs, pointing in my direction.

"No, I just like the word, smartass. Besides, not everything great comes from the TV," I fire back at him.

"Oh, really? Where else then?" he says, quirking an eyebrow.

"Ever crack open a book?"

"Ever crack open a smile?" he retorts, then scrunches up his face. "Okay, that didn't work as well as it sounded in my head."

We both laugh and I reach for the flask again, giving him a side eye.

"So, when did you move here?" I finally ask.

He sighs heavily. "Last week."

"Happy move, then?"

Shrugging, he takes the flask back and has a sip. "Depends. I'd say it's looking up."

He catches my eye, holding my gaze for a few extra beats. My face flushes and I glance down at the unexpected eruption of butterflies in my stomach.

"What about you? I assume this is home turf. So, will I catch ya around town?" he asks.

"Yeah, I work over at the—" I stop myself, realizing this could be an added layer of complexity I'm not sure I need right at this moment.

"At the...?"

Standing up quickly, I brush off my jeans and slowly back away.

"Yeah, you know, I better get going. My mom and I didn't leave on the best of terms and I think I should go have a word with her. Besides, if I don't make it back soon, she'll have the cops out looking for me," I say, pointing toward the way I came in.

"I didn't mean to upset you," he starts, standing up and gaping at me.

Shaking my head, I say, "No, it's not you. Just gotta run. It was nice to meet you, Angel."

Without another word, I half walk, half run my way out of the older part of the cemetery.

In the distance I hear, "Catch ya around, Dru."

Anxiety blossoms through me and I sprint through the rest of the cemetery. I slip past the opening, and when I've reached the safety of the street, I lean against the gate and run my hands over my face.

Nothing exciting has happened to me for weeks—

months, even. Making the decision whether or not to go to the Windhaven Academy isn't easy as it is. Why would the universe curse me with meeting a guy now? And not just any guy, either. One who gets my dorky television references and feels drawn to hang out in the cemetery, too.

Forget fate. The universe is just cruel.

CHAPTER 3

THE WINDS OF CHANGE ARE COMING

After the worst night of sleep I've had in a long time, I reach over and cease the annoying buzz of my phone's alarm clock.

Instantly, memories of last night rush at me like a raging bull and I bolt upright in bed.

I'm nowhere closer to making a decision about Windhaven Academy, and the run-in at the cemetery certainly isn't helping. It's been nearly two years since my best friend moved to England for college. While we both promised to talk often, the time difference has pretty much dampened our communication. A deep part of me longs for someone who just...gets me.

Even if they believe in something as ridiculous as ghosts.

I brush my hands over my face, then throw the covers back.

By the time I got back home, my mom was fast asleep, so there was no resolution there. She's never been the type of parent who would wait up in a dark room, ready to pounce. She values her sleep too much and knows waiting wouldn't make a difference anyway. If anything, it would mean a big blow-out with no joy at the end. Instead, it would just keep everyone awake and pissed off. I suppose morning makes as good a time as any to pounce.

Dressing as quickly as I can, I throw on a pair of ripped-up skinny jeans, a form-fitting t-shirt that says *Be the Change,* and my dark-gray Vans. Pulling my thick auburn locks into a haphazard ponytail, I give myself a quick glance in the mirror and rush out the door.

I don't need to be gobbed in makeup or have my eyebrows drawn on like I'm paying homage to Groucho Marx. Other girls in town have that covered, anyway. I'd rather stand out by being the opposite of all of that insanity.

Tiptoeing down the stairs, I make my way to the kitchen as quietly as possible. As I reach the heart of our home, I'm surprised to find it devoid of the usual activity. Not only is Mom not waiting to dive into a conversation, she isn't even rushing around trying to make a healthy breakfast before she bolts out the door to her office.

"Mmmkay, this isn't good," I say aloud. I walk over to the kitchen window, leaning over far enough to see if her Subaru is still in the driveway.

Its shiny black paint glistens in the early-morning sun and its windows are still fogged over with a hint of frost.

A lightbulb goes off in my head and I spin around, racing to the kitchen cupboards. If Mom's overslept, she's going to be freaking about not having a decent breakfast to start the day off right.

Yanking the fridge door open, I grab the eggs, bacon, spinach, garlic, and those weird tiny tomatoes she loves. I chuck them all at the counter and spin around for an avocado and her gluten-free toast.

My eyes flit to the clock on the stove: 7:11 a.m. Plenty of

time for me to get this thing rockin' before I have to bolt out the door, too.

"May as well make some for both of us. Nothing like totally surprising her by eating healthy along with her," I chuckle, grabbing the whisk and going to town. "She'll be totally convinced."

I dice up the garlic and onions the way I've seen her do almost every single morning of my teenage years, and throw them into a frying pan of olive oil.

And she thinks I never pay attention to her. Pft.

I turn the burner on high and walk back to the spinach, tomatoes, and avocado. Scratching the back of my head, I realize I have no idea what she does with those. I must have tuned her out at that point as I engaged on Insta.

I cut up the tomatoes into fours and wash the spinach. I assume it's a salad, right?

Before I realize it, the garlic and onions are smoking and I race back to the stovetop, fanning the noxious odor as the beginnings of the eggs go up in flames.

"What on earth are you doing?"

I jump, pushing the pan to the back burner as if I'd been caught doing something I wasn't supposed to. Staring at her with wide eyes, I've drawn a completely blank.

"Were you—were you trying to make breakfast?" she asks, her face a bundle of surprise.

I shrug sheepishly.

"Wow, I expected you'd want a continuation of yesterday's discussion, not deliver some ass-kissing," she says, blinking rapidly. "I'll take it."

"Yeah, well, I think I screwed up the eggs." I point to the charred remains.

She nods, a hint of a grin sparkling in her eyes. "They certainly are beyond resuscitation."

My gaze falls to the floor and I scrunch my face.

Mom sets her briefcase down on the counter and takes the handle of the frying pan and the wooden spoon. "Looks like you just had the oil too high. How about we start over?"

Walking to the small countertop compost bin, she scrapes the contents into it and rinses the pan out in the sink.

"Yeah, okay." I nod.

"You did a great job with the dicing, though. How about you do that again and I'll start the toast," she offers.

I set to work and before we know it, a newly cooked version of the meal is laid out before us. She's right. I definitely had the oil on too high. The eggs, too, come to think of it.

"Thanks for getting this going. I was planning on swinging through Panera on the way to work," Mom says, reaching for my hand and giving it a squeeze.

"Thanks for teaching me how to make eggs without burning the house down," I grin.

A smile lights up her face, but her eyes glass over. Instead, tears work their way to the surface.

"C'mon Mom," I say, tipping my head, "don't do that."

She takes a deep breath. "I'm—I'm okay," she whispers. But her voice cracks, betraying its sentiment.

"What's wrong now? I thought this was a good morning."

"It was—*is*."

"So then, what?"

"It's just—I'm going to miss you so much," she says, her lip quivering.

I sit up straighter and lean in. I search her eyes, pleading with my own.

"Mom, I haven't decided on anything yet."

Her greenish-hazel eyes, just like the ones I've acquired

from her, blink slowly as a single tear falls. She swipes at it and shakes her head.

"I wish I could believe that, sweetie. But I know you. I know how stubborn you are. You're just like your—" her words break off and she holds my gaze for a moment.

"Even if I am like Dad," I whisper, "I really haven't decided yet."

A twinge of guilt punches me in the gut, but I ignore it.

She gives me a knowing look, but nods. "Well, thanks for a nice breakfast, sweetie. I—I gotta get to work," she says, pushing away from the table.

"Yeah, uh—me, too," I say, blinking back the surprising spring of emotions.

Each collecting our things, we trod down the front steps, one after the other. Mom heads to her SUV and drives off with a small wave, but I keep walking. I move in a haze past the garden of flowers I'd normally stop and admire and onto the sidewalk. Hiking my purse strap up, I consider heading to the cemetery again to clear my head and relieve some of the guilt I have over trying to make this all about Mom. I should be opening the craft store in the next fifteen minutes, but no one will notice if I'm a couple of minutes late. Most of the locals don't even stroll in until well past nine, anyway.

"Eh, why not?" I say, walking straight past work with a shrug.

As I turn the corner, I hear someone yell, "Hey—Dru! Drusilla."

My insides trip all over themselves, and I chance a glance over my shoulder. Jogging after me, his dark hair flopping up and down with his steps, is the same guy from last night. Surprisingly, his features are even more striking in the daylight. I'm oddly excited to see him again.

I continue walking, but despite myself, slow my pace a

wee bit, just in case he really wants to catch up. After a moment, I feel a tap on my shoulder.

"Hey, didn't you hear me back there?" he asks, matching my stride as we walk shoulder to shoulder.

"Yeah, sorry. I, uh, didn't realize you were talking to me. Sorry, forgot about the nickname," I lie, trying to sound more confident than I feel.

"Ouch. You already forgot about our tit-for-tat in the cemetery?" he says, pretending to jab a knife into his heart. "That hurts."

"That's life," I say, quoting my mom without thinking. She says that no matter what crap thing goes wrong. Who knew I'd already be turning into her this young?

"Well, all right then," he says.

I turn to look at him. He's dressed in a casual button-down shirt beneath the same leather jacket as before. It splays itself open nicely, revealing an outline of his trim torso. His ripped-up blue jeans certainly suit his shape.

Goose bumps flash across the back of my neck and I shiver involuntarily. Most of the guys in town think they look like God's gift in their baggy Champion shorts and t-shirt that could fit three of them inside.

"So, you look like you're on your way to the cemetery again. Are you still sorting out whatever was bothering you last night?" he asks, watching me closely with those discerning silver eyes.

I nod. "Yeah, a lot on my mind."

"Anything I can do to help? I'm a good listener," he says, grinning broadly.

"No. Thanks, though," I say, my gaze surveying the expanse in front of me.

"C'mon. Nothing I can do? Are you sure?"

"Nope. I think it's pretty much screwed," I say, covering my mouth with the crook of my pointer finger.

"That sounds dire..." His eyebrow twitches upward.

I let out a slow sigh and curse under my breath.

"Well, see, I just got a full ride to the Windhaven Academy, but my mom doesn't want me to go. Last night we got in a big fight over it. I was trying to figure things out, but this annoying guy sorta derailed my thought process," I blurt out. Shifting my gaze from his expectant one, I continue, "Of course, the fact that I don't have an ounce of supernatural ability isn't helping either. So, there's that."

"Hold up," he says, grabbing my wrist. "You're thinking of moving?"

I grin in a painful, wincing kinda way.

His eyes are serious, and he genuinely looks disappointed. "So, did you meet another guy? Or?"

I slap him across the chest with the back of my hand.

"It's you, doofus," I say, snickering softly to myself.

He breathes a sigh of relief and nods. "Oh, okay, good. That's good."

I can't help but chuckle.

"So, Windhaven, huh..." he says, kicking at the ground in front of him.

"Yep."

"Well, why do you think they want you then? I mean, if you haven't shown any supernatural signs by now, I would have thought they would have passed you up."

"Your guess is as good as mine," I say, shrugging.

"Well, aren't you the least bit curious? I mean, I know I would be."

"Obviously, yes," I say, turning forward again and continuing down the sidewalk. "It's all I've been thinking about since I found out. Well, *almost* all I've been thinking about."

He narrows his gaze, but doesn't dig deeper, thank goodness.

When we reach the cemetery, he pulls my arm back and stares at me with the kind of serious expression that makes me self-conscious. "I know we just met and maybe my impression doesn't amount to much, but here's my two cents worth anyway. You need to figure out why you've been accepted, Dru. I mean, the Windhaven Academy doesn't make those sorts of mistakes."

"That's what I was thinking too, to be honest. It's just... my mom is pretty adamant I don't go. She hates everything supernatural," I say, scrunching my face.

"Are you living for you? Or are you living for her?"

I stare at him for a moment, unable to form words. It's like he's in my head.

"Fair point," I finally say.

"A damn good point," he laughs, pushing back strands of black hair from his eyes. "Besides, it would be pretty convenient for me since I'll be going to Windhaven Academy soon, too."

A strange sense of relief floods through me and I take a step back.

"Really? You're supernatural?" I say, my mouth dropping open in surprise. He seems so...normal. Well, sorta.

"Yeah. I guess so. I mean, I don't really know much myself. I guess I get psychic vibes, but they tell me I have to develop it," he says.

"So, what are you waiting for? Why not go this year, too?" I say, quirking an eyebrow. "It would be nice to know another first-year student."

His tongue grazes his lower lip, drawing my attention. "Unfortunately, I can't. I have a few things I have to take care of here in Mistwood Point first."

I tilt my head. "Like what? What's more important than developing your gifts?"

He inhales deeply, then lets out a sigh. "Like caring for my grandfather until he dies. He's on hospice and I can't let him die alone. He's the only family I have left."

"Oh. Oh—I'm so sorry. Is that what brought you here?" I whisper, not really knowing what else to say.

He nods.

"Well, this conversation has taken a turn," I say, staring out over the tombstones beyond.

My responsibilities are niggling at the back of my mind, and I know I won't be able to spend much longer here, let alone head deeper into the cemetery—or the conversation for that matter.

"Sorry, I didn't mean for—" he begins.

I raise a hand. "Hey, no...no worries. I'm glad you told me."

"Well, the point was to let you know that even though I won't be at Windhaven this year, I will be there eventually. And if it were me, I would want to unravel that mystery of yours," he says, reaching out and tucking a loose strand of hair behind my ear. "I hear orientation is coming up in a few weeks. I could go with you, if you want."

"Yeah, they've made a pretty big deal about it in my letter, actually," I say, biting the inside of my cheek.

"So, it's a date then?" he asks, standing so close I inhale a heady mixture of Dove soap mixed with sandalwood.

I consider for a moment, realizing that if this has the chance of going any further, I no longer want to be talking to an alter ego.

"Angel, er—" I splay out a hand, asking silently for his name.

He narrows his eyes, as if trying to decide whether or not to release his trade secrets.

"Wade." He blinks slowly, his dark lashes fluttering against his cheeks as they mound from his smile.

"*Wade*," I repeat. My pulse quickens as his real name crosses the threshold of my lips. "I would love to check out Windhaven Academy with you."

"Excellent. I'd love to unravel the mystery of your superpowers with you," he mimics my gesture from before, trying to suss out my own name.

"Autumn," I whisper.

Wade grins broadly. "*Autumn*. I like that. It suits you."

"Well, I better..." I jab a thumb back toward the way we came. "I actually have to get to work."

"Ah, no problem," he says, taking a small step back. "But... since we're going to check out Windhaven together, maybe we would have dinner or something to get to know each other a little better. Whatcha doing tonight?"

His face is open as he beams back at me.

Nervous energy blossoms through me and my words catch at my throat. I flit my gaze to the headstones again, and despite my worries, I say, "Meet me here at seven and find out."

Wade nods in approval and I turn around to head to the craft store before I can talk myself out of this.

Relationships and I have a sketchy history, at best. As I walk away, part of me wants to jump for joy, but a darker, more sinister part of me wonders if this is really too good to be true.

CHAPTER 4
BARELY EXISTEDNESS

After my parents' separation and watching my mom struggle through the years, I always swore I'd learn to be more self-reliant than she was. There were plenty of times when my father had to bail us out—not that she'd ever admit that to me. I'm not even supposed to know about it. But each time, I'd heard her crying afterward. It was like speaking to him was the hardest thing she'd ever had to do. It was clear to me she still loved him, but for whatever reason, they decided they couldn't be together. I grew up knowing that loving someone, *really* loving them, means suffering for it.

Now, I feel as though I'm running headlong into a train, and happily anticipating its wreckage.

As I walk up, Wade is standing in the same spot I'd left him earlier in the day, waiting for me. The grin that graces his face could light up the setting sun.

"Hi," he says as I approach.

"Hey," I respond, ignoring the sound of my runaway pulse. "I have something I wanted to show you. Are you game?"

"Of course," Wade says, a hint of surprise and confusion lighting his face.

"You're new in town, right?" I shoot him a mischievous grin and wait for him to nod. "So, obviously, there is no way you could be in charge of this date, silly fool. I've taken it upon myself to show you the sights before you're fully assimilated into the overwhelming monotony that is Mistwood."

"Assimilated? Wow, that's very Borg." Wade grins.

Butterflies erupt from my solar plexus and I can't help but laugh. It's nice to have someone else around who gets the stupid, random stuff I end up referencing. Especially when it's not about Fortnite, Call of Duty, or some other video game guys can't seem to get enough of.

"So, *Wade, not Angel*...where did you live before coming to Mistwood Point?" I ask, venturing a sideways glance as we continue down the sidewalk.

Wade turns his gaze straight ahead, suddenly very interested in the concrete in front of us. "Oh, trust me, it's nowhere noteworthy."

"Oooh, that bad, huh? This could be fun. Let me guess..." I say, thrusting my hands out in front of me, interlacing my fingers, and giving them a good crack. "Your old town was really a traveling circus tent and you never really set up shop anywhere."

He chuckles, shaking his head.

"No? Hmmm... I was so sure about that, too. Okay, okay... let me think." I place my fingertips to the sides of my head in mock concentration. "You're actually from the future, but you came back in time because you know the Antichrist is about to be born in Mistwood Point and it's your mission to end him before the Earth falls into total annihilation."

"Warmer," he snorts, his lips curving upward, despite his not wanting to meet my gaze.

My eyebrows tug in.

"Really? Warmer... Hmmm. Okay. How about, you were stolen as a baby because your parents were really serial killers and they liked to hang out with dead bodies," I say, grinning like a goof at my insane prediction.

"Uh..." He glances at me, narrowing his eyes and looking away. "No, not quite."

"Okay, I'm out. Where'd you come from, man?" I ask again.

Wade finally turns to face me, grabbing hold of my arm. His face is suddenly a hundred percent serious. "I never really had a hometown, if you know what I mean. I've sorta been on my own since I was fourteen."

Chills run up my spine, but definitely not the good kind. "Really? Why? That's gotta be like, what, six years?"

"Nine, actually," he says, shooting me a glance. "I'm twenty-three. Er...hope that's okay."

I swipe my hand in the air. "Totally fine."

"Good," he exhales a puff of air. "Anyway, my dad died when I was fourteen and I couldn't bear to live with my grandparents. Yes, the same grandpa I'm living with now. Ironic, I know. I mean, I loved them, but I was just not in a good place. Hell, what fourteen-year-old is, even without that sort of thing happening? I didn't want to drag them into it. You know?"

"Oh," I sputter, grasping for words that could possibly make any of that better. "I'm—I'm so sorry, Wade. What about your mom? Is she in the picture?"

"No, she died when I was really little. It's not really a big deal. Not anymore," he says with a shrug.

I fight the urge to say, 'Suuuuure it's not.' Instead, I face forward again, leading us onward in utter, awkward silence.

After a couple of minutes, I ask, "How did it happen, if you don't mind me asking."

"My dad? Or my mom?"

I nod solemnly. "Either?"

"Well, for my dad it was a brain tumor. One day he was fine, the next he was really sleepy and sorta off. His balance wasn't right, his words were slurred. At first, the doctors thought it could have been a stroke. He went in to get checked out and we found out he had three separate masses growing on his brain. He was gone in less than a month," he says, his voice trailing off.

"Wow, that totally sucks."

Wade nods, his eye going distant. "Definitely weren't the funnest days ever."

"Do you know what happened to your mom?"

His eyebrows knit together and he shoves his hands into his pocket. "She drowned. I guess she really loved to kayak and one day, she never made it back. They found her body in the river a few days later. At least, that's what I was told once I was old enough to understand."

"That must have been terrible. Losing both of your parents. I mean, I don't always get along with mine, but..."

"Yeah, it was hard at the time, and definitely in my teenage years. Luckily, I'd like to think I've grown beyond it. I mean, the past only has control if you let it, right?" he says, shooting me a sideways glance.

"Very true." I nod. "Well, so how are things with your grandpa? Do you guys get along?"

"He's a good guy. Sweet. *Old.* He doesn't even have internet in his house. So, that's fun," Wade chuckles under his breath.

"Oh my god, it's like being plunged into the Dark Ages. How are you gonna survive?"

He shrugs. "I'll probably just have to call the phone company and get it brought in. It was on my agenda for today, actually. But I got distracted by a beautiful woman and spent some time daydreaming about her."

I stop walking to narrow my gaze at him. My cheeks flame, but I can't help but smile.

"Well, you better get on it, Mr. Wade. If I do go to Windhaven, we need a way to stay in contact, don't we?"

He places his eyes on me, his pupils widening until his irises are nothing more than a thin silver line around the edges. I suck in a deep, but jagged breath, trying to calm my sudden flare of nervous energy.

"I wholeheartedly agree," Wade says. "Does this mean you've decided to go?"

I shift my gaze to my feet. "Yes? No? I don't know. I want to go...but..."

"You have to think long-term, Autumn. What is it you really want?"

"But my mom..." I begin.

"Your mom will be fine. If you've got powers, ignoring them isn't going to do you, or her, any good. You need to figure out what they are. Trust me. Living with the knowledge of latent potential kind of sucks."

I don't know what to say to that, so I just clamp my lips tight and nod.

He reaches out, grabbing hold of my arm. I stop walking and he lifts a hand, gently stroking the side of my cheek. The sensation of it catches me off guard, and makes my back go rigid.

"I'm really glad I bumped into you at the cemetery. I really am," he whispers. "This might be kinda out of place, and honestly, I can't believe how dorky I sound in my head, but would you mind if I come out to visit you?"

My eyebrows tug in.

"I mean, if it's too forward..." he says, backpedaling.

"No, it's not that. It's just... I haven't given much thought to where I would stay. I've never been much for crowds and I'm not a party girl. I don't think I could stay on campus. So, the logical next step would be to stay at my dad's."

"Why does that sound like it's a bad thing?"

"It's not that. In fact, the more I think about it, the more I think it could be a good thing. He'd probably love it. I just haven't heard from him in a long time and to be honest, it's been a while since I stayed out there. Plus, I'm not too sure my mom will be keen on it."

"How long has it been?" Wade asks.

I make a face. "I guess the last time I was there was when I was seven."

"Wow, that's been a while, then. What, twelve years?" he says, wagering a guess the way I had.

I snicker. "Add a year and you'd be right on target."

"So, twenty, huh?" Wade says, raising his eyebrows high.

I stop walking to place a hand on my hip. "Am I too young for you now?"

He snorts, taking my hands in his. "Actually, just right."

"Hmmm...and when exactly is your birthday, might I ask?" I grin, poking him in the arm.

He watches me from the corner of his eye, but keeps his mouth pinned shut.

"Come on now, don't hold out on me. When does the world celebrate the day Wade was born?"

"Sorry, I only share that kind of privileged information with people who stick around," he says, smirking.

Holding up a pretend knife, I jab myself in the heart. "Oh, ouch. That was a brutal takedown, man. I mean, really. Right to the heart. I had just been leaning toward going and now this?"

Wade laughs. "I call it like it is, what can I say?"

"Hmph. Well, still unfair. You're the one encouraging me to go."

"Very true," he concedes.

"So, you'll tell me?" I say, my face brightening.

"Nope, not a chance."

"Ugh. I'll find out. So help me, if I have to stalk you on Insta, I'll hunt down your besties and learn of your secrets."

"Best of luck with that. I actually encourage you to try."

"Really?" I say, surprised.

"Sure," he shrugs.

I narrow my eyes and tease, "Why do you sound so glib about this endeavor?"

He rubs at the spot beneath his lip. "Well, for starters, what's my last name?"

I open my mouth, only to close it again.

"Dammit."

Wade grins broadly.

I wave a hand dismissively. "No matter. Where's the fun in that?"

His eyebrows rise to his hairline. "Oh, it's a challenge now, is it?"

"Why yes, yes, it is, Wade. I will learn of your last name and the date your mother pushed you out into this world."

"Eeew. Now that's taking things a step too far," he says, shuddering and sticking out his tongue.

I chuckle. "What can I say? *I* call it like it is."

"I don't know about all that. I prefer to believe I had a Superhero birth. Made, not born."

"Nice try, fair boy. Nice try," I laugh.

We turn left, bringing us down a small footpath that leads

us to the river. It's not an open or heavily trafficked area, which is why I love it.

"It's really pretty down this way," Wade says, his gaze all over the wooded area.

I nod in agreement. "Yeah, this is another one of my favorite spots. I like to come down here when I want to be alone. Well, here and the cemetery, but that seems to be more crowded lately."

"Oh? Did I ruin your sacred space?" he laughs.

"No numpty, you're now invited," I say, rolling my eyes. "But don't get cocky about it."

"Cocky? I wouldn't dare," he says with mock surprise.

I slowly raise an eyebrow. "Hmmm."

We walk out into a small clearing before it transforms into the bank of the river and continues to walk the narrow trail. When we reach the edge where the rocks begin to jut out and the natural flowers spring up, I find a good place to take a seat.

"I didn't even realize this river was down here. It's not very big, is it?" he says, taking it in with wide eyes.

"No, it's more of a creek, really. But I love its barely existedness. I found this spot when I was twelve or thirteen and I've been coming back ever since."

Wade takes a seat opposite me, crossing his legs as he watches my every move. I can't seem to get enough of those big, silver eyes of his.

"What?" I ask after a few moments under his scrutiny.

"Nothing. I just—you have ridiculously amazing eyes," he says, the corner of his lips twitching upward.

I squint at him. "They're just green."

"No, they aren't. They're way more than that. When the light hits them just right, they sparkle with hints of golds, browns, and even some blue in there. I've never seen anything like it."

Heat rises up my neck and nestles in my cheeks.

"Ah, and a little color does her some good," he grins, leaning back onto his elbows.

I rub at my cheeks and shake my head.

"Yeah, well, you have pretty spectacular eyes, too," I say, realizing I sound utterly stupid, even though it's true.

"Doesn't count. I told you first." Again he smiles, but this time he winks at me. That crazy wink that suits him so well.

I shift my gaze away but can't seem to wipe the grin off my face.

"So, what does the infamous Autumn Blackwood do when in her secret hideaway in the woods by the nonexistent river?"

My eyes widen and I tip my chin down. "Have you been asking around about me?"

He shrugs. "Maybe a little."

"Well, see, now that's not fair. You know my last name and I don't know yours. It gives you an unfair advantage."

"I can't say I'm all that bothered," he smirks.

I shake my head, "How on earth did you get my last name already? I mean, it's only been a few hours. Did you knock on every door until you narrowed it down?"

"Perhaps," he says.

"Yeesh, you move fast."

"Only when necessary," he says, shooting me a knowing look.

"And this was necessary?" I ask, kicking my legs out so they land to the side of him.

He does the same, then places a hand on my shin. The contact immediately sends goose bumps flashing across my body, making me shiver. "Of course it was."

The creases of his eyes crinkle and his dark hair seems to move in slow motion in the breeze. He's like one of those male models, only he's here, in real life, sitting with me for some godforsaken reason. And I'm seriously thinking of leaving him soon, because he's right. Even if I don't like it.

Dammit.

"I, uh, I'm not sure what to think of all that," I stutter.

Wade leans in a bit closer. "Don't think too hard. It's really very simple."

"It is?"

"Of course. Boy moves to new town. Boy meets girl. Boy likes girl. Boy tries to learn more about girl so he can see her again," he says. The smile beaming from his face could light this entire pocket of nature, even if it were night. "See? Simple."

"You forgot the part about 'Boy learns girl could be moving away, so he probably shouldn't bother.'"

He grins sheepishly. "Eh, the heart is a fickle thing. It wants what it wants. Have to accept it and bend to its will."

"Oh." I raise my eyebrows. "Now you're getting the heart involved?"

"Aren't you?" Wade smiles slowly.

Everything inside me is screaming yes, even if my brain isn't so sure it's wise. I narrow my eyes. "Maybe?"

A hearty, deep laugh erupts from his lips. "Maybe is good enough. We have some time to work on that."

We lock eyes and for a moment, it's almost as though time stands completely, utterly still—just for us. Light streams through the branches of the trees in thick, beautiful beams as flying insects meander in and out of the intensity. The green around us even seems to fluctuate with its deep hues.

Switching to a more upright seated position, Wade shifts

forward, and scoots his body so his torso is inches from mine. My breath hitches and my pulse quickens, but I don't move a muscle. I simply watch him, mesmerized.

His eyes lock with my own before he bends in to claim his kiss. One of his hands gently caresses the side of my face, tracing at the area where my eyebrow meets the corner of my eye, and I can't help but breathe into him.

When our lips touch, the entire world falls away, and all I can think about is... if I go to Windhaven, how am I going to make it through any time apart?

CHAPTER 5

GOING BACK IN TIME

When you have little-to-no contact with someone, the last thing you want to do is call up and ask for a favor. I never expected my first call to my dad in forever would be to tell him I got a full ride to the Windhaven Academy...and that I need a place to crash. I sure as hell hope the open-door policy still stands, but things aren't looking good. The deadline for finalizing my Windhaven plans is looming.

"Still not answering, huh?" Wade asks, taking a seat on my computer chair.

I toss my cell phone on the bed and sit down. "Nope. It doesn't seem like him, either. I'm hoping he's just busy and not completely avoiding me."

"Do you really think he'd do that?" Wade asks, throwing me a surprised look.

I shrug. "Hope not. But at this point, who knows. If I don't get ahold of him in the next hour or so, I'm paying him an impromptu visit later on."

"That seems like a good idea. I mean, it's Saturday, so maybe you'll catch him relaxing at home and he'll be open to your questions. Want me to come with as moral support?" he asks, tapping the edge of my computer desk and glancing at me sheepishly.

Thinking for a moment, I slowly shake my head. "No, for some reason, I feel like I better go alone."

"Are you sure?" Wade asks, holding my gaze for a beat longer than expected. He leans forward slightly, resting his elbows on his knees.

My back stiffens slightly, but I make it a point to lean back a bit on my bed. I break his mesmerizing gaze and look away. "No, I mean yes. I need to do this on my own. It's been ages since I last went to see my dad. It's terrible, really. I mean, I'm an adult now. Keeping in contact is just as much my responsibility as it is his. So, I think it would be weird if I showed up asking to stay there and brought along my..." My eyebrows scrunch in as I realize we haven't defined what we are.

"Your..." Wade says, a lopsided grin emerging.

I narrow my eyes and purse my lips.

"Ooohh, do you have trouble saying it?" he chuckles.

I give him a sideways glance, noticing he hasn't technically defined what we are, either. "Regardless..." I say slowly, changing the subject.

A smug look of satisfaction slides across his features and he leans back in his chair, watching me closely. He crosses his legs, placing his right ankle on top of his left knee.

Pressing my lips into a thin line, I carry on. "This really is something I need to do on my own. But I appreciate the gesture, Mr. *Hoffman*."

Wade's eyes open wide and I grin broadly, knowing I hit the money. It pays to know every old lady in town. They knew exactly which grandpa was on hospice, who also had a new grandson in town to help. Plus, the fact that we've practically spent every waking moment together for the past few days helps.

"Ah, so you've done your homework, I see."

"Of course. I told you I would," I smile.

"Well played, Ms. Blackwood. Didn't take as long as I thought it would."

"Oh, ye of little faith," I say, lying down on my side and propping my head on my hand.

"Well, I hope I get to meet your dad soon," Wade says. "I mean, I don't know about you...but I don't plan on going anywhere soon."

"Was that a jab at me leaving?" I say, quirking an eyebrow.

"Of course not. I'm still lazily tip toeing around the previous subject. Poorly, obviously," he laughs.

My heart lightens, but I remind it to chill out. Things don't need to be defined right away. It's kind of nice to settle into the energy of a new relationship—if that's what this is.

Of course, that's what this is. Who am I kidding?

"Hmmm... Well, you will definitely meet him. If I do end up staying at his place, you better damn well come and visit me. But we'll do the introductions right," I say, sounding more independent and self-assured than I actually feel.

"Sounds like a most excellent plan," he says, tipping his head in acknowledgement.

"Did you just go all Bill and Ted on me?" I say, covering my laugh.

Looking over his shoulder, then switching to the other side, he presses his fingertips to his chest. "Who? Me? How old do you take me for, miss? I'm not forty."

"I'm not entirely convinced," I say, shooting him a sideways glance and dialing my dad's number for the sixth time. Again, it goes to voicemail.

I stand up and grab my purse from the hook by the door.

Wade drops his laid-back position and stands. "Going already?"

"Yeah, may as well. I want to get this over so I know where I stand. Besides, my mom's gone, so it'll be easier to head out without a thousand questions."

Without another word, we make our way downstairs. Once outside, I lock the front door and follow the sidewalk to the driveway. When we reach my Ford Escape, I turn to face him, leaning against the blue door.

"So, is your mom working today?" Wade asks.

I shake my head. "No, she went shopping. Something about a big conference coming up in a couple of weeks that she has to attend."

He nods. "Does she know about you going to Windhaven?"

I grimace.

"Oh, intrigue. Why didn't you tell her?" Wade asks.

"You know why. She doesn't understand the whole Windhaven draw. The last thing I want to do is get her riled up right now. She'll assume I want to take over the world with superpowers or something." I kick off the door so I can open it and toss my purse onto the passenger seat.

Twisting around, I turn to face him and he wraps his arms around me. He pulls me in tight, turning a simple hug into something borderline sexy. Chills race across the surface of my skin and a part of me wants nothing more than to forget going to Windhaven and, instead, bring him back inside and do unspeakable things to him.

"Get the answers you need, beautiful," Wade whispers in my ear.

As he pulls back from our embrace, his hands make their way to my face and he guides me in close. Electricity sparks between us and, like a magnet, I'm drawn to him. My hands rise to his hair, weaving themselves into his dark locks.

When he pulls back, my world is spinning.

"Mmmm..." he says dreamily. "Have I mentioned I'm glad I went to the cemetery that night?"

Involuntarily, I lean back against my car door, and smile.

He beams, taking a tentative step backward. "You'll let me know when you're back, right?"

Still unable to form words, I nod.

He seems to understand as he reaches around to open my car door for me. Nodding at the gesture, I sit and roll down the window. Reaching for the ignition, I start my beat-up SUV.

"Are you sure this thing will get you there?" Wade chuckles.

I've had Big Blue forever, but her time is coming to an end, of that I have no doubt.

"I'll be fine," I say, still grinning to myself.

"Okay, well, text me when you get there. And if you need me, just say the word. I'll come find you," he says, placing his hands on the windowsill.

"I will," I whisper.

Wade bends in, planting one last gentle kiss on my lips through the open window.

"All right, then, see ya around, Dru," he says, backing up and flashing his trademark wink.

Despite my desire to stay, I ground myself to my better judgment, and put Blue into gear. "See ya in a bit, *Angel*."

As I drive off, he taps the back of my vehicle. I turn on my hazards; a final good-bye before I drive out of sight. My eyes flit to the side mirror to get a final glance of him. He waits, standing in the middle of the road, until I can no longer see him at all.

Leaning back into my seat, I let out a low groan.

"Oh my god, I am in so much trouble with him," I say aloud, unable to ignore the desire beginning to build inside me.

Despite myself, I don't spend the two-hour drive to Windhaven thinking about what I need to ask my dad, or what I'd like to learn from him about our family history. Instead, I spend it fighting myself about how soon is too soon to hop into bed with Wade. Oddly enough, it's a welcome distraction.

As I make the final turn down my dad's extended driveway, nervous energy erupts in my stomach, and I realize I'm walking into this totally unprepared. The last time I was here wasn't the most pleasant of times, to say the least. I spent more than a few weeks in bed—and even more of that confined to my room, despite it being a large house.

The trees on either side have a mysterious air about them as the sunlight filters through the branches arching over the road. There isn't another house anywhere in eyeshot and a hint of anxiety trips into my consciousness.

It's like going back in time.

Or at least what I imagine going back in time would be like.

I sit up straighter, clutching the steering wheel a bit tighter as I search for any signs of sentient life. Suddenly, the trees give way to a large clearing and the overgrown dirt driveway gives way to an older, cobblestone one.

As the enormous ancestral home comes into view, memories flood in. There weren't just crappy times here. I do remember some happy ones. Ones when we were all a family, but they're hazy. However, there's still a piece of me that loves the house and wishes I could go back to those simpler times.

Now that I'm older, I definitely admire the architecture and style of this old Georgian manor. Its entire presence commands the landscape to embrace it and hold it safe, and it's utterly breathtaking. The barely turning leaves are still in contrast with the gray stonework, making the front façade pop. The oversized windows adorn much of house, and I remember fondly that when the curtains are pulled back, it lets an incredible amount of light into the home.

I continue down the cobblestones at a slow pace until they start to loop around in front of the main entrance. An old statue of a weeping angel rests in the middle of the loop, surrounded by vines and flowers starting to die back from the colder weather. Tilting my head to the side, I put the vehicle in park and kick open my door. Before heading to the house, I walk up to the statue to have a better look. Interestingly, the angel is male, not the stereotypical female. But like many of the others, his face rests into his bent arm as he leans against a stone pillar.

I don't know why I didn't take much notice of it as a kid, but it creeps me out a bit now.

Blowing out a puff of air, I turn around and my chin tips upward as I take in the sheer size of the home.

"This is definitely bigger than I remember it," I whisper to myself, surprised. Usually, it's the other way around. Swallowing hard, I straighten my shoulders and walk up to the entrance.

Its massive front door is crafted from heavy oak beams and full of stained-glass figures and geometric shapes that are hard to distinguish from this side. Taking hold of the large cast iron knocker, I tap it against the doorframe three times.

I take a step back, clasping my hands behind my back and wait. After a minute or two, Dad still hasn't come to answer the door, but I swear I can hear movement just inside.

I reach out and knock again, this time louder.

"Come on in," a voice answers from the other side.

My eyes widen, but I pull my shoulders back and push open the door.

"Hello?" I call out, a strange seed of excitement blossoming inside me as I enter the entrance hall.

In a weird, alternate universe kinda way, it's like stepping into a movie version of my life. Even at seven years old, all I wanted to do was explore this house and the mysterious grounds. It seemed like a big, glorious adventure, only to be squashed by my dad's overprotectiveness. Now that I'm older and it's even more massive, the pull is definitely real. The house and this entire location has a strange, magical energy all its own and it resonates with the reason I'm here in the first place.

The main entry is an enormous, open space—the kind you see in movies. An expansive chandelier hangs above the entryway, illuminating a small, round table in the middle of the space. Beyond that is an impressive staircase with a bottom that flares outward, inviting you to continue your journey up to the second story, and the landing that wraps around the upper level.

"Whoa," I whisper, taking it all in.

"Do you like it?" Dad asks, joining me in the entryway from the sitting room on the left.

I let out a yip and nearly jump out of my skin.

"Sorry, I didn't mean to startle you, sweetie," he says, chuckling. His blue eyes look tired, with far more wrinkles than I remember.

"No, it's okay. I just—this entry is...wow. I mean, it's just you in here, right? Why do I not remember it being so big?" I ask, unable to help myself.

His shoulders inch toward his ears and he says, "I've been

restoring much of the house, adding my own touches to it. It is bigger. Something to do in my spare time, I guess. I'm a homebody, when time allows. Plus, I've always loved this era of old, historic homes. They have more character than the matchstick boxes of late. I suppose you could call it my legacy."

"I can definitely agree with you about the house design," I say, stepping beyond the entrance table and letting my hand rest on the wooden banister leading upstairs. "It certainly is beautiful."

"Thank you. You know, this home has been in our family for generations," he says, taking a seat on the steps.

I glance down at him and hold my breath as an awkward silence fills the space between us. I'm not sure how to start this bizarre conversation. I don't know how he'll respond to any of it. In fact, for all I know, he's as hellbent against Windhaven as Mom is.

Dad narrows his gaze. "Not that I wouldn't love to talk your ear off about the house, but why are you here, Autumn? Did something happen? Is your mom—?" he asks, shifting his eyebrows up.

"Oh no—she's fine. Everything's, fine," I say, shaking my head.

Letting go of the railing, I walk away from him a few feet and begin to pace. I can feel his eyes on me, and it makes it hard to find the right words.

"Dad, here's the thing... I was sorta, well, I'm thinking I..." I begin, unable to get the words to come out in actual sentences.

His eyes narrow and he runs his hand through his strawberry-blond hair as he waits.

I clear my throat.

"What I'm trying to say is, I've been accepted to the

Windhaven Academy and I want to go. I know it's strange and makes no sense because I'm a complete mundane human, but..."

"But you need a place to stay," Dad says, a hint of a smile lighting up his eyes.

I exhale with a bit of relief. At least he's not as supernatural-opposed as Mom.

"Yeah."

"You are always welcome here," he says, standing back up. "In fact, I insist."

"I can?" I say, picking at the edges of my fingernails. "Are you sure?"

"This is your home, too," he nods. "There's so much I've been waiting to show you..."

CHAPTER 6

I DON'T WANNA GO...

The next couple of weeks fly by like they've been sucked into the Hellmouth. Between stolen moments with Wade and packing up my life's existence, I oscillate back and forth between utter bliss and total panic. There is no way to explain the sick perversion I feel knowing regardless of how much pain I'm going to be in when I leave him behind—it's all worth it right now.

"You're going to forget me as soon as I'm gone," I mutter, entangling my fingers in Wade's dark strands as he rests his head in my lap.

He glances up at me, twisting around on my bed. His penetrating eyes lock with mine and instantly my worries are suspended.

"That will never happen," he whispers. "If anything, you'll get to Windhaven, become the talk of the town, and lose touch with the strange guy you used to know back home. I mean, how can I compete with the supernatural guys you're about to meet?"

I shake my head, snickering to myself. "First of all, you

give me far too much credit for being the talk of anything. Second, you're a supernatural guy I've already met."

"Yeah, but my powers are latent and the ones I do have barely work. It's not like I can fly or phase through walls or anything," he says, frowning. "I'm just straight up strange."

"Wade, you're about as far away from strange, at least the bizarre-o kinda strange, as you can manage. You're strange in all the right ways. Seriously," I say, trying to stress the point by holding our gaze. "Besides, you're going to be visiting me so often, it'll seem like you're already there. Right?"

I search his light gray, damn near silver, eyes. His pupils widen as he leans up on his left arm.

"I will be there every possible moment. I've already made arrangements to have a substitute personal care assistant come in to look after my grandfather on Saturdays and Sunday mornings. So, as long as you don't get sick of me—I'll be there every weekend. Think your dad will let me spend the nights on Saturdays? He's not one of those uber-overprotective types now that you're an adult, is he?"

"Not as far as I know...and that sounds like heaven," I say, reaching out to run my index finger over his eyebrow. "I'm sure Dad'll be fine. There are like a billion rooms in the manor. Even if you pick one and we tell him that's where you're going to sleep, he should be fine."

I give him a slow, sexy smile.

"Well then, wild horses couldn't keep me away, Dru," he says, shifting all the way to a seated position.

My heart flutters at his nickname for me—the one he still uses when he wants me to remember where we began.

Wade leans forward, his scent of sandalwood and hand soap wafting between us. I suck in a quick breath as his face inches toward mine and his lips lightly press against my skin. His tongue skates across my bottom lip in a silent request and my pulse quickens. He knows me so well, it's like he can read my mind.

I sigh into him and pull him closer. Without question, he scoots up as I lay back. Maneuvering so he presses down on me, I feel the weight of his body and the excitement building between us. His tongue dives in deeper, enticing me to give in to him, and I'm so ready to offer up everything.

Wrapping my arms around him, my hands trace from his hips up to his shoulder blades. His strong back muscles are taut, and I can't help but tip my hips up to meet his.

A deep growl erupts from his throat and he breaks our kiss to plant little nibbles down the side of my neck. Instinctively, I arch back and offer more of myself. Raising his right hand, he pulls back my cardigan and continues to plant soft kisses along my exposed collarbone. A deep desire sweeps over me and I'm nearly caught off guard by the intensity of it.

I can't help but wish I could freeze time right here and now—to take in the whole moment forever. The way he feels, the way he moves, the way he smells—*everything*.

Before I know it, tears stream down my face.

"What is it? What's wrong?" Wade says, pulling back, his face clouded with worry.

I wipe frantically at my cheeks, feeling utterly stupid. This was a beautiful moment, and who knows where it could have gone had I not let my fears get in the way.

"Nothing. It's...it's nothing," I stutter.

For a moment, he doesn't move a muscle. Instead, he watches my every movement as if it might give him some magical insight into my mixed-up mind. He slides off to the side of me, propping himself again on his left elbow. Then he tucks a strand of hair behind my ear as he rests his right hand just over my heart.

"This isn't the end, you know," he finally says, his gruff voice barely a whisper.

Another traitorous tear threatens to fall from my right eye and I bite my lip to keep it from quivering.

"Then why does it feel like it? I mean, logically I know it's not, but I wish you... What if *you* find someone else while we're apart?"

Wade's eyebrows tip upward in the middle and he wraps his arms around me, pulling me in close.

"I've been trying to be strong, but it feels like we'll be in two locations forever," I whisper, trying unsuccessfully to keep my cool without going full on crybaby. "What if—"

"Hey, hey—come on. We'll see each other again this weekend. Your head will spin by how fast it will be," he murmurs in my ear. "Like you said, you won't even have time to feel like we're apart. I promise."

"Maybe I should wait. I mean, I could talk to them and start next fall when you—"

"You cannot put your life on hold for me. No," he says, shaking his head. "No way. You need to figure out what you are—what they see in you. I may not have a ton of powers, but at least I know what I am. Sorta. Trust me, we'll be fine. Get things set up so I can be impressed when I come visit you next weekend."

"Orientation isn't for another week. Maybe I should just wait until—"

"Woman, you chose this weekend for a reason. Remember? You wanted time to get settled before diving into all the craziness about to come at you. Don't start second-guessing yourself now."

"But—"

Without letting me finish, Wade kisses me again, effectively cutting off the rest of my excuses. I breathe into his longing and can't help but relax into his energy. In the short period of time we've known each other, I cannot even imagine a time when he wasn't in my life. I'm edging precariously close to never wanting to be without him.

My heart takes a leap into my throat at the thought and I break from our kiss to pull Wade in closer. I bury my face in the crook of his neck and breathe in his scent. He doesn't move a muscle. Instead, he holds as still as I do. I close my eyes and try to memorize the sound of his heartbeat.

"Come on, Autumn," Wade whispers in my ear. "We got this. It's a week and I'll be there. I'll have all of orientation with you, too, which will be amazing. Then, we can text every day and I'll FaceTime you every night before bed. Hell, we can shut off the lights and pretend we're in the cemetery together."

Despite myself, I smile.

"I'd..." I begin, wiping at my face again. "I'd love that."

"Then it shall be done," he says softly, winking in the crazy-sexy way only he knows how to pull off. Releasing his hand from my chest, he slides off the bed. With a quick motion, he extends his right hand out, flipping the ends of his fingertips as he suggests I take his hand.

I grab it and scoot off the bed after him. My eyes widen and I shake my head. "I really don't need to go just yet."

His fingertip clamps down on my lips. "Yes, you do. And it's okay. Now, later—it's not going to get any easier. In fact, I guarantee the longer we're here together, it will only get harder."

I shake my head, smiling. "How can you be so calm about all of this?"

Taking a moment to think about the question, Wade's

eyebrows knit together. He finally says, "I guess, when you're around someone whose life is ending, it's easier to put things into perspective. Don't get me wrong. I don't want you to go. Far from it. But as much as I want to spend every waking moment with you, and believe me, I do... I also know that we're better together when we are still ourselves. I have my grandfather to think about right now and you have Windhaven Academy. Our time together will come, and I am more than happy in the knowledge that it's on its way."

"Wow, that was really...profound, actually. I feel like a silly schoolgirl or something," I say, biting down on the inside of my cheek.

"Not in the remotest. You have an incredible heart and a healer's energy. You just want people to feel supported. You don't want to say good-bye. *It's who you are*. And I love that about you."

Tears brim in my eyes again as he seems to strip me down to my bare essence without even trying. Swallowing hard, I blink them away.

"But trust me, before you can heal the ones around you, you have to heal yourself. That starts with taking care of the dynamic between you and your dad. *And for the love*, even if you're not curious, *I* want to know why Windhaven Academy wants you there," he says, nudging me with his shoulder.

"Oh, so now the real truth comes out," I laugh, despite myself. "All those beautiful words and really it boils down to you wanting me to figure out what kind of supernatural nerd I am."

"I won't lie, that's totally mixed in there," he grins.

"Well, when you put it all that way..." I say, sticking out my tongue at him. "I wanna know what kind of supernatural nerd you are, too. You've barely explained."

"That time will come," he grins. "I gotta keep a little mystery between us, right?"

"Totally not fair," I say.

Wade bends forward until his breath tickles the side of my cheek. "And yet, it will all come out in the end and you know it," he whispers into my ear. "Come on, let's get you on the road. You'll feel better once this part is done."

I tip my chin to look him in the eyes and despite his words, my own angst is mirrored back at me. He feels it too —this pull to stay together. He's just better at setting it aside than I am. Maybe it's because of all he's had to let go in his past. Losing your parents at such a young age can't be easy. I place my hand over his heart to mimic back his energy. Then, taking a deep breath, I grab my backpack and lead the way.

Everything is about to change in ways I'd never be able to imagine. The strangest part is feeling like I'm closing a chapter of my life that I'll never return to. I mean, how often will I really return to Mistwood Point? A few times a year to visit my mom? Things will never be the same.

A sudden wave of regret washes over me. My mom's not even here to say good-bye—not that I expected her to. To say she wasn't pleased with my decision would be an understatement.

My legs are shaky as I meander down the narrow stairs with Wade. The muted thud of my footsteps as they fall on the wood are haunting. Like they're nothing more than echoes of the past. When we reach the bottom, I take a quick glance around the only place I've known as home for the past thirteen years. The small living room to the left houses the bazillion books and DVDs my mom and I have spent countless hours perusing. To the right, the dining room table is empty, with the exception of a single placemat and table setting.

She's already put mine away.

"Ready?" Wade whispers, placing a hand on my shoulder.

I smile weakly and nod. Without looking back, I open the front door and walk out onto the porch—and into the unknown.

CHAPTER 7
WELCOME HOME, AUTUMN

The entire drive to Windhaven is a strange mixture of elation and despair. Leaving now is one of the hardest things I've ever done. But Wade was right about one thing—saying good-bye isn't my forte. It's like it's not even in my DNA. Had he not been the guiding force, encouraging me to go out the door, I'm almost certain I would have decided to stay in Mistwood Point.

However, the more distance I get, the more clarity washes over me. There are answers I need, and a part of me realizes there are mysteries I need to unravel. At the very least, I need to rebuild my relationship with my father.

When I pull up to the manor, darkness has descended and the landscape looks far more ominous than it did when I arrived the last time. Gone is the beautiful sunlight and inviting trees. Instead, I'm met with gnarly branches, moonlight, and abrupt, twisty turns along a long drive.

Lights are on inside the home, however, casting a warm glow across the cobblestone driveway and inviting me to come within. I put Blue into park and hop out. I take a deep, cool inhalation and stare at the moon. It's barely a sliver and about to disappear completely in the next day or two.

The angel statue in the middle of the circle still draws my attention and the deep grooves and shadows that are cast upon it by the landscape lighting. The evening hours certainly give it a haunting aura. Twisting around, I grab my backpack from the passenger seat and head up the stone stairs.

Lifting my hand to knock, I hold there with my hand in the air. Instead, I drop it to the handle and open the door. After all, if this is about to be my home, I guess I should start acting like it.

The massive door creaks open and I peer inside.

"Hello?" I call out. "Dad? Are you here?"

Silence greets my echo, but as I take a few steps into the main entry, Dad appears around the corner.

"Hi there, sweetie. I was wondering when you'd be here," he says, a bright smile gracing his face. It lights up all of his features and lifts my spirits. There were so many times when I wished I had a better relationship with him. Or when I wished I could understand what happened between him and my mom. Hopefully, now's that chance.

"Yeah, I, uh, it was hard to leave Wade and Mom. Harder than I expected—"

He nods. "I get it. Saying good-bye isn't easy."

"It really isn't," I agree. I take a deep breath to clear my energy, and I shuffle the backpack on my shoulder. "Well, I'm here now." I smile back at him, trying to emulate the same level of enthusiasm.

"Excellent," he says. "What would you like to do? Did you want a quick tour? Or do you just want to get settled for the night?"

"A tour would be great, actually. I didn't get the chance to see much the last time I was here," I say, casting my gaze around the space with curious eyes. Despite being here not long ago, it still looks vastly different from what I remember as a kid.

"Well, all right then. Let's do the tour," he beams.

I nod, waving my hand out in front of me.

Dad takes the lead, speaking over his shoulder like a proper tour guide. "So, I don't know how much about this house you remember...but the manor, it's been in our family for generations."

"I remember being here as a kid, but it definitely looks different."

"Yeah, when your mom and I had moved in, it had fallen into some disrepair over the years. I felt like it was my purpose, my mission, to restore it to the type of glory it deserved," he continues, as we make our way up the massive front staircase.

"You've done a lot from what I can tell," I say, unable to pick a single place to look. Everywhere is something to see—beautiful sconces, decorative woodworking, old pictures, and knickknacks. Each item looks like it was plucked out of another era, but still somehow manages to look like they belong.

"The original structure's still in here—it's just received a much-needed facelift."

"You've done a really beautiful job, Dad," I say, and I truly mean it. I can only imagine the kind of work this place has needed to look so good.

As we reach the second level, Dad turns left and follows the corridor around the corner, as the house curves into its U-shape. Ornate glass and bronze sconces hang from the walls in intermittent intervals, glowing dimly like candlelight. I can't help but feel like I've either walked into a fairy tale or some sort of horror movie.

"We'll start on this wing and work our way backward to your bedroom. Sound good?" Dad says, shooting me a grin from over his shoulder.

"Works for me," I nod.

"Well, up here is a lot of the miscellaneous rooms. Some are bedrooms, but others are just useful for the view," he begins. "The interior rooms, these ones to the right, overlook the pond and courtyard, so they're nice for reading, relaxing, and whatnot. Since it's pretty much pitch-black outside, it'll probably be better to take another look in the morning."

I nod in agreement.

The house is laid out more like a hotel than a home, with a good ten or so doors along both sides of the massive hallway. Most of the doors are closed, so we keep walking to the end and an enormous bay window with two massive chairs that face it.

"This faces the pond, right?" I say, pointing out the window.

Dad nods. "Indeed. The middle and both ends of the house face out toward the pond. Everything else faces the interior of the courtyard or out into the woods. So, the other wing looks almost exactly like this one. It's where my bedroom is and at the top of the stairs was my study. So, let me show you those quick before we head downstairs," he says, turning around and going back the way we came.

Old paintings and mirrors adorn the walls, like remnants of the past. None of it looks like something a modern day dad would buy, so I'm pretty sure they came with the house. As we pass the main stairwell, I stop to look out over the entryway. From the landing, the large chandelier somehow looks even bigger at this angle. Its light ricochets off in all sorts of directions and is absolutely stunning. Holding onto the railing, I lean forward, looking at the space from this near-bird's-eye view.

"Pretty, isn't it?" Dad says, walking back to me.

I nod. "It really is."

"You know, I wish... I never wanted you and your mother to leave. It's been hard living here all alone." His words are barely a whisper.

I turn to look at him over my shoulder.

"Dad, you don't need to—" I begin. "I mean, it's not that I'm not curious."

"You must have a lot of questions about what happened," he says, the middle of his light eyebrows tipping up. His blue eyes sparkle with emotion.

"I guess I do," I say, grabbing hold of the railing for support. I wasn't expecting to get into a heavy conversation so early, but since it's presented itself...

A strange chill rushes past me, making my neck hairs stand on end. I raise my hand to my neck, surprised by the sudden goose bumps flashing across my skin.

Dad's eyes widen, and he takes a step back.

"Um, you know, you must be hungry. Did you have supper?" he says, changing the subject and going down the stairway a few steps.

"I, uh," I begin, surprised by the shift in conversation.

"Come on, let's get a snack." Dad turns on his heel and practically bolts down the stairs.

Looking over my shoulder, I drop my hand and shake my head.

"Sure, but can I drop my backpack off in my bedroom first?" I call out.

"Oh, yeah, you bet. It's this way," he says, taking off in the lower level.

I race after him, trying to keep up as he turns right at the bottom of the stairs and takes a quick turn down the left corridor.

"Dad, is something wrong?" I ask, trying to keep up. "Did I say something wrong?"

"No, not at all. I just realized how late it is. I don't always keep track of time very well. Hazard of living alone, I guess."

We reach a bedroom door on the right and he stands off to the side, waiting for me to open it. As I walk up, memories start rushing at me. They are a strange mixture of mystery, happiness, and unpleasantness.

"Is this the same bedroom I had as a kid?" I ask as I open the door.

"Yes, I hope you don't mind. I thought maybe you'd be the most comfortable here," he says, standing by the opening.

I tip my head in acknowledgement as I walk inside.

The space is lit with small lamps all around the room. They sit on every flat surface—the dresser, the end tables, a large desk, and even a bookshelf in the left corner. Directly in front of us, a wooden king-size bed rests in the middle of the left wall. Beyond that, and straight ahead of us, is an enormous picture window alcove with a window seat. Just like he said, it's pitch-black outside, but thanks to my memories, I can imagine how beautiful it will be come morning. The view of the garden and trees is pretty well etched in my mind.

Along the upper edge of the wall, a shelf runs the entire circumference of the room. There are knickknacks and dolls, old toys from my childhood, and picture frames filled with images of me, Mom, and Dad during the first seven years of my life. In the far right corner, the door is open to a large walk-in closet.

I blink back my surprise, trying to form cohesive thoughts. It's beautiful and mysterious for sure, but anxiety washes through me and I can't seem to shake it.

"It's almost exactly like I remember it," I say breathlessly.

Dad grins broadly.

"Do you still like it?" he asks.

"Of course," I say, trying to hide my sudden trepidation. "What's not to love?"

"Good. Good...this was the room you picked out when you were little. You said it had the best view, so it was yours," he says, chuckling softly. "Well, how about we head to the kitchen and grab that snack?"

"Sure," I say, dropping my backpack on the bed and turning around. "Let's do it."

Leaving my bedroom behind, Dad stops at the doorway across the hall from my bedroom and points. "I don't know if you remember, but this is your bathroom, by the way. It's not attached or anything, but at least it's close."

I peek inside, marveling at the spaciousness of it. It's bigger than my bedroom back at Mom's. Large windows along the main wall are composed of frosted panes of glass, but have no curtains. In the middle of the room stands a big soaker tub with old-fashioned clawed feet. To the right is the toilet and large double-sink vanity.

"Whoever built this home certainly didn't do things small, did they?" I laugh.

"I'm kind of with them. Go big or go home, right?" Dad says, his eyes sparkling.

I smile, shaking my head as we step back into the hallway.

"You'll get used to it. It's really not as big as you might think. You're just used to your Mom's place and—"

I shoot him a sideways glance.

"Sorry, I wasn't meaning it in a bad way. N-nevermind, let's—here, let me show you the kitchen," he mutters.

Dad takes a sharp turn to the left. For a brief moment, the small hallway actually looks like something I would expect in any other ordinary home. But then we enter the spacious, open kitchen, and that pretense falls away.

"Holy crap, you could practically fit Mom's whole house in this kitchen," I say, my mouth agape. Angst sweeps through me unexpectedly. Why on earth would she have given all of this up? What was so bad between them? Most kids remember their parents fighting all the time, so a separation and divorce doesn't seem unusual. But for the life of me, I still have no idea what went wrong.

Dad rakes his fingertips at his eyebrow, but he walks across the expanse to a large double-doored refrigerator.

"We, uh—I didn't know what you'd like to eat or drink, so there's a lot to choose from in here," he says, gesturing for me to come closer. "If you want something else, just let me know. I'll make sure it gets added to our shopping list so James can pick it up."

"James?" I say, quirking an eyebrow.

His face darkens a bit as he says, "He's the housekeeper. You might not think it, but keeping this house running can be a lot of work. So I hired him to help out with some of the tasks."

I raise my eyebrows, surprised. Mom had to work full-time with two different jobs to make ends meet. And here Dad is, living in practically a mansion with a butler. Okay, *housekeeper*. In a weird way, it doesn't seem right. While Mom never complained about Dad or what he did or didn't do, a tiny well of resentment kicks me in the stomach.

Why didn't he help us out more?

"Inside there's juice, milk, soda—you name it," Dad says, pointing at the fridge and pulling me from my internal dialogue.

Opening it up, I stare into its depths for a moment, and reach for a can of Red Bull.

"That won't keep you up all night, will it? I hear it's got some kick," he offers.

I shrug. "Tomorrow's Sunday. It's not like I'll be going anywhere."

"Good point," he laughs. "Are you hungry? What do you want to eat? We have—"

"Actually, I should probably check in with Mom and Wade. I want to let them know I made it safely," I say.

"Right," he nods. "I suppose you'll need the Wi-Fi password. It's YBGon3. Wanna write that down?"

"Nah, I'll just add it to my phone now. Hang on," I say, taking my phone out of my pocket.

As soon as I get it entered and logged in, I lean against the edge of the breakfast bar, unable to truly grasp the sheer size of this place. I mean, I knew my Dad had a big house, but for some reason, I didn't realize that translated into having money. It's weird how when you're a kid, you don't think of those things. But now, it's like moving in with a secret superhero or something.

"Our last name isn't really Wayne, is it?" I blurt out.

Dad pulls up short and snickers. "Ha—no. Blackwood's as good as it gets, sweetie."

"Just checking," I say, grinning sheepishly.

The two of us stand in awkward silence for a moment before I crack open the Red Bull and take a sip.

"So," I start.

"So—" Dad repeats.

"I guess, I'll head back to my room and get situated."

"Of course. Yeah. You do what you need to do," Dad nods.

I cast a tiny wave his direction. "Thanks, Dad. See you in the morning."

"Night, sweetie," he says. I can tell he'd like me to stay a bit longer, though, because his smile doesn't quite reach his eyes.

I make my way out into the entryway and down the hallway leading to my room. Suddenly, the same cold sensation from earlier flashes over me. I shudder and turn to look over my shoulder.

This old house must be super drafty.

I turn back around, taking a few more steps, when I swear I hear a woman's voice whisper, "*Welcome home, Autumn.*"

CHAPTER 8

DO YOU THINK I'M NUTS?

Twisting back around, I see absolutely no one in the hallway. It's just me, myself, and I. Blinking away the shock, I clutch the ornate door handle to my bedroom and step inside. Two strides into the room, I place my Red Bull on the closest nightstand and sit down on the cushy bed. I stare out into the dim light of the hallway.

Did I just hear what I thought I heard?

"Maybe you need sleep more than you thought, Autumn," I whisper, eyeing the Red Bull with suspicion.

Shaking away the strangeness, I pull my phone out of my pocket and text Mom.

I made it in one piece. Getting ready for bed. Talk tomorrow. Love you. <3

She's probably fast asleep by now. It's well past 11:00 p.m. and the likelihood she'd still be up is next to nil. If there's one thing Mom doesn't mess with, it's her sleep.

Before I call Wade, I walk over to my backpack and pull out my charger. If past conversations have any bearing, there's a good chance our call will go on all night—even if we're just sleeping. So, it's imperative to have it charging. I plug it into the outlet beside the bed and pull out the nightshirt I packed in my backpack. Tomorrow, I'll grab the rest of my stuff from Blue. After what just happened in the hallway, there's no way I'm wandering outside to my vehicle now.

Clutching the shirt to my chest, my eyes flit around the room.

Despite the strange well of anxiety cropping up, the room isn't half bad. A little old-fashioned, maybe, but nothing some fresh paint or new decorations couldn't cure. I mean, I'm not seven anymore.

I walk over to the large oak desk on the right hand side and sit down in the plush chair. Clearly meant to be more for a study than a bedroom, it doesn't have the kind of lumbar support a person would need if they were doing homework or something on a computer. But it sure is comfy.

Running my fingertips along the polished wood surface of the desk, I take a deep breath and try to relax. This is not at all what I was expecting.

Granted, I'm not entirely sure what I expected, so maybe that's all this is.

Somewhere in my gut, there's a strange feeling about this room, and I just can't shake it. I remember hating it here. Hating the room, hating being stuck here. But now that I look at it with fresh eyes, it *is* really a nice room. It's got a lot of character, even if it's got an old-school vibe.

I get undressed and slide into the tank top I like to sleep in. When I pull my phone out again, upon closer inspection, there are three texts from Wade.

Hey Dru~ watching you go was the worst. But trust me, it's gonna be great. I hope things go better for you than you expect. Thinking about you. ~Angel

I was thinking...isn't this how things started in Twilight? Girl being shipped off to live with her dad? Maybe I should call you Bella. Too geeky? Come to think of it, probably not any more than Dru. Ha! ;-)

So, you there yet? I hope everything's okay. Call me when you're in. Can't wait to hear from you, beautiful. Miss you already. <3

My heart both soars and constricts. He's such a nut, but adorably so. And I totally miss him already.

I walk around the room, flicking off all the lights except the one right next to the bed. Then I set the phone on the stand and pull up his name. It only rings once before Wade answers.

"Hey there, gorgeous," he beams, leaning back in his chair. His dark hair is disheveled, like I just pulled him out of bed. His exposed upper chest muscles flex as he pulls his legs into a cross-legged position.

A small gasp escapes my lips before I can stop myself.

"You okay?" Concern sweeps across his features as he leans in closer to the screen.

"Yeah, oh yeah. Just *fine*," I say, melting internally and grinning. It's a cheesy *oh my god he's got great pecs* kinda grin. But I can't help it.

"Excellent," he nods. "So, how was the drive? Everything go okay with your dad?"

"Yeah, the drive went fine, I guess. I mean, I had to crank some music and get my mind off of things. You know?"

"I get it. It was really hard seeing you go," he says, his eyebrows tipping up in the middle.

"Bet it was harder leaving," I say with a smirk. "On the upside, Dad's been great. I can't wait for you to see this place, too. It's massive—way bigger than I remember."

"Did he add on to it or something?"

"Yeah, I guess? Plus it's an old manor home. They liked to build big back in the day," I say. "But it feels like I just moved into Hogwarts."

"Oh, we're busting out the nerdery now. I like it." Wade grins, his eyes lighting with amusement.

I narrow my eyes and stick out my tongue. Of course, I knew he'd love it, though.

He chuckles. "I'm looking forward to seeing it, too. Wonder which house I'll be sorted into."

"Oh, you're definitely a Hufflepuff." I chuckle.

"Pft." He laughs, resting back in his chair again with his arms behind his head.

I sigh wistfully. "How's your grandpa doing?" I ask, trying to drag my mind anywhere besides the gutter.

"He's doing okay. This afternoon, he even sat up and ate something. So, that was good," Wade says, trying to let optimism light his features. But there's a hint of sadness hidden in his eyes.

"That's good. Did he recognize you today?" I ask.

"No, not really. He still thinks I'm my dad," Wade says, shrugging.

"Really? I'm sorry, Wade. That must be hard. Isn't that a little weird for you?"

"It was at first, but I'm kinda used to it now," he says, keeping his expression neutral.

My lips press into a thin line as I try to imagine taking care of someone who didn't know who I was.

"That's gotta be a little hard, though, right? I mean, with your dad being—"

Wade shrugs, dropping his hands to his lap. "I just think of it as a job and ignore the weird emotional stuff. Does that seem cold?" A quizzical expression blossoms across his features.

"I don't know. I guess not. Then again, it's still hard to think of you as the personal care assistant...*type*?"

"There's a PCA *type*?"

"Definitely," I say sternly.

"All right, you have me curious. What is a PCA type?" His eyes narrow and he tilts his head slightly.

"Big burly dude with a nurse's uniform?" I offer.

"Nice," he snorts. "Do I have to have a big wart on my chin and hair poking out, too?"

A laugh bursts from my lips and I can't help but shake my head. "So, I don't think I ever asked you... Where did you work before taking on your grandpa, then? Hot Topic? Forever 21? Oooh, I know—it was one of those dorky board game shops that sell Dungeons and Dragons stuff and hoards of dice?" I say, flicking my tongue to the roof of my mouth.

He bends in close to the screen, then, blinking slowly, he says, "The bookstore, sweet thing."

My eyes raise to the ceiling as I nod. "Oh, right. *Bookstore*. I forget about those sometimes. Mistwood Point never had a good one. They all went the way of the dinosaur when ebooks came about."

"Hey now, Mistwood has the Alcove. Though, in saying that, I think they sell more used books and incense than anything hitting the market in the past ten years."

I nod with mock seriousness. "And don't forget, they do aura readings every third Saturday."

He chuckles. "That, too."

Crossing my legs under the covers, I sit up a bit straighter. "Well, when you get a few free moments tomorrow, sneak me a call. Okay? I'm sure I'll be dying for some company after a full day alone in this enormous house with my dad."

"I will be both ready and willing. You can count on it," he says, his signature wink making its first appearance for the night.

My cheeks flush. He's so dang sexy without even trying.

"What time do you start your day tomorrow?" I ask, clearing my throat.

"Seven-thirty. Grandpa needs to take his meds and I'll have to check his catheter."

"Fun times," I say, flicking my eyes to the clock on the wall. "Wade, it's almost midnight. You better get your ass to bed."

"Psh. It's no big. As long as I get a few hours of sleep, I'll be fine," Wade says with a smirk.

I shake my head. "Huh-uh. Absolutely not. I won't be the reason you slept through your alarm and your grandpa missed his catheter change. Get to bed. We can talk more tomorrow."

"Really, it's no big deal. I don't mind," he protests. "How about—how about you just go about your business and I'll go lie down. We can just, I dunno, fall asleep together?"

"That might be the sweetest, weirdest thing you've said to me," I say, running my fingertips over my forehead.

"Is that a yes?" he asks, his face brightening.

"Fine, but you better go to sleep. No trying to chitchat your way outta this. Otherwise, I'm gonna tough love you by hanging up," I say, narrowing my eyes and pointing a finger at the screen.

"Ugh, fine," he says. It's almost a pout, but not really. Getting up from his chair, he lifts his laptop and brings it to the nightstand beside his bed. For a moment, he's out of view as I hear some clothing drop to the floor.

A shiver skitters through me as my mind goes into overactive-imagination mode. Placing both hands over my mouth, I tap the side of my cheek with my fingertips.

The fabric on his bed pulls back and he jumps into bed like the Flash. I didn't catch anything definitive, but I'm pretty sure he was naked.

Oh my god.

He props himself up onto his right arm and leans into the camera. "Night, Dru. I'll be thinking about you. If I don't get to see you in the morning, I hope you have a great day tomorrow."

"Thanks, *Angel.* You, too. Hope your grandpa has a good day tomorrow," I say, blowing him a kiss. "Hope he remembers it's you. Now, get some sleep."

He blows a kiss back, then leans deep into the pillow. Rolling onto his side, he faces the camera, grinning like a fool.

I do the same, lying down so I can face the camera. I don't know how I happened to get so lucky, but I really am.

I sigh contently.

"You are so beautiful, you know that?" Wade whispers.

"Shhhh...no talking," I say, narrowing my eyes. Despite myself, my heart flutters. "But thank you."

Silence floods the space for a moment.

"One last thing, I promise," he says, shifting up onto his elbow. "I'm looking forward to going to the Witching Stick orientation with you next week. It should be a lot of fun."

"I'm looking forward to it, too. And stop trying to sneak

your way out of sleeping. I'm on to you, mister."

Somewhere in the darkness beyond the foot of my bed, a weird scratching noise pulls me from the screen. I peer to the other side of the room with wide eyes.

"Everything okay?" Wade asks, worry painting his tone.

"I—there was just a weird scratching noise," I mutter, still trying to look for the source.

"It's an old house. It's probably just a mouse or bat or something."

That makes total sense. Not that it makes me any happier.

I shudder and make a face. "Yeah, you're probably right. I just..."

"What?"

"It sounds completely dorky, but I've had a couple of weird experiences since I've been here. I guess I'm just being jumpy because it's all new," I say, returning my gaze to the screen.

"Weird how?" he asks, quirking an eyebrow.

"They're nothing, really. Probably just my overactive imagination."

"Indulge me, would you, woman?" he says, propping up further and allowing the blanket to fall down to his waist.

I sigh internally. A couple more minutes of talking couldn't hurt...

"Well, when I was upstairs, there was a strange cold pocket that sent a chill straight through me. Dad was there when it happened, and he got really weird. Like, changed the subject abruptly and everything. Then..."

I think back to the voice and I shake my head. It's ridiculous. I'd sound completely mental.

"Then...?" he prompts.

"It's nothing really. You'll think I'm nuts."

"Woman, I live with a man who thinks I'm my father. I seriously doubt that," he says, lowering his eyebrows.

"It sounds completely crazy out loud, but before I came in here to call you, I swear I heard a woman's voice," I say, scrunching my face.

"Like, your dad has a woman in the house and hasn't told you?" Wade asks, his eyes wide.

I shake my head and narrow my eyes. "Nah. I don't think so."

"Are you sure?"

"Pretty sure," I nod. "She said, 'Welcome home, Autumn.'"

Wade's lips part, then close again. His eyes dart downward as he thinks. "So, what? You think there's a ghost?"

"Don't be ridiculous. Ghosts aren't real. But I am a little concerned about my mental health. There's a lot I haven't dealt with from my past and I wonder if maybe I'm seeing or hearing strange things that aren't really there."

"I don't think so. I know you're very science-minded, but you also live in a supernatural world. You're going to a supernatural school for godsake. Is it really that unheard of to think you might have ghosts?"

"Honestly, I don't know. Growing up, my mom forbade me to look into the supernatural. She always pointed me to scientific theory and the explainable. It's part of the reason I wanted to be a forensic scientist. I wanted to be able to understand death, not make excuses for it. Besides, have you ever seen a ghost?" I ask, narrowing my eyes.

Wade shakes his head. "Well, no, but I believe they exist."

"How can you be so sure?" I snicker.

Wade's eyes go distant and a thoughtful expression paints

itself across his face. "Let's just say, in my line of work, it's almost part of the job."

"That makes no sense," I say.

"It would if you've seen what I have," Wade says, laughing softly.

"What? What's so funny?" I say incredulously.

With a mischievous twinkle in his eye, he says, "Maybe you really *did* move to Hogwarts."

CHAPTER 9
THE WITCHING STICK

Extremely loud calls of crows echo from somewhere nearby. My eyelids flutter open and take in the morning light as it streams into my bedroom through the large window. Rolling over to my side, I lazily stare into the blue expanse beyond the glass. Red, gold, and green leaves flutter at the edges of the panes, and a smile slides across my lips. I've had a week to get used to this view and it still hasn't gotten old. Instead, I find each day I'm more and more fascinated by the beauty of this place.

My heart flutters in my chest. Wade will be here soon so we can go to the Witching Stick orientation together.

Despite the craziness from the first night, everything since has been completely and utterly ordinary. If anything, I feel foolish for even allowing myself to get freaked out or think there was something more going on. Instead, I probably just needed a good night's rest and to get over my anxiety over the move.

Reaching for my phone, I tap to open the text message left by Wade an hour ago.

Have I told you, you're beautiful when you sleep? I'm leaving now. See you soon. xxx

Blushing slightly, my right hand floats to my cheek. I type out a reply quickly.

Hey, Angel. Thinking of you. <3 Drive safe, okay? Can't wait to see you! PS—> You're cute when you sleep, too. ;)

I hit send, shut off the screen, and clutch the phone to my chest as I fall back into my pillow. A contented sigh escapes my lips and I find myself grinning like a lunatic.

The crows caw again, drawing my attention back to the window.

Throwing my feet over the side of the bed, I cast my blankets aside and stand up. I walk over to the window and take a seat on the large cushions of the window seat. The wind blows against the branches in the courtyard, and for a while, I'm mesmerized by their dance.

In the distance, fog rolls off the pond, reaching its tendrils toward the sky. I find myself smiling broadly but my eyes land on a dark figure standing well beyond the confines of the courtyard. Bending toward the window, I narrow my gaze. As if sensing me, the figure turns toward the house. His face is shrouded by the fog, but it's enough to make my blood run cold.

Without thought, I head over to my dresser and pull on a pair of jeans and a sweatshirt. I throw on a pair of hiking boots, slide my phone in my pocket, and run down the hall. The house is eerily quiet, so I make my way through the kitchen to the closest door I know that leads to the courtyard.

Flinging it open, I race out into the crisp autumn air. The crows continue to call, as if tattling on the intruder and hoping he gets caught.

My heart thumps loudly in my ears as I make my way through the fall splendor. From this vantage point, the pond is almost obscured by the smaller trees and shrubbery. Keeping my eyes trained on the area I last saw the figure, the cold air cracks in my lungs as I race to the pond's edge.

"Hey—hello? Who's out here?" I call out when I think I'd be within earshot.

I freeze, even holding my breath so I can hear better.

The only response is the growing cacophony from the crows.

Walking out to the small dock area, my eyes sweep across the shoreline, but other than two swans swimming peacefully at the edge, there's nothing here.

Exhaling slowing, I walk the shoreline to the spot where I saw the figure. Bending down, the grass is flattened and the semi-frozen dew is gone. I glance up, surveying the nearby trees and bushes, but there's no sign of footsteps having traveled anywhere else. It's like whoever was here simply up and vanished.

Chills rush up my spine, and my phone vibrates in my pocket, making me squeal out loud. Pulling it from my pocket, I'm relieved to see Wade's smiling face shine back at me with his call.

"Hello?" I answer, my voice shaking more than I'd like.

"Hey there, beautiful. I think I'm nearly there. You almost ready to head out?"

Clearing my throat, I glance around one more time and

walk toward the manor. "Uh, yeah, almost. How long until you're here?"

"Siri says ten minutes. So, probably five?" he laughs.

"Okay, I'll be ready. See ya in a few."

Hanging up, I race to the house so I can run to the bathroom and freshen up.

When I enter the house, Dad is still nowhere to be found, so I beeline to the bathroom. In record time, I've done everything I need to do and head back to the front of the manor just as there's a knock on the front door.

Taking a deep breath, I straighten my shoulders. Suddenly self-conscious, I step back to look myself over in the large entryway mirror, tousling my crazy auburn hair a bit and pinching my cheeks so I don't look like death warmed over.

Turning back to the door, I fling it open. "Hey there," I say, unable to stop the massive grin spreading across my lips at the sight of him.

His dark hair blazes with red and gold streaks in the morning sunlight and just seeing him threatens to melt me into a puddle at his feet.

"Wow, this house...it's something," Wade says, raising his eyebrows. His eyes sparkle mischievously as he adds. "But if it's not Hogwarts, are we sure it's not the Winchester mansion?"

I roll my eyes, pulling him inside. "No, it's just the Blackwood Manor, smartass. But in honor of your observation, I will say, good pop culture commentary. Did you just watch the horror film?"

"Actually, no. I've visited it in person, thank you very much. It's creepy. And totally awesome."

"Well, all right, then," I say, totally impressed.

"Ready to embrace the Witching Stick?" he asks, trying hard not to stare into the depths of the house.

"Sure, but do you want a quick tour before we head out?" I ask, knowing full well what the answer will be.

"Oh, god, yes," he purrs, relaxing his shoulders and having a look around.

"All right, come on," I laugh, linking my arm in his. After a quick tour through the rest of the manor, I finally stop outside my bedroom door.

"And this...is my room," I say, leaning my back against the heavy wood with my hand resting on the knob behind me.

Wade steps forward so he's directly in front of me. His silver eyes are almost crowded out by the intensity of his pupils. Heat rolls off of him and it takes all of my strength to stay put and not open the door.

"Well, are you going to show me?" he finally asks, leaning in close.

I grin and tilt my head slightly to the side—an offering as I consider.

He takes the hint, gently placing his lips on the space just under my ear. "Pretty please?" he whispers against my skin.

Sighing with contentment and more than a little longing, I twist the knob and open the door. We step in together and he walks into the middle of the space with a certain air of satisfaction.

"So, this is where you spend your time now, is it?" he says, circling the room. He walks over to my dresser, his fingertips grazing one of the red petals from a large floral arrangement of roses Wade had delivered the other day.

"Well, thankfully not as much as I used to, but yes." I nod.

"Used to?"

"Long, boring story," I say, waving my hand and trying to avoid casting my gaze to the bed.

Orientation...must get to orientation...

"You'll tell me, though, right?" he asks, turning back

to me.

"If you have trouble sleeping," I tip my head tersely, "then sure."

"Excellent," he says, walking to me and offering up his bent arm. "Shall we, then?"

My eyes fall one last time on my bed and take hold of his arm. With a little less pep, I lead us back to where we started. Wade's black Impala is parked in the loop, right behind Big Blue.

He tips his chin toward the statue in the middle of the loop. "Interesting decor your dad has there. Don't you think?"

"I know, right? I kinda like it though," I say, walking down the steps.

Wade's eyes flick back to the weeping angel one more time. Then his hand sweeps out toward our two vehicles. "Which carriage would you like to take, my lady?"

I chuckle. "Well, seeing as this is my new town and I need to learn the way, I'll drive."

Hurrying out in front of me, Wade opens my door and waits for me to sit down before he closes it. Then he runs back around to the passenger side and hops in.

"Thank you, sir," I say, putting the keys into the ignition and firing up the engine.

"Of course." He tips his head curtly.

Placing my phone on the in-dash holder, I punch in the coordinates to get us to the school. Once they're up, I put the SUV in drive and head out. For the most part, the scenery is nothing more than trees, rolling hills, and wide open roads. As we enter town, older houses with a mix of Georgian and Victorian flare begin to scatter the roads in increasing density. Other buildings begin to come into view, as well. The library, a bar, a pizza joint, two churches, and a burger place called the Bourbon Room. It takes us roughly fifteen minutes to reach Windhaven Academy and as we enter the parking lot, it's clear the school is what dominates this town.

The parking lot itself extends the length of a couple of football fields put together. All around us, people are rushing in and out of the gothic-looking building, adorned with old stones, covered with red ivy. As we come to a stop, I can't help but take in the looks on people's faces. Rather than excitement or nervousness, most of them have wide eyes as they use large gestures.

"Wow, these supernatural folks take orientation really seriously around here," Wade mutters, eyeing them as well.

"I don't think this is normal. Do you see their faces? They're scared," I say.

"Of what? Finding out what lessons they have?"

I shrug. "Only one way to find out."

Both of us kick open our doors and make our way toward the building. Everyone is engaged with someone else, but the snippets of conversation I catch as we pass by are all the same.

"...missing..."

"...creature..."

"...water..."

"...could it be back?"

I don't even have time to take in the grandeur of the academy, which, even in my periphery is impressive. As we enter the wide main hall of the school, a man wearing a suit and tie is ushering people back out the door. "Sorry, everyone. This year's Witching Stick has been canceled because of what's happened. Please know we'll be doing our best to get everyone situated as soon as we can."

Wade turns to me with alarm written across his face. "What do you think happened?"

I shake my head. "I don't know. Let's go ask."

Together, we walk up to the man in the suit.

"Excuse me," I begin.

The man's arms are splayed out wide as he flicks his wrists and tries to get everyone to stay on the other side of him.

"You need to go home, Miss. Things aren't safe right now," he says.

"What's happened?" Wade interjects.

"Two ten-year-olds have gone missing near our lake. We need all available faculty to use their gifts in order to help us search for them," he says.

"Professor Lambert, we need you out back, sir," a woman with short, curly blond hair says, tapping him on the shoulder.

"Will you excuse me?" Professor Lambert says, turning and heading down the hall.

The blond-haired woman remains behind, taking up the role he vacated.

"You need to head home," she says as her dark brown eyes fall on us.

"Do you think the kids are okay?" I ask, trying to wrap my head around all the confusion.

"We have our best trackers on this. That's all you need to know for now. Please, both of you, head home. I'm sure this will all be resolved before school on Monday."

"Come on, Dru, let's go," Wade says, wrapping his arm around my shoulder and leading me down the hallway.

The number of people at the school has dwindled, but those who are still here run back and forth as if they don't know what direction to head.

"Talk about a weird orientation," I mutter as we leave the main entrance hall.

"I'm sure it will all get worked out," Wade offers.

I shake my head. "If they need the teachers, do you think

it's a supernatural problem?"

"Maybe? I suppose that would make sense." Wade agrees.

My mind whirls through different scenarios as I try to come to a conclusion of what could be happening. My mind instantly goes into bleak.

Did the children drown? And if they did, what could any of the teachers do about it?

"Don't let this freak you out. I'm sure it's all just a precaution. Okay?" Wade says, intertwining his hand with mine as we walk through the parking lot.

"I'm trying not to. It's just so weird. You know?"

"I totally get it," Wade nods. "Dang, I was looking forward to learning what they think your superpowers were, too. I mean, what if you can summon storms or zap things with your mind? How cool would that be?"

I shoot him a sideways glance.

"Sorry, I know...you're worried. I was just trying to lighten the mood," he says, grinning sheepishly.

As we get close to where we parked, a guy with spikey white-blond hair pops up from the back end of my vehicle. When he sees us, he starts running into the tree line. Instantly, alarm bells go off in my head and I start running after him.

What if he's involved with whatever is going on?

"Hey—hey, what were you doing?" I yell.

Wade's on my heels, keeping up as if an impromptu sprint after a fiasco like today's orientation is no big deal. I race past my SUV, but the white-blond guy bounds into the tree line and I lose sight of him completely. Twisting back to Wade and Blue, I get a good glimpse of what the guy must have been doing.

Etched into the paint of Blue are the words: *veritas vos liberabit.*

CHAPTER 10
VERITAS VOS LIBERABIT

Thrusting open my bedroom door, I stomp over to my desk and drop into the chair. Flipping up the lid to my laptop, I immediately fire up Google.

"Don't be too upset. I'm sure it's nothing bad, Autumn," Wade offers, placing a hand on my shoulder as I type feverishly.

I tap the edge of the desk, waiting for the page to load. "And maybe you're right. But who knows in this town? I mean, who does that sort of thing? You know? Especially with what just happened at the Witching Stick. What if it's a clue to the missing girls?"

"Maybe it was just some jerk who was drunk and thought he was being funny? I mean, it's still a college."

"I suppose," I nod, considering.

After searching through a few of the Google results, I point to the screen and lean back in my chair, more confused than ever.

Wade leans in, narrowing his gaze. "The truth shall set you free?"

"Yeah, what the hell?" I mutter, anxiety and anger welling

up inside me. "Why would anyone bother keying something like that on my vehicle?"

"Looks like it's also the motto for a bunch of colleges, but none of them are nearby. It's not Windhaven Academy's either," Wade says, confusion mirroring back at me.

I shrug. "Right? At least I feel a little better knowing what it says."

"I hate to ask, but...is there anything you've been hiding? I mean, something that you'd be targeted for?" Wade says, his face crumpling.

Shaking my head, I push away from the desk. "No, not even remotely. Until I got the invite to Windhaven Academy, I've led the most vanilla life ever."

Wade breathes out slowly through his nose. "Well, until you can find the guy who did it, anything we come up with is all just speculation. So, what do you want to do? Go hunt him down? Do some sniffing around town?"

I chew on my lower lip for a moment. If we go out, there's a good chance it will go nowhere. I don't know anyone in this town yet and the likelihood of finding the guy right now is pretty damn low. Plus, there's the whole issue with the missing kids. If there's something out there, something mystical or supernatural, I don't want to get caught up in it. Or worse yet, be a suspect because we're roaming around when we've been told to go home.

"I never got to tell you," I say, glancing up and looking into his concerned gaze. "Before you showed up today, I thought I saw someone out by the pond."

Wade takes a seat on the edge of the bed, placing his elbows on his knees, and clasping his hands. "Okay..."

I stand up, pacing. "What if...what if maybe he had something to do with the missing kids?"

"Wait a minute. I'm all for a good conspiracy theory, but

that's taking a pretty big leap. I mean, what would even give you that idea?"

"I've never seen him before. He looked"—I break off, thinking back to the hidden, almost ghoulish appearance—"*off*. Like he was out of sorts. Ripped-up clothes. I couldn't really see his face. Then when I went outside, he was gone."

"Well, you haven't been here long, so everyone would be new to you. Maybe they were just homeless?" Wade says. "Didn't your dad say he has a housekeeper? What if it was him?"

I think on that for a moment. There's a sliver of truth in there, since I haven't met James yet. However, I doubt he'd be dressed like that. Shaking my head, I continue to pace. "No, I don't think so. Why would he look like he was homeless? I just keep thinking about the fragments of stuff I was hearing at the school. About the water and creature..."

"Well, do you want to take it to the police? See if the guy matches the description of whatever they're looking for?"

My fingertips fly to my face and I blow out a puff of air. "I sound ridiculous, don't I?"

"No, not at all. Something weird is definitely going on. I get it. You're just trying to make sense," he says, standing up and taking me into his arms.

"No, I sound crazy," I say, running my fingertips over my forehead. I take a deep inhalation and close my eyes. "Maybe you're right. We should just chill here. Enjoy our night together and come Monday, if it seems relevant, then I'll say something."

"That sounds like an excellent plan," Wade says, pulling me closer. "With that all resolved, what do you think we should do next?"

"Well, I could show you where I saw the creepy dude?" I say, playing coy.

Wade pauses a moment. "We could, but it's sorta not what I had in mind."

I glance up into his mischievous eyes. "And just what did you have in mind, sir?"

His eyebrows make their way toward his hairline and he grins. "For starters, I was hoping to meet your dad..."

"Oh, right. My dad," I say, nodding. That was so not what I thought he was implying. "We can go hunt for him. I would think he'd be home."

Wade kisses the top of my head and takes a step back. "Lead the way, beautiful."

We make our way out of my bedroom, down the hall, and into the main entry. With the exception of the large grandfather clock chiming noon, the house has settled into relative silence.

"Dad? Are you here?" I call out, hoping the central location will broadcast far enough.

Wade tips his head, listening.

"Hmm, strange," I mutter, looking around the space. "He's always here somewhere."

I walk over to the antiquated intercom station in the main entry, but when I push the button, all I get is static.

"So much for that," Wade laughs. "Ya gotta love old technology."

"Right? It worked the other day when Dad showed it to me. Oh, well, I guess I'll take it as a sign we're meant to grab a bite to eat and just spend some quality time together instead," I say, walking past Wade and heading toward the kitchen.

After a quick lunch comprising turkey sandwiches and Red Bull, we find ourselves back in my bedroom.

"I'm kinda bummed I haven't been able to meet your dad yet. On the upside, it looks like we have the house to ourselves," Wade says, walking over to the window seat. He pats the space beside him and I drop into the cushy pillows and cross my legs.

"Looks like," I nod.

"What should two young college kids do with such an opportunity? Skinny dip in the pond? Race around the house naked?" Wade chuckles, his arms splaying out to suggest the whole of the house.

"Hmmm...seems like you have nakedness on the mind, Mr. Hoffman," I say, quirking an eyebrow, as my lips slide into a smirk.

I'm both elated about that prospect, but also hella nervous. It's been over a year since I was alone with a guy I liked and things got hot and heavy. But damn, I could use the distraction and I'd be kidding myself if I hadn't been daydreaming about what it would be like to feel his body against mine.

Wade's eyebrows tug down in mock seriousness. "Hmmm, fascinating. I hadn't noticed until you pointed it out."

"Sure, sure..." I tease.

Without giving him an opening to redirect, I bend in, placing my lips against his. He tastes like a mixture of sweet and savory—a remnant from our lunch, but his intoxicating scent of sandalwood and soap is what melts me.

A rumble moves through his chest and he pushes himself closer, taking my face in his hands. My lips burn from the intensity, yet I can't help but respond with the same. His tongue sweeps across my lower lip and there's not a single drop of reservation holding me back. Parting open my mouth, his tongue entwines with mine, bringing a rush of excitement right along with it.

Wade's hands slowly drop from my face, to my collarbones, resting there for a moment and sending tendrils of desire coursing through my upper body. In a swift movement, he wraps his arms around me, lifting me from my cross-legged position on the window seat and carrying me over to the bed. I let out a squeal of surprise, groping at his shoulders to hang on. His back muscles move underneath his dark t-shirt and all I can think about is how much I want to be skin on skin. My thoughts leave the building entirely as I tug at the fabric, lifting it up, then over his head. He shakes himself out of the shirt and I flick it to the floor. For a brief moment, he stands there between my legs, looking like a Greek God and reflecting the same desire consuming my every cell.

His eyelids blink slowly, opening to half-cover his silver slivers.

"I don't know how I got so incredibly lucky to find you, Autumn," he whispers, shaking his head.

I prop up on the backs of my forearms, but he bends in, taking my face in his hands again, his lips crushing down on mine. Dropping back, I pull him to me, straddling him between my legs. I dance my fingertips along his upper back and his torso pulses forward.

My hands make their way from his upper back to his waist. I loop my fingertips into the inner edge of his jeans, running them between the fabric and his skin. He arches up, pulling his body from mine for a moment. His dreamy eyes lock with mine and I take the opportunity to unbutton his jeans.

He inhales sharply, holds the breath for a beat, then exhales slowly. Without a word, he reaches for my top. Lifting it at my waist, he slides his hands inside and pulls the shirt over my head. Before I can make an attempt at anything else, his mouth traces a trail along my collarbones and make their way down my cleavage.

His left hand traces my right side, teasing at the purple

lace fabric of my bra. My breath hitches and I arch my back slightly, wishing he'd go there—do what he wants. Consume me.

Suddenly, I'm ripped from the momentum of desire as an insanely loud crash makes us jump apart. Wade stands back, his eyes surveying the room.

"What in the..." I say, clutching at my heart and sitting bolt upright on the bed.

Beside my dresser, the large vase of roses is sprawled across the floor. Shards of glass, pools of water, and bits of blood-red roses are everywhere.

"Shit," I say, racing to the destruction and trying to collect the broken fragments of glass into one of the larger pieces. "How did this happen?"

"Maybe it was just too close to the edge? Do you have a broom, Autumn?" Wade asks, bringing over the small garbage bin by the door.

"I—I think so," I say, pulling my hair back so I can see better. "It would be in one of the pantries in the kitchen."

"Okay, I'll find it. Be right back," he says, buttoning up his jeans and walking out of the room shirtless.

Rattled, but starting to calm down, I pick up one of the roses and twirl it in my fingertips. Petals hang from odd angles and some of the leaves are broken and dangling from the stem. Staring at it a moment, I'm mesmerized by its beauty, even knowing now that it will never be the same. I wish I had paid closer attention to where I'd placed the vase. It's a shame to see something so beautiful wasted before its time.

Suddenly, as if sensing my desire for it to be the way it was, the petals begin to lift and the leaves right themselves. I blink back my surprise and set the rose to the side, stacking each of them together. Perhaps I'll be able to salvage them and put them in a new vase.

I move on, picking up as much glass as possible. It's everywhere. Thank goodness the floor is mostly wooden. It should make cleanup a lot easier. When I've picked up as much as I can, I take a deep breath and sit down on my haunches.

Things were intense there for a hot minute, but I feel like the moment has unfortunately passed. Standing up, I tug on my shirt and sit back down on the edge of the bed.

Despite the pristine nature of the room, and the damn near identical appearance from when I was a kid, a seam of wallpaper beside the dresser is slightly beveled. Thanks to its age, the wallpaper has clearly seen better days, and it's finally unhinging itself. Perhaps the added moisture from the vase breaking had something to do with it?

Walking back to the scene, I'm careful not to step in the mess on the floor. I reach forward, my fingertips trailing the edge of the wallpaper. A small rip along the seam has separated with time. I wouldn't have even given it a second thought, only...there's a glint of metal behind the paper façade. It's just a tiny thing, really, but it's enough to capture my attention.

Cocking my head to the side, I lean in closer, but it's hard to get a good look with everything in front of it. I push the dresser a little more to the right so I can sidestep the mess. Then I bend down and have a closer look. Again, I run my fingertips along the slightly frayed edge of the wallpaper and debate whether or not I should pull it back completely.

Glancing over my shoulder, I half expect Wade to come back in.

Confused, I gently pull back the paper as far as I dare.

"What in the world...?" I whisper, leaning in to get a better look.

Beneath the delicate wallpaper is the plate to what looks like a super-old door handle. The bronze-looking plate has an antique vibe and it's unlike any of the other handles in the house. Ripping the paper so I can see the handle clearly, I stick my fingertip in the gaping hole where the doorknob should be.

"Found the broom and dustpan," Wade says, reentering the room. "Did you know, this house has way too many cubby holes, pantries, and cupboards?"

Letting out a squeak, I jump at the sound of his voice, twisting around to face him.

"Well, that was both adorable and slightly hilarious," he says, chuckling. "Whatcha find there?"

He walks over to me in only a few big steps.

"I'm not sure..." I say, trying to cram my heart back into its proper place.

Wade drops the broom on the floor, bending in to have a look. "Is it a door?" He twists back around to look at me.

I nod. "Looks that way to me, too."

"Weird. Why on earth would it be hidden?" he asks. "Did you know it was here?"

"I had no idea," I say, shaking my head and pressing the back of my thumb to my lips.

"Wonder where the handle is," Wade says, echoing my own thoughts.

My heartbeat thumps in my chest. "I don't know that one, either."

More importantly, where does it lead?

CHAPTER 11

FIRST DAY OF SCHOOL & OTHER STRANGE THINGS

The first day of school arrives before I know it, and despite the alarm clock on my phone going off as planned, I still find myself running late.

Go figure.

You'd think of all the days to be wired and anxious, the first day in a new school full of supernatural beings would be it. But with all the questions circling about the house, the missing kids, not to mention Wade's visit and all the complexity he brings to my emotions, I haven't really had time to worry about it.

Grabbing a coffee to go in my travel mug, I race out the door without even trying to find Dad so I can say good-bye.

I make it to Windhaven Academy in under twelve minutes, but I'm still five minutes late to the start of my first class. Hopefully, they'll cut new students a little bit of slack on their first day.

Exiting my driver's seat, I make my way to the front of the building as quickly as my feet will carry me. The crisp autumn air rushes at me and I breathe it all in as I race to certain doom. I'm not the only one coming and going, but I feel like I'm the only one who doesn't really belong. After the fiasco at the Witching Stick orientation, I never got to undergo the Divining Rod part, which was supposed to tell me what kind of supernatural being I am. Or at least point me in a direction. With a little luck, things will be sorted out in the next few hours.

In all honesty, Wade's not the only one dying to know what kind of powers I may have.

Staring at the façade of the old building, I admire the old-fashioned gargoyles and embellishments that adorn the outside of the school. I hadn't noticed them the other day, but they add a certain level of mystique to the whole academic process here in Windhaven. In a way, it almost reminds me of being back in the old part of Mistwood's cemetery. It had all sorts of statues, too.

Hoisting my backpack up on my shoulder, I take one last deep breath and swing open the massive front door.

The school is a hustle and bustle of kids and teachers as I walk in and head toward the main office. When I get there, I push open the door and a woman with thick, black-rimmed glasses glances up with the kind of slow motion that makes you wonder if she's part sloth.

Hell, in a school with wereanimals and shifters, maybe she is, I remind myself.

"Can I help you?" sloth lady asks.

"I uh—yeah," I nod, leaning against the tall wooden front desk and setting my backpack at my feet. "I'm Autumn Blackwood. I'm new—"

The woman's eyebrow twitches, as if trying to decide if it's too much work to actually arch over those massive rims. Instead, she sits up a bit straighter, and runs a hand over the piled-up, mousy-brown bun on the top of her head.

"Ah yes, Ms. Blackwood. We've been expecting you," she

says. Shuffling through the piles of paperwork on her desk, she pulls out a manila folder and flips it open. "You never completed your orientation. Is that correct?"

I nod. "Yeah. I mean yes. By the time I got here, the school was being evacuated. I was wondering if I can still—"

"Here's your schedule," sloth lady says, cutting me off and sliding over a stack of papers, "a map of the school, details about upcoming campus events, and a list of faculty who can help you get situated. This one is rules and regulations on cell phone use during school hours, as well as the student Wi-Fi password. My name is Ms. Cain. You can come to me with any questions regarding the school. I make it my job to know and *see all*. Welcome to Windhaven Academy."

A creepy smile spreads across her lips, like it's the first time she's attempted one for the past decade.

"Thanks," I say, reaching for the stack of papers.

Ms. Cain spins her chair, lowering it a bit so she can reach the floor, and walks around the broad wooden desk.

"Allow me to show you to your first classroom," she says, stiffly walking straight out the door.

Clutching the papers to my chest, I grab my backpack and follow her.

She's a full head shorter than I am, but surprisingly, the woman has some speed to her when not sitting behind her desk. It's all I can do to keep up as she leads the way through the wide, twisting hallways.

Inside, the school is as architecturally interesting as the outside, and I find myself slowing to admire some of the oversize windows with stained glass art and interesting pillars or stairway embellishments.

"Try and keep up, Ms. Blackwood. This is a large school and without the advantage of the Witching Stick, you'll likely be confused for quite some time. It will do you some good to find someone you can team up with who can show you the ropes," Ms. Cain says. We pass a large open area with cushy chairs and she points in their direction. "This is the commons area. You'll find students will mostly chitchat here, because the serious students tend to congregate in the library."

She eyes some students lounging lazily in the chairs as we pass by and I can't help but smile to myself.

"Okay, good to know."

Ms. Cain stops abruptly, twisting on her heel to stare at me over the top of her glasses. "This school has its history, Ms. Blackwood. Be sure to bring your map with you at all times if you plan to *explore* alone. It's not like you're a clairvoyant or anything, I can tell that just by looking at you. Finding your way out of messes could prove quite difficult for you."

My eyes widen at the seriousness of her tone and I nod in lieu of any other response. Not psychic. Check.

Sweeping her arm out, she points at the door beside us. "Your first period is in here. Intro to Essential Life Energies with Mrs. Karlgaard."

"Thanks," I say, stepping inside.

As I walk in, the attention of the entire class shifts from a woman with a floor-length dress and intricately laced granny shawl. Mrs. Karlgaard's wavy brown and gray hair floats to her mid-back and she looks like she could make the pieces of the room dance with a flick of a wand.

She raises her hands to the class and turns to me. Her bright-blue eyes scrutinize my every move before they crease in their corners. "Thank you, Ms. Cain. You must be Autumn Blackwood," she says, her cheeks transforming into pink mounds as she smiles. She walks around her desk, her finger floating down a piece of paper. When she's satisfied, she scribbles something and looks back up.

I nod, and flit my gaze around the room. Every student in the classroom either has their eyes on me or is leaning to someone closest to them and whispering. The cliques are evident immediately, and I can't help but feel extremely exposed. These people probably know exactly why they're here, what powers they have, and why. Not to mention, the advantage of growing up around each other. Most supernaturals do.

"Okay, go ahead and grab a seat, Ms. Blackwood," Mrs. Karlgaard says, waving an arm out in front of her. "We're just getting started so you haven't missed much."

Whispers erupt around me, but I ignore it all and take my seat, thrusting my backpack into the space under my feet.

"Hi, my name's Caitlyn, but everyone calls me Cat," the girl beside me whispers as she ventures a tiny wave.

Her dark skin is in deep contrast to the buttery yellow shirt she has on and her black hair is braided in the most beautifully intricate way. She has an almost regal air about her, and I know instantly she's well-liked. It would be hard not to like her, come to think of it.

"Hi," I say, nodding. The morning sunlight streaming in the large picture windows sparkles in her dark eyes as she grins and I can't help but return the gesture.

"Are you excited to develop your powers?" Caitlyn asks.

I nod, keeping my lips pursed, knowing full well what the next question will be. Explaining that I don't know what I am yet is going to get old super fast. However, Cat surprises me by not even going there.

"You'll love it here. Windhaven's more than just a school, it's really a close-knit community. We take care of our own. If you need any help with anything, just let me know," she whispers.

"Thanks, that's really—"

"Okay class, now that Ms. Blackwood is settled, let's return to our discussion regarding the seven Chakras..." Mrs. Karlgaard begins. "Autumn, it appears you and Ms. Gilbert have already broken some ice. Why don't the two of you work together for this lesson."

"You got it, Mrs. K.," Cat says, nodding and giving her a thumbs up.

Mrs. Karlgaard tips her head in acknowledgement, then turns back to the screen behind her. The juxtaposition of the old architecture with the modern tech screen in place of a blackboard is a little bit strange to settle into at first. We didn't have such fancy stuff in Mistwood Point. The best technology my high school had was the old television they'd roll in for movie days and it was at least twenty years old and still used a VHS player.

I settle into the talk on energy work, healing via the Chakras, and more. It's super interesting, but also clear that it's a basic requirement for most students at this school. As the hour goes on—the ambiance from the school puts off an almost steampunky vibe and I find myself actually admiring the divergence of it.

When the hour wraps up, I quickly grab my backpack and head for the door. The moment I step into the hall, the realization slams into me that I have no idea what my next class is, let alone where to go.

"Need some help finding your next class, don't you?" Cat declares, stepping up beside me with a knowing smile.

"That obvious, huh?" I mutter, moving to the wall and digging for my schedule.

"Only a little."

Shaking my head at myself, I pull out the piece of paper, staring at it like it's in a different language.

"Mind if I take a look?" Cat asks, holding out her hand.

"Be my guest. Hopefully it makes more sense to you," I say, thrusting the paper into her open palm.

Her forehead crinkles and she bites her lip as she studies the parchment.

"Mkay, looks like you have Mr. Reed next for Powers & Technology. I'm in that class too. I can show you where it is," she says.

"Thanks, that would be really helpful. I missed the Divining Rod portion of the Witching Stick this weekend and I'm pretty new to the idea of being supernatural. By the time I got here, they were ushering everyone out. So, I feel like I'm at a total disadvantage."

"Don't worry about it. You'll get the hang of it in no time. Besides, the Divining Rod isn't always accurate. It's just a prediction tool. Most of the time, we have multiple powers to develop and which ones we actually take on are up to us," she says, handing my schedule back. "Like with me, for instance, I can conjure fire." Opening her hand, palm-side up, a tiny golden flame ignites in the center of her hand. Then, as she closes it, the flames vanish. "But every time I get too close to electronics, stuff goes on the fritz. So, this next class ought to be interesting."

My eyes widen. "That's incredible. I mean, at least you know what your powers are. Sort of."

"You'll figure yours out, too. It's what this place is all about," Cat says, patting my shoulder.

I glance back down at my schedule, trying to decipher how she figured out my next destination.

"They vomit your entire year's schedule onto one piece of paper. See, this is semester one, hour one," Cat says, pointing at the section with my current classes. "You just need to follow the hour, and cross-reference it with the semester and day, and you're set."

"Thanks, I don't know why they can't just simplify it," I say, shaking my head and folding the paper into a tiny square so I can cram it into my pocket for easy access.

Cat shrugs. "Who knows? Maybe it's just a sadistic rite of passage?"

I chuckle. "Yeah, sounds about right."

A guy with the same dark skin, but a much softer demeanor walks up, placing a hand on Cat's elbow.

"I'm gonna have a word with Ms. Cain about something. Meet ya in Powers and Tech," he says to her. His eyes lock with mine for a brief second before he drops his gaze to the floor.

"Okay, Colt. Be right there," she says, nodding.

"Yeah, all right," he practically whispers. For a split second, he hangs back as if there's more he wants to say, but he drops his head, pulls up the hood on his hoodie, and walks off.

I quirk an eyebrow. "He your boyfriend?" I ask, watching him turn the corner.

Cat snickers, covering her face. "Uhm, no. Ewww," she laughs. "I guess I should have introduced him. That's my twin brother, Colton. But pretty much everyone calls him Colt. It's kind of a big joke around here. I'm Cat, he's Colt. Funny thing is, neither one of us are wereanimals."

"Oooooh," I say, dragging the 'o' out, thinking. "So, twin, huh? That's pretty cool," I say, trying to shift the awkwardness.

Cat tips her head, suggesting I follow her, and she starts walking. "Yeah, it's pretty awesome. Colt and I have been inseparable since—well, conception, I guess," she laughs. "He's the only one who really gets me. Just like I get him. We can practically communicate mentally, no powers needed."

"That's really awesome. I'm an only child, and so far,

there's only one person I feel really gets me. But that's okay, he's pretty awesome," I say, smiling.

"Ah, so my turn to take the leap. Boyfriend?" Cat says, leading the way.

I nod. "That obvious?"

"Well, only because of the shitty grin you have on your face right now. I'd say you're pretty enamored."

"Definitely," I say, blushing.

"Well, I'd love to meet him," she says. "I've lived here my whole life and let me tell you, it's nice to see some fresh faces."

"What are you doing this weekend?" I say, shooting her a sideways glance. "He has standing plans to come up to Windhaven Saturdays and Sundays."

"By the sounds of things, I'll be stopping by to meet a new friend's boyfriend," she says. "I take it he doesn't live here?"

I shake my head.

She presses her lips tight. "Eh, absence makes the heart grow fonder and all that. Maybe we can all go hunt for the creature they think is loose in the waterways together," Cat says, wiggling her fingertips in the air in front of her.

"The what?" I say, scrunching my face.

"Didn't you hear?" Cat says, her mouth slack-jawing open. "There are two kids missing. That's the big deal that was going on during the Witching Stick."

"Oh, yeah. I did hear that. Do they know what kind of creature?" I ask, remembering back to the snippets I heard when we first arrived on campus.

"They're not a hundred percent. But evidently, there are rumors about the disappearance being similar to one a while back. So they think it might be the same one since it got away. I've heard the magical community has been called in on the hunt because time is critical. From what I hear, it's not the kind of creature that kidnaps to have tea and crumpets." She sticks out her tongue and makes a face.

"Whoa. That's—I didn't realize how big of a thing that was. Creatures, I mean," I say, my words stumbling out.

Cat smirks. "You're in a school for magical abilities and you're surprised there are creatures out in the world? Where have you been living, Autumn?"

"Under a rock, I suppose. Until recently, I was pretty sure I was just a human of the non-magical variety," I laugh. "Don't get me wrong, I knew there were creatures but I guess I'd just never come in contact with any of them."

"Ah, well, that explains a little bit. Just be careful if you're near any of the waterways—things like rivers, streams, lakes... ponds," she says, stopping in front of a classroom door.

"Okay, good to know."

Ponds? My hypothesis from before suddenly doesn't sound so out there.

"Don't worry. I'm sure everything will be resolved soon," Cat offers with a sincere grin. Without another word about it, she heads inside the classroom.

The rest of the day flies by in record time. Between getting a bearing for my new lessons and trying to figure out the layout of the school, there isn't much time for anything else. Luckily, Cat's in four of my six classes, and the two she's not in, her brother Colton is, so she still knew the way. My mind continues to circle around the news of a water creature snatching kids and for some reason, I just can't seem to shake an eerie familiarity of it. I hope they find the two kids soon, *and in one piece.*

As the last class of the day ends, I make my way to the commons so I can try to gather up my thoughts before heading home. I sit down in one of the big, cushy red chairs, trying to discern whether or not a pattern emerged from today's schedule that might clue me in on what kind of powers I could have. Unfortunately, everything is pretty generic. Intro to Essential Life Energies, Power & Technology, History of Supernaturals, Spellcasting Basics, Intro to Conjuring, and Grimoire Crafting.

I wonder if I should just go back to Ms. Cain in the front office and ask her. She seems like the kind of lady who knows a lot more than she lets on.

"Hey, do you need a lift home?" Cat asks, flopping into the seat beside me.

I look up, blinking at her. "Nah, I drove myself. Thanks, though."

"You're not gonna get lost trying to find your way home, are you?" she says, grinning at me.

"No, I think I can handle it. Besides, I can ask Siri." I hold up my phone and wave it.

Cat nods in approval. "Nice. What kinda car do you drive?"

"Ford Escape."

"Wicked. I wanna get a Honda Civic, but my dad made me get a four-wheel drive SUV, too. Because, winters. Ugh, anyway. Can I come see?" she asks. "I have some time to kill before Colt gets done chitchatting with Mr. Reed. He's a tech geek. Probably because he knows it's the one thing I suck at." She rolls her eyes.

"Be my guest." I shrug.

Standing up, I throw my backpack over my right shoulder and lead the way. It takes a while to get to Big Blue. Since I was late, I had to park at the outskirts again.

"Jeez, where did you park? Siberia?" Cat huffs. "Dang good thing we're nowhere near water anymore. I'd be worried we'd be snatched next, for sure."

I shudder away the thought. "Well, I was running late,

remember. So I had to park a ways out," I say, trying to stay lighthearted. "Come on. We're not far now."

"Had I known I had miles to go, I would have changed into my running shoes," she chuckles.

"Behave," I say, shaking my head. Her flippant attitude does wonders for setting me at ease about running into anything nefarious out here—creatures or otherwise. Plus, it makes me feel a little less self-conscious about being here at all.

"So how far is your house from the school?" she asks, hiking her backpack up on her right shoulder.

"Mmm, not super far. Twenty minutes if I drove the speed limit, I suppose."

"Me, too. Where are you at?" Cat asks, quirking an eyebrow.

"I'm out on Lone Oak Boulevard."

"Hey, me too," Cat says, grabbing my arm. "Which house are you?"

"Erm, 17535. I think?"

Cat stops dead, butting her head with the palm of her hand. "Oh my god. I don't know why it didn't click sooner. Blackwood."

I nod, "Yeah, that's my last name."

She stares at me with her mouth agape.

My eyebrows tug in. "What?"

She shivers, "N-nothing. It's just—I didn't think anyone lived at the old Blackwood estate anymore."

I snort. "Really? Why?"

She blinks rapidly and licks her lower lip, "I, uh, live across the pond. Honestly, I haven't seen anyone come and go from that place in ages."

"Ah. Yeah, my dad kinda likes his privacy. He's more of a homebody," I nod.

Cat's eyebrows tug in and she takes a moment to think. "Yeah, he was always kinda like that. I guess I haven't seen him for a while. Weird."

I narrow my eyes, trying to make sense of her reaction. When she doesn't say anything else, I turn and point to the bright blue hood beside me. "Okay, anyway, here's Big Blue."

"Not too shabby. This blue is electric. I love it, " she says, circling the vehicle. "Did you have it custom painted?"

"Nope, I got it this way. It's actually why I bought it."

As she reaches the back of the car, she stops dead in her tracks. Her fingertips reach out and she touches the etchings left from the other day.

"Autumn—"

I race over to her side, my hands flying up and shaking in front of me. "Yeah, I know. Some jerk did that when I came in for the Witching Stick. It's going in next week to get fixed."

Clearing her throat, Cat backs away.

"Do you know who did it?" Her voice is barely a whisper.

"I wish I did. I saw a guy with white-blond hair run off into the woods, though. Wade, my boyfriend, and I figure it was probably a prank or something and they just got the wrong car. Because, seriously, no one knows me in this town. I used to live in Mistwood Point."

Cat's face turns red and her jaw clenches. "You know, I better... I gotta go. Colt doesn't know where I am and I'm his ride. He's probably done with Mr. Reed by now. I'll see you tomorrow, okay?" she says, backing away.

"Everything okay?" I ask, alarm rising with the hairs on the back of my neck.

She nods a bit too enthusiastically and looking down at her empty wrist. "Yeah, yeah... I just need to get moving. I didn't realize what time it was."

"All right. See you tomorrow, then," I mutter, taking a tentative step toward my driver's side door.

"Okay, yeah. See ya tomorrow," she says, shooting me a quick wave and turning on her heel.

I open the driver's side door and fling my backpack over to the passenger seat.

Cat stops walking and twists around. Her eyes are serious, dark pools. "Keep an eye out for anything strange, Autumn," she says. "Don't go outside by yourself. *Especially* near the pond."

CHAPTER 12

OKAY, THAT WAS UNUSUAL

Cat's bizarre statement set off a burst of anxiety coursing through me and even though I know I'm safe, I feel like I should be doing something to find the missing kids. I don't know what, though. Surely they have people far more qualified to be out there than I am.

When I get home, the house is still relatively quiet. I'm beginning to think it's just the way of things here, but I'm still not used to it. At Mom's house, there was always some noise. Whether it be her running in and out, or a radio left on somewhere.

The silence pulls on my thread of anxiety until it's woven tightly around my mid-section. Taking a deep breath, I kick off my shoes and make my way up the grand staircase to hunt for Dad and let him know how the first day of school went. Afternoon light streams in from various directions, gifting a beautiful, magical energy to the space. When I reach the second floor, I take a beat, looking out over the massive entry.

The ornate carvings along the stair rails look centuries

old, and maybe they are. The upper windows on the second level bleed beams of light onto the stairway, illuminating the dust particles as if glitter rains from the rafters.

I can't believe I didn't appreciate this when I was little.

Grinning and shaking my head, I grip the railing and look over the edge. As I do, flashes of a woman dressed in a blue floor-length dress sprawled out on the floor, her body bent at an awkward angle, rush up at me. I squelch a startled scream and back away.

"Everything okay?" Dad asks, rushing toward me from the other end of the hall.

I trip backward, slamming my back into the wall behind me.

"I—uh—yeah," I stutter, trying to shake away my surprise. "There was just—I think I..."

"What did you see?" Dad presses, watching me intensely.

My fingertips trace my eyebrows and I shake my head.

"Uhm, nothing. It was nothing," I mutter.

"Are you sure, honey? Your scream kinda said it *was* something," he says.

"Yeah, I think I just got too close to the edge of the rail—"

His blue eyes darken and he narrows them at me.

"Seriously, Dad. I think I just startled myself. I—I'm gonna go do my homework," I say, no longer sure I want to engage in a long conversation with him. I need to regroup.

"Wait a second. How did your first day of school go?" he asks.

"It was fine. Good. Definitely good," I say, feeling like the air around me is closing in. God, I'd do anything to go to my room and just breathe for a minute.

"Good, good. Glad to hear it," he says, his head bobbing up and down slowly.

"Yeah," I say, running my hand across the back of my neck.

"All right, well... I guess I'll let you go. I'll be out in the garden for a bit, if you need me. Dinner should be soon. Maybe you can tell me more then?"

"Yeah, that sounds like a plan," I nod, feeling more appreciative that he can read my need to be alone for a bit. Mom would have pressed me and continued until I spilled everything. "Thanks, Dad."

He shoots me a sideways grin. It's not necessarily a fake smile, but one that doesn't quite reach his eyes.

I take a tentative step onto the staircase, unsure if I really want to go down to the main floor and past the spot where I saw the woman.

Without another word, Dad makes his way past me and down the large staircase. When I can tell he's out of earshot, I step forward gingerly and peer over the edge of the rail. My fingertips dig into the railing, but the only thing at the bottom is the huge decorative rug.

Relief floods through me and I make my way down the rest of the stairs.

"Weird," I mutter, shaking away the tendrils of terror when I reach the spot where the body was laying. There's nothing there, not even a hint that anything may have been there at one point. "Get a grip, Autumn. Or more sleep." I rush past the location, half running down the hall to my bedroom.

As I open the door, the natural light lacks the intensity from the front of the house. Instead, it illuminates the backyard and its various shades of fall. Walking to the large picture window, I take a seat and stare out into the beauty beyond. The view of the pond in the distance is somewhat obscured, but still beautiful, as is the rest of the courtyard. It almost hugs the blazing trees in the middle with a welcoming embrace.

Settling into the stillness, my cell phone buzzes in my pocket, making me jump. I tug it out, flipping it over to see who's calling.

I grin, pressing the green phone icon. "Hello?"

"Hey there, beautiful," Wade says, his voice like a melody from a song I forgot I loved.

"Hey, I'm so happy to hear your voice," I say, clutching my phone to my ear.

"Same here. I know I coulda just texted, but I...dunno." He takes a deep breath. "I missed you."

My heart flutters. After everything that's just happened, my emotions are whiplashing and I blink back the tears brimming in my eyes. "I miss you, too. Are you still planning on coming at the weekend?"

"Definitely. Wild horses and all that. Will your dad be there this time?"

"Yeah, I think so. I mean, I can ask him, for sure," I say, swallowing hard and nodding to myself.

"Do you think he'll let me stay there again? Or do I need to sleep in my car?" he asks, chuckling under his breath.

"You are *not* sleeping in your car. I'm sure it will be fine. Besides, I'll sneak you into my bedroom if I have to," I say, glancing over to the big king-size bed.

"Well, that sounds promising," he says, a twinkle of mischievousness playing at his tone.

"Hey now, don't make me regret that statement."

"Oh, trust me, there would be no regret," he laughs. "Well, of course, unless your room decides to throw more stuff."

"Yeesh, right? I'll make sure everything is strapped down if I have to."

"That also sounds promising," Wade says, his voice smoldering even through the phone.

"It does, does it?" I tease, letting the wave of desire wash over me unexpectedly. "Is that a promise?"

He pauses for a moment, his breath slightly ragged on the other end of the line. "Only if you want it to be."

Goose bumps flash across the back of my arms; dancing their way up my neck and into my scalp. I bite my lower lip and shiver.

Wade clears his throat, "So, uh, anyway..."

Swallowing hard, I blink away the daydreams his words have conjured. They've almost all but erased the strangeness of the day.

"Yeah—uh, so anyway," I repeat, sighing loudly, "first day of school was a bit weird, and being home hasn't been any more normal."

"Oooh, do tell. Anything has to be more exciting than changing a grown man's diapers."

"Where do I even start?" I say, pulling my legs up and crossing them on the bench. "I still feel kind of out of place. So that doesn't help."

"Still no hint on what kind of powers you have, huh?"

I shake my head, looking back out over the courtyard, "Not even the faintest."

"Dang."

"I know, right? Then there's this weird chick. I mean, she's great, actually, but..." I trail off, thinking about how Cat reacted to the back of Big Blue.

"But?" Wade urges.

"Well, she lives on the other side of our pond, I come to find out. That was actually kind of exciting, but she acted really strange when she saw the etching on my vehicle."

"Strange how?"

I think back to her expression of rage. "Well, at first, she seemed pissed. Which makes no sense to me. But then she got really skittish and made an excuse to run off and get her brother."

"How do you know it was an excuse?" he asks, his voice soft as he urges me through the conversation.

I let my gaze drift to the outer courtyard. "Just a feeling, I guess."

"Well, give it some time. I'm sure if there's anything to it, it will all come out. Any more news on the missing kids?"

"Not really. But they do think there's a creature involved. So far, they don't know what kind, but I did hear rumors that this has happened before. So, that's creepy."

"I'd say. Hey, speaking of creepy... Have you raced around the house yet, looking for a doorknob or key to that hidden door in your room?" he asks, laughing softly.

"No, not yet. I just got home and talked to Dad for a bit. He wanted to know how things went, too." I sigh quietly, trying to decide whether or not to tell Wade about what I saw from the top of the stairs.

"You should be exploring the rest of the house to hunt for them. If it's going to be a while before we know what powers you have, I gotta at least satiate my mystery seeking by knowing what's behind that door."

"I'll see what I can do," I say, floating my gaze to the tattered wallpaper. After the weird vision in the entry, I can't say opening a hidden and locked door is the first thing I want to do alone. I've seen enough horror movies to know that's never a good idea.

"What are you waiting for? The mystery would be killing me," he chuckles.

"What are you talking about? It's already killing you,

nutball. Besides, this incredibly sweet guy called me, so I figured I'd answer the phone," I say, leaning back in the window seat and grinning.

"Very true," Wade says. "I regret nothing."

My lips curve upward. "Well, I probably should get going, though..."

"Already?" Wade says, a hint of shock in his tone.

I sit up straighter. "I'm sorry, did you have more you wanted...? Oh, I should have asked you about your day—"

"No, I'm totally teasing. Go, go... But if you do go exploring, call me if you find anything."

Standing up, I nod. "You will be the first to know."

"Excellent," he says. "So, can I call you before bed tonight?"

"Of course."

"Until then, beautiful. Talk to you soon."

Before I can respond, the call ends and I pull my phone back, gaping absently at the picture of the Mistwood graveyard I have as my background. My teeth dig into my lower lip as my gaze drifts from my phone to my backpack. My eyes linger there for a moment, then they flit out to the courtyard and other areas of the house.

"Eh, a half-hour looking for the doorknob wouldn't hurt," I whisper to myself, flitting my eyes to the garden, where my dad should be. "It's not like I need to open it, even if I do find it."

I stand up, thrusting my phone into my pocket. Without another thought, I walk out my bedroom door. Even though I live here, at least for now, it feels like I'm sneaking about. Dad never said I couldn't explore, but it sorta feels like an invasion of privacy. Like I'm in a big hotel and I'm entering into other guests' rooms.

As if carrying themselves, my feet move of their own accord, and I turn to the right and follow the rest of the hallway. The space continues with the same grandiose architecture—high ceilings, ornate carvings and curving and embellished trim work. Some of the windows even have stained glass that casts a colorful glow into the space.

Practically tiptoeing down the hallway, I reach for the first door handle to the room on the right. The door is unlocked, and I open it. Inside, the room is dark and dusty, with white sheets covering the furniture. Along the left wall is a massive fireplace that looks as though it hasn't seen a fire in a century.

Stepping tentatively into the room, I lift one of the sheets. Underneath is one of the most beautiful loveseats I've ever seen. Its decorative pattern woven into the red fabric, ornately carved woodwork, and curves make me wish I lived in a different time.

"Wow," I whisper.

Moving on, I go through similar rooms, all with their own furniture buried under sheets and covered in layers of dust. But room after room, nothing stands out in terms of a doorknob or key. If anything, they're devoid of any extra embellishments beyond the furniture. In addition, none of them seem to have a doorway that resembles the one that was hidden.

In some ways, it's strange to think only one man lived in this massive house all these years. Of course, now there's the two of us, but...why would anyone need so much space? Why not just sell it and get a boatload of money?

As I reach the end of the hallway, I stand at the large picture window at the end that faces out to the pond. The view of the pond isn't obscured like it is from my bedroom and I could see myself coming down here to study from time to time. There are so many rooms to be searched and I'm not closer to finding anything useful. Besides, it's pretty evident that if there was a doorknob or key—it's been deliberately hidden or lost with time.

Shaking my head, I whisper, "I should just head back..."

"Ah, there you are," Dad says from behind me.

The sudden, abrupt interjection makes me jump. I clutch at my chest, bending forward. "Oh, my god, Dad. You scared the daylights out of me."

"Sorry about that. I went to your room to let you know supper was ready and you weren't there. So, I went looking for you. I didn't mean to startle you," he says, quirking a finger over his lips and trying not to laugh.

"I—I hope you don't mind me exploring a bit. I just figured I've been here a while now, but I don't think I ever really got used to it."

"I don't mind at all. It's your home, too," he says, a sense of nostalgia lingering in his gaze as it goes slightly distant.

"Thank you, I appreciate that. You know, you're so different than I remember," I say, pressing my lips tight. "I mean, I hope that doesn't sound rude..."

"Don't worry about it. I get it. You were a seven-year-old girl who only wanted to watch TV and play near the pond unsupervised," Dad says. "Things were different then."

"You know, you could have trusted me to stay out of trouble, instead of locking me in my room," I say, holding his gaze. "Even if you and Mom were fighting, or whatever was going on..."

Confusion flitters across his features and he takes a seat in one of the arm chairs beside me. "Autumn, I never locked you in your room."

"What do you mean? Of course you did. I only got to leave for meals. It was torture," I say, my eyebrows tugging in.

"Is that what you think was going on?" Dad says, shaking

his head. "No, sweetie. That was you. After the...*accident*, the only way I could coax you out of your room was with food. There were even plenty of times when you wouldn't come out for that, so we had to bring your meals to you. Your Mom and I—"

I snicker. "What on earth are you talking about? Accident?"

Dad's eyes narrow. "Are you—you're not serious?"

"Dad, honestly, I have no idea what you're talking about."

Rubbing his fingertip across his lips, Dad's eyelashes flutter furiously. "You know, dinner's getting cold. I think we should get moving so we can enjoy it while it's still hot," he says, abruptly standing. "Hope you like barbecue ribs."

"I—yes. I do, but Dad, what in the hell are you talking about? I'm so confused. You need to stop and tell me what's going on," I demand, crossing my arms.

Sighing deeply, Dad waves a hand dismissively. "It's nothing, honey. I'm probably just the one getting confused. Let's get a bite to eat. James will be devastated if it gets cold. We can chat more about everything after we've had some food."

Swallowing hard, I nod. He may think I'll let this go, but he'll be sorely mistaken. I do have a bit of Mom in me, after all. But I do have enough of Dad in me to know when to find the opportune moment. "All right, I'll be right there."

"Okay, sweetie. Don't be long. I'll tell James to get everything dished up."

"Sounds good. I'll be right behind you."

Nodding to himself, he turns quickly and heads down the hallway. In his absence, I'm left with the disorienting sense he's one more person who's hiding stuff from me.

Shaking my head, I look out one last time over the wooded space. My eyes scan the landscape, hunting for something, anything to clue my mind in on what he was talking about.

Making a face, I rest my gaze on the shimmering surface of the pond.

Could I really have locked myself in my bedroom and just...*forgot?*

CHAPTER 13

HOLY HELL—IT WAS YOU!

Before I moved to Windhaven, the biggest mystery in my life was whose grave was I sitting next to. There are so many strange things that have happened since I moved here, and it's making my head spin.

When I pull into the parking lot for school the following day, I spot Colton and Cat right away. I straighten my shoulders and try to act totally normal. Between my own inner confusion and their strange behavior, I just gotta find some common ground.

"Hey, Autumn," Cat says, waving as I get closer. Her smile is broad and open, like nothing strange happened at all yesterday.

Colton briefly smiles, but drops his gaze to his feet. His left hand reaches up, running across the back of his neck. "I uh, I gotta go," he half-whispers. "See ya later, Cat."

Without so much as a hi to me, he stomps off.

My eyebrows rise on their own accord. He's one of the stranger people I've met, for sure.

"Okay, see ya, Colton," I say, mock-waving. "Yeesh, still haven't had the chance to introduce myself properly to him."

Cat shakes her head, chuckling under her breath. "He's socially inept and not super good around the opposite sex."

"You aren't kidding," I say, watching him enter the school. "Though he seems just fine with you."

"I'm not dating material," Cat says, giving me a knowing look that stops me in my tracks.

"Uh, what?"

"He's not gonna date his sister. That would be gross," she reiterates.

"Oh, yeah, that would be super weird..." I say, my voice trailing off.

I make a mental note to mention Wade when Colton's around.

Shaking it off, I turn back to Cat. "So, ready for class?"

She gives me one of her broadest smiles, wrapping her arm around my shoulders. "Sure am."

Cat leads the way, giving me clues and tips on the best way to get through the school to various classes. Different routes we hadn't tried the day before. As we turn the last corner to Intro to Essential Life Energies, I'm bowled over, landing hard on the tiled floor.

"Ouch. Watch where you're—" I begin.

Hovering over me is a tall, slim guy with white-blond hair. Instantly, I know it's the same dude who carved up my car.

"You..." I say, my breath a rushed whisper.

Taking a step back, he quirks an eyebrow like he's God's gift. He smirks and I have the sudden urge to kick him in the shin while I'm down here.

"You know Dominic?" Cat asks, offering me a hand to get back up.

"You wanna explain how we know each other?" I ask, glaring into his crystal-blue eyes.

Widening his stance, he adjusts the collar on his leather

bomber jacket. "Sorry lady, I think you must have me confused with—"

"Like hell I do," I interrupt, brushing off my ass. "You're the jerk who keyed up my car."

"Wait, what?" Cat says, flitting her gaze back and forth between us.

"Yeah, this is the guy who carved *veritas vos liberabit* on the back of my damn car," I spit, jabbing a thumb his direction.

"Dom, was that you?" Cat sputters, her lips making a large o.

He holds his hands up. "I have no idea what this crazy chick is talking about."

"Oh, don't be coy. You know damn well you're the one who did it," I fire back.

People disappear into the classrooms all around us, pretty much announcing it's time to get our collective asses to class.

"It's been real, but I gotta bolt," Dominic says, grinning like the psychopath he is. He sidesteps the two of us and continues on his way.

"Come on, Autumn. We can deal with this later," Cat says, grabbing me by the arm and dragging me along to our classroom.

Dominic winks at me—a move that instantly reminds me of Wade. My cheeks burn in anger and I have the sudden urge to go back and punch him in the nose.

"It was him... I know it was," I begin.

"Okay, okay. We can sort all of this out later," Cat says, pulling me behind her.

"How do you know that guy? He's such a jerk," I protest in her wake.

"Later," she says, rushing into the classroom.

We take our seats just in the nick of time, but she turns to me and says, "If it was him, we'll get this all sorted out, okay?"

"Sure," I mutter, trying to seem more upbeat than I actually feel.

Cat nods. "Look, I know I was acting a little weird yesterday. I hope I didn't—"

"Don't worry about it," I mutter, swiping my hand in the air. "I have bigger things to worry about."

"Good. I mean, not that you have other things going on. It's just that... I'm really worried about this water creature thing. I was a kid the last time something like this happened, so I don't remember much, but I do remember it was terrifying there for a while." She shoots me a significant glance.

"Don't worry about it. I totally get it," I say, pulling out my notebook and pen.

She sucks in a ragged breath, nodding to herself, and turns to face the front of the class.

We spend the next hour, sitting in silence as Mrs. Karlgaard discusses the Root Chakra and its effects on the way our powers manifest and why it's the gateway for everything. Cat even gets to show off her ability with fire, as Mrs. Karlgaard uses her as an example of how to connect to your source of power. While the discussion has its fascinating moments, my mind doesn't stray far from Dominic and how I can make him pay for the damages to Blue.

The bell rings and I'm the first one up—ready to bolt out the door and interrogate Cat some more. Cat's quick too, as she grabs her bag and chases after me. When we get out in the hall, Colton joins us. His hands are in his pockets, and his eyes are still cast to the floor.

"Hiya g-guys," he mutters.

"Hi Colton," I say, tipping my chin upward and extending my hand. "I'm Autumn, by the way."

"Yeah, I know who you are," he mutters without looking up.

"Okay, good." I nod to myself, pulling my hand back, and turning to his sister. "Cat, you gotta explain the guy from earlier. How do you know him? How can I find him? He's gotta pay for the damages to my vehicle."

Cat pulls up short, staring me in the eye for a moment before sighing loudly. "Look, Autumn, I get it. I would be pissed, too. But I wouldn't go after Dom. He's not the kind of kid you want to mess around with. He's popular and rich—not to mention he's got some mental powers that could cause some serious problems down the road if you get on his bad side."

"Popular and rich. That explains the idiotic, entitled behavior then," I say, rolling my eyes. "I don't care who this guy is, or thinks he is. I want to know why the hell he would do that to Blue and I want him to pay for it. If he's got money, he should be able to afford it, right?"

"Dominic won't confess," Colton says, raising his intense, dark eyes to mine for the first time since we met.

"Uh, okay. I don't know why that matters. Maybe it's time someone teaches him to take responsibility," I say, crossing my arms.

Cat rolls her eyes. "Yeah, okay. I know you're new and all, but that's..."

"...*not* wise," Colton finishes.

My nostrils flare. "Why is everyone protecting this asshat?"

Colton and Cat exchange a significant glance.

"Oh, fine—yeah, yeah. I get it. Autumn's an outsider, so why bother filling her in. You know what? Whatever. I'm outta here," I say, turning on my heel.

The farther away from the two of them I get, the more panic begins to build in me. Not only because of the odd exchanges and bizarre attitudes, but also because I still have no idea how the hell to get to my Powers & Technology class. Cat brought me the other day and I totally wasn't paying enough attention. I'll be damned if I give them the satisfaction of knowing that, though. Instead, I find a quiet offshoot and quickly pluck the crumpled map from my backpack and try to orient myself.

"Ah, so you like dark, quiet halls to yourself?"

My head jolts up, and I come face-to-face with Dominic's flashing blue eyes.

Thoughts tumble around in my head like one of those BINGO letter pickers.

"You know, if you wanted to be alone with me, you coulda just asked," Dominic says, taking a step closer like a predator on the prowl.

Suddenly, the air in the space around me is extremely suffocating.

"Do you mind?" I say, thrusting an arm out to keep him at bay.

He chuckles. "Ah, playing hard to get, huh?"

"What in the hell are you even talking about? The only one playing at something is you," I spit.

"Oh, come on," he snickers. "Don't be like that."

There's a heady sort of energy surrounding him and despite myself, I can't help but want to lean into it. It's almost as if he's drawing me closer with just a look. Somewhere in the back of my mind, music radiates, like something from a different time in history.

Shaking my head, I gather my headspace and let it wash off me without sticking.

"I know it was you," I say, jutting out my chin.

He shrugs nonchalantly. "So what if it was?"

"Why?"

He arcs a perfectly trimmed white eyebrow. "That's for me to know and you to...well, you know the rest."

I roll my eyes.

"You don't even know me. We hadn't even met. Why did you target my car? You know I have to have the back end repainted now, right? You're gonna have to pay for it," I say, clutching the school map in my right fist.

"Oh, I do, do I? Who's gonna prove it was me?"

"Really? That's how you wanna play this? My boyfriend was there and saw you, too. Are you really that much of an entitled ass? You think you can just do stuff and never pay the price?" I say, taking my own step toward him. Anger wells in my gut and I want nothing more than to make this creep cry 'uncle,' regardless of how unlikely it might be.

His eyes widen for a split second, almost as if something I said actually hit its mark.

"Look, Autumn, it might do you a little good to worry less about me and about, well, what I carved said it all," he says, his voice dropping to practically a whisper.

"How did you know my name?" I say through clenched teeth.

He grins. "Just follow the message. It has meaning."

"The truth shall set you free? What truth?" I fire back.

"Ah, so you did your homework?" Dominic says, leaning back in surprise.

"Of course I did," I spit back.

"Good," he says, nodding.

"Would you stop with the cryptic and explain what in the hell you're getting at?"

The hallways start to clear around us.

"Shit. I gotta get to Astral Projection," Dominic says, twisting around toward the main hallway before turning back to me. "Look, meet me at the back of the cafeteria at lunch."

"And why in the hell would I do that?" I say indignantly.

"Because if you wanna know *why*, you'll be there," he says, flicking his eyebrows in acknowledgment.

With that, he's gone—racing down the corridor with expert precision.

Finding my classes throughout the rest of the morning is tedious, at best. But, regardless, it flies by, despite my constant state of confusion. Before I know it, lunchtime has rolled around.

"So, whatcha gonna do?" Cat says, meeting me outside History of Supernaturals.

I hike my backpack up and shake my head. "Go talk to Dominic, obviously. I need answers..."

"Just...be careful, okay?" Cat says, tipping her head toward the salad bar as we reach the cafeteria.

My eye catches Dominic's white head of hair in the back of the cafeteria and we lock gazes. For a moment, it's like the entire roomful of people fades away and zooms out. Or like he's managed to use a homing beacon and is calling me in. He waves an arm, trying to coax me toward him.

"I—I think I'm gonna..." I begin, starting to make my way toward Dominic.

"What about lunch?" Cat says, frantically trying to pull me back. "You'll miss it."

Twisting back around, I glance at her ebony hand clutched around my forearm and she tries to pull me back. "It's okay. I won't starve. I'm just going to talk with him and then I'll get food. Now, are you coming or not?"

I spin around, making my way to Dominic. Behind me, Cat whimpers, but I'm positive she's right on my heels. Making my way through the crowd, all eyes feel like they're on us as we beeline to Dominic's table. But I don't care. I barely take my eyes off of him the entire time, and oddly enough, he does the same. There's a weird magnetic energy between us and, for whatever reason, I don't think I could make another decision if I tried. Perhaps it's part of his power Cat tried to warn me about. Instead, I follow its lead and come to a screeching halt opposite him at the table.

"So, you wanna talk? Talk," I fire at him.

His blue eyes widen, but he leans back in his chair. "Ladies, so nice to see you again," he says, drawing out his words as he splays his arms across the chairs beside him.

"Come on, Dom. Just tell Autumn what she came here for so we can go grab a bite to eat," Cat mutters, looking over her shoulder longingly at the salad bar.

I cock an eyebrow and rest my hands on the back of the seat in front of me.

"Well, see, this could take a while," he says, smirking. "Might as well grab a seat."

CHAPTER 14

I JUST HOPE YOU'RE READY

Who the hell does this guy think he is?

"I'm not here to socialize," I spit. "Are you gonna fill me in on what the hell I'm supposed to be aware of? Or are you just gonna jerk my chain for the rest of the lunch period? Pretty sure Cat here wants to get some food."

Cat snickers beside me, and I know instantly she's impressed with my bravado, or perhaps stupidity. Maybe both.

"Trust me, it's not something you want me calling out across the table. If you'd just sit down—" he says, eyeing the seat beside him.

I have the sudden urge to sit, but I fight it and stay on my feet.

"Anything you gotta say to me, you can say in front of Cat," I mutter, clutching the back of the chair harder, and refusing to give into his mental suggestions.

"I ain't talking about Cat." His eyes flit around the space of the cafeteria.

My eyebrows tug in, and alarm bells blare in the back of my mind.

"What in the hell is going on here? I mean seriously. I just moved here, and I get the distinct impression there's more going on behind the scenes than I have a clue about," I say through clenched teeth.

"What gave it away? Was it what I carved in the back of your car?" he says, arching a knowing eyebrow.

"So it *was* you?" Cat says, leaning in. "Dammit, Dominic..."

"Of course it was me, Cat. For the love," he says, rolling his eyes. "You of all people should know why she—"

Cat's eyes widen and she shakes her head in the slightest of ways.

"What's he talking about?" I say, rounding on her.

"N-nothing. I don't know, Autumn," she sputters.

"Come on, Cat," Dominic warns.

"If you're talking about what I think you are, this isn't the time and place for this," Cat says, her eyes wide and nostrils flaring. "I know what you're trying to do, but this isn't the way."

Dominic snorts.

My stomach clenches and I'm overcome with the need to either hear something useful or go find somewhere quiet to think. Too bad the cemetery isn't closer.

"You know what? Screw you. Keep your secrets, both of you. I'm...I'm out," I sputter.

Spinning around, I push my way past the gawking spectators and out into the hallway. I continue walking, allowing my feet to take me wherever they like, as long as it's far, far away from the mind funk that is Dominic and Cat.

Here I thought I might actually learn something about what's really going on. Stupid.

Pushing open the doors to the school's courtyard, I walk out into the cool, crisp autumn air. I don't stop walking until I reach the edge of the football field, and I do what I would have done back at Mistwood High. I make my way to a quiet spot under the empty bleachers.

To my surprise, the space isn't empty at all. Instead, Colton drops the sandwich he was about to bring to his lips and shoves a book to the side.

"Well, hey. I wasn't expecting... What are you doing here?" I say, trying to sound like I'm not as surprised as I feel.

His eyebrows tug in and he wipes at his mouth with the back of his hand. "I was going to say the same thing about you."

I take a deep, cleansing breath, swiping at the air and taking a seat opposite him on the ground.

"Yeah, it was kind of impromptu. Dominic's messing with my head. And your sister—" I shake my head.

Colton watches me intensely, but doesn't say a word. It's the first time where I felt like he's actually seen me, not just a brief glance so he can run off.

"I've only been in this school for two days and I already feel like I'm going crazy. I mean, there's a lot of weird nuances here and I feel like I must have stepped into some cluster of a dynamic. You know?" I admit, eyeing the book he was reading.

He nods, but shifts the book behind his back so I can't see the title.

I narrow my gaze.

"So, what's your deal?" I ask, tipping my chin up.

His eyebrows skirt his hairline, but he says, "Deal? What do you mean?"

"I dunno. You're kinda quiet, and a little weird," I chuckle.

"I'm not a huge...people fan, I guess," he offers.

I shift around so I can lean my back against the chain-link fence to the left of us and nod. "I totally get that."

"You do?" he says, surprise painting his face.

"Uh, duh. Yes. People suck. Did you not just hear about Dominic?" I chuckle.

Colton snickers, glancing down at the sandwich in his hand.

"Can I ask you a question?" I say, shooting him another significant look.

He shrugs.

I take a quick beat, trying to decide what it really is I want to ask.

"Do you know why Dominic would have written 'The Truth Shall Set You Free' in Latin on my car? I tried to get it out of him just now in the cafeteria, but all I got was the runaround."

Colton taps his lips, but nods.

"You do?" I say, tucking my legs in tighter so I can sit up straighter.

"Yeah. Everybody does," he whispers. "Well, pretty much everybody."

"You've got to be kidding me," I say, leaning closer.

He scratches at his left eyebrow for a moment before finally saying, "I dunno if it's really any of our business, to be honest. It really should be something your..." His voice trails off.

I roll my eyes. "Not you, too. Your sister tried the same line of B.S. Come on, throw me a bone, would you? This is killing me."

Colton's eyes widen, but he clears his throat and puts his sandwich back into his lunch sack.

"How much do you know about the history here in Windhaven?" he finally asks.

"Erm, I know this school is a big deal and my dad lives here..." I pause, thinking. "Yep, that's about the gist."

His face tightens as he winces.

"Well, if I were you...I would start there," he says, holding my gaze. The significance in this simple gesture makes the hairs on my arm and neck stand on end. "It will shed a new light on things. Then we can talk more."

Exhaling slowly, I nod and pull my knees up toward my body. Wrapping my arms around my legs, I bite the inside of my cheek. "Fine," I say, a bit more tersely than originally intended.

"I know this is all really confusing. I just don't feel like it's my place to—really, you should talk to your Dad... Or do some digging on your own. But don't rely on Google. It won't help. You'll wanna go down to the county library if you're going to look to external sources."

I gawk at him. "I don't even know where the county library is."

"I can...uh, show you sometime," he says, looking at his lap. "I mean, if you want."

I nod. "Yeah, that would be great."

Watching him closely, I can't help but feel a certain amount of connection with him. He clearly has his own thing he's into, but others don't understand. It actually makes me want to get to know him a bit better.

"So, come on. Whatcha reading?" I ask, trying to get a glimpse of the cover.

Colton stares at me like a deer in headlights.

I narrow my eyes.

"Come on, it can't be that bad," I laugh, pushing my way around him.

After a little bit of a struggle, I pull the book from behind his back.

"Oh, Frankenstein," I say, clutching the cover and sitting back down. "Well, I mean, sure—"

"Yeah, I'm—"

"I get it. You're one of *those* kids," I laugh, handing it back.

"And what kind is that?"

"The kind who reads ancient stories the rest of the school wouldn't dream of touching, of course," I laugh.

"Ah," he nods. "Yeah, I guess I am."

I shrug. "Yeah, me too. At least to a degree. I haven't read this one, but I have seen the movie, obviously."

"It's totally different," he says.

"Of that, I'm not surprised," I say.

We sit in silence for a minute, listening to the sounds of birds and mostly peaceful quiet. It's a blissful break when there are no kids outside. They're all enjoying their lunches, or still in class. And for whatever reason, no one is using the field.

"You know, this whole move has been nothing but a weird, confusing mess. I mean, don't get me wrong, I kinda like here better than I expected. But it's just been so weird," I say, talking to myself more than anything.

"Yup," he agrees.

"How would you know?" I ask, chuckling to myself.

For the first time that I can remember, Colton actually smiles.

"Wow, he does have a grin," I say, pointing.

He laughs quietly, "Yeah, well...don't get too used to it."

I snort, shaking my head. "In all honesty, you should do it more often. It suits you."

For the briefest of moments, I swear Colton's face flushes —but in the darker light under the bleachers, it's hard to tell.

He clears his throat, grabbing his lunch sack, and pushing to a stand. He holds out his free hand to me. "Lunch is nearly over. I'll walk you to your next class. You know, if you want."

Nodding, I smile at him. "Yeah, I'd like that."

I take his offering, and he pulls me to a stand.

Together, we walk back to the school in a strange, comfortable silence. Oddly enough, I'm overcome by this strange sensation, like I've known him forever. Despite barely saying two words to one another before today, there's just something familiar about him. Maybe it's because I'm already sorta used to his sister?

When we get to the doors leading inside, Colton turns to me and says, "You have Spellcasting Basics next, right?"

"Wow. Uh, how'd you know that?" I say, turning to him in surprise.

He runs his hand across the back of his neck. "I uh..."

I pull up short, "Have you been...keeping tabs on me?"

"Well, when you say it like that..." he begins.

My mouth drops open, "Oh my god, you have—"

"Really, it's not as creepy as it sounds," he says, waving his hands in front of his body. "I just know where Cat is and since she's with you..."

I narrow my eyes at him. "Oh, right."

He shifts uncomfortably and nods his head. "Really, I'm totally not stalking you. I just noticed is all. Promise."

He crosses his heart with a pointer finger.

"Hmmm," I say, a small laugh bleeding through my façade. "All right, all right. Don't get your panties in a bunch. I believe you."

A relieved smile breaks across his face, lighting up his brown eyes.

"Well, I better—uh, I gotta go," I say, pointing down the hall to nowhere in particular.

"Still want me to walk you to class? Or do you remember how to get there?" he asks, biting on the inside of his cheek.

"Oh, right. Yeah, yeah. Lead the way," I mutter, thrusting my hand out to suggest he move out in front.

We walk the hallway in silence as students flood the halls, disrupting the awkwardness between us.

"So, how are you liking Spellcasting?" Colt asks.

I shrug. "I have no idea. It's only been one day. I wish I understood more. This whole supernatural thing is new to me."

"Oh, right," he says, scrunching his face.

"Hey, you two," Cat says, bounding down the hall and pushing her way between us.

"Hey," I say, trying not to let the ice in my voice turn too frigid.

"Oh, come on. You're not mad at me, are you?" she says, her forehead wrinkling. "Honestly, I only have your best interests at heart, Autumn. I really wish you knew that."

"I'm not mad, but I am a little busy. Right, Colt?" I say, twisting to him.

He shoots an apologetic glance at Cat and nods to me. "Oh. Yeah, okay."

Cat's mouth pops open as I take his arm, practically pulling him down the hallway.

After a second, Colt leans close and says, "You know we're heading the wrong way, right?"

I exhale and roll my eyes. "Of course we are."

"Want me to take you on the scenic route so we don't have to double back?"

"That would be lovely, yes," I nod. "Anything to allow me to save face."

His laugh sounds like music as he relaxes. "You know, she really does mean well."

"I know. I just gotta give it a little time before I can let it slide. You know? I don't like being yanked around. I appreciate you at least pointing me in a direction. I hope you know that," I say, shooting him a sideways glance.

He grins. "Sure."

After walking around in circles—at least, that's how it feels, we finally end up back at the Spellcasting hallway.

"And now, I'm thoroughly lost," I laugh. "I have no chance of finding my way back here tomorrow."

"I can walk with you again, but show you the normal way next time," he says, a hint of a smile hidden in the mounds of his cheeks.

"Sounds like an excellent idea," I nod. "Thank you."

Colt turns away, heading to wherever he needs to go next, but I run over to him and tap him on the shoulder.

"Hey, do you... I mean, would you have time to hang out after school? I'd like to learn more and maybe you could show me where this library is."

His eyes widen in surprise, but he nods.

"Great. Do you want to meet at my place at, I don't know, 4:30 p.m.? I need a few minutes to drop all my stuff at home and..."

"Sure, 4:30 works great," he says, his eyes sparkling.

"Here, let me write down my address," I begin, scrounging though my backpack for a piece of paper and a pen.

He shakes his head. "No need. I know where you are."

My head snaps up, "You do?"

"Well, yeah. We're practically neighbors."

"Oh right. You live across the pond."

He steps back, surprised.

"Don't get excited. Your sister told me," I say, tipping my head.

"Ah."

"Speaking of which, I suppose I better go make up with her in Spellcasting or she'll be on me for the rest of the day. See ya later," I say, waving.

He nods and turns on his heel like a toy soldier sent on a mission.

Walking into class, I take my seat beside Cat. She glances up as I sit down and I manage a smile.

"Hey, I'd be pissed too, if I knew people were withholding information from me. I'm sorry, Autumn," Cat says, her eyebrows tipping up apologetically.

"I know. Look, let's just say going forward, no more secrets. Okay? Colton's going to come over tonight to show me where the county library is. Wanna come with?"

Her eyes widen. "I—are you sure? I mean, you aren't leading him on, are you?"

I snort. "Of course not. What's that supposed to mean?"

"N-nothing. You know, nevermind. Yes, I'd love to come, too. Especially since I'm the driver," Cat says, smirking. "Colton has, as of yet, to get his license. He's just not in a big hurry, I guess."

"Okay, it's settled. Colton's promised to point me in the right direction to get answers. If I can get my bearings, I can figure out what Dominic's problem is."

"You'll probably find more than you bargained for..." she says, her voice trailing off. "I just hope you're ready."

CHAPTER 15

LIBRARY & DEAD ANCESTORS

Do you ever know when you're ready to face big truths? Is there an internal clock of knowing? Or is it more of a slap in the face that puts you on the path of discovery?

Racing to the front door, I swing it open to face Colt and Cat's wide eyes.

"Hey guys," I say, trying to ignore the way their stares at my house make me totally uncomfortable. "Ready?"

The pair of them nod, but no words escape from their mouths.

"Erm...you guys okay?" I ask, unsure how else to respond.

"Ah, yeah. Fine. It's just...*wow*, Blackwood Manor," Cat says, an air of awe lingering in her voice.

Colton's expression is identical to his sister's and I scrunch my face

"I know, it's actually pretty cool," I say, closing the door behind me, "right?"

They both blink back their surprise, but nod.

"Yeah...uh, it is," Cat mutters, turning to face her SUV.

Walking up to their Pontiac Torrent, Cat opens the

driver's side door and hops inside. Colt walks around to the passenger side and opens the door. Rather than hopping in, as I expected, he stands beside the door, looking at me expectantly.

"Oh," I say, realizing he's holding it for me, "thanks."

Grinning awkwardly at him, I hop in the front and reach for my seatbelt. The gesture mimics something Wade would have done and I can't help but wonder if it's a guy thing, or if Colton is hoping it will put him in my good graces.

Colton nods silently as he closes the door for me and gets in the back.

Cat exchanges a significant glance with me, her eyebrows popping up in surprise.

Mental note: introduce Colton to Wade. Just to be sure.

"Okay, so to the Grove County Library we go..." she says, turning the vehicle on and putting it into gear.

"Guess so," I say, buckling my seatbelt.

Silence floods the vehicle for the first few minutes on the road, but eventually, Cat leans over and flips on the radio.

"Too quiet," she says, shrugging at me.

"Agreed," I laugh.

The music is a weird combination between '90s pop and techno, and I have absolutely no idea what on earth they're singing about.

"Who...uh, who's this?" I ask, pointing at the radio.

Cat shrugs, "No idea. I was hoping you'd know."

Colton snickers in the backseat.

Twisting around, I grab hold of my seat and ask, "What about you? Any idea who this is?"

He shakes his head. "I couldn't even wager a guess."

"Lord, woman, why on earth are we listening to music none of us have a clue about? Yeesh, leave this to me," I say, cracking my knuckles outward and reaching for the dial.

After flipping through damn near every station in the vicinity, I shut off the radio entirely and lean back in the seat.

"There is literally no good music out here," I declare.

Cat laughs. "There really isn't, is there?"

"Next time, I'm grabbing my aux cable and we'll plug into YouTube or something. Because *that* was ridiculous."

"Oh, YouTube... Good point," Cat says, her eyes suddenly wide, like a lightbulb had gone off inside them.

Colton snickers under his breath and I can't help but laugh, too.

"Well, luckily, we won't have to endure anymore awkward silence. We've arrived at our destination," Cat says, splaying one hand out above the steering wheel and dashboard.

As she pulls into the parking lot, I lean as far forward as I can, trying to take in the architecture of the library. The old, damn near ancient stone façade instantly reminds me of the academy and my mouth drops open.

"Wow. This is the library? It looks more like an out-of-place castle," I say in awe.

"It's not big enough to be a castle," Colt chuckles, opening his door.

I kick open my car door and get out.

"Well, good point, but the stonework sure does remind me Windhaven Academy—and that looks like a castle, too. I mean, look, it even has gargoyles like the school," I say, pointing to the creatures atop the uppermost parts of the building. "I bet the same architect who built Windhaven Academy built this, too."

"Very true," he says, nodding his head. "It probably was."

I grin triumphantly.

Cat walks over, clicking the button on her car remote. It beeps loudly as all the doors on her Torrent lock.

"The two of you are adorably dorky," Cat says, walking past us and up the stone steps.

My eyebrows tug in at the odd phrasing, and I shoot Colt a sideways glance. He runs his hand along the backside of his neck and rolls his eyes.

"Okay. Uh, come on," he says, following her.

The double wooden doors groan as he pulls them open for us to enter. The open entryway is adorned with a mixture of stone and wood, continuing on the semi-castle motif. Beyond is a large desk with only one station for a single librarian to sit. It's nothing massive, but certainly impressive.

"Wow, back in Mistwood, they had at least three librarians working all the time. Kinda quaint in here, huh?" I whisper.

"Three? How big was your library?" Cat gasps.

I shrug, "Not super big. But they did a lot of community outreach stuff, though."

"Well, here, our library does books. *Old* books. And that's about all..." Cat whispers back.

"Alrighty then..." I say tipping my head in acknowledgement.

"Come on, I'll show you the section you'll want to start digging into," Colt says, walking out in front and leading us past the librarian's desk and deeper into the library's depths. The smell of old, musty books and papers assaults my senses, but I breathe it in deep, like it's a familiar scent of home.

"I love that smell," I say, inhaling deeply. "Don't you love that smell?"

Cat cocks an eyebrow, but Colt's lips curve into a genuine smile.

"I do, too," he says, leaning in close. He smells like aftershave and a hint of something else...burnt wood? Cinnamon? Colt straightens up, adjusting the collar on his jacket and picking up speed again so he can show us the best place to research.

Oddly enough, we leave the confines of the normal-looking library, as we take a set of stairs in the back, leading down to the lower bowels of the building.

"Okay...because this isn't creepy at all," I mutter, taking the stairs slowly so I don't trip.

"You'll see why everything's down here in a minute," Colt says.

Cat wraps her arms around her body, but doesn't say anything.

As we enter the lower level, the old-books smell gives way to ancient-books smell. The thickness in the air actually borders on decomposition.

Colton flips on a light switch and a series of low-hanging incandescent bulbs flicker to life.

"Jeez, are we even supposed to be down here?" I ask, taking in the shelves of old tomes, newspapers, and goodness knows what else.

"Yeah, I come down here all the time. It's where the old histories of Windhaven are kept," Colt says, clearing off some space on a dusty table in the center of a small enclosure of shelves. "Well, anything older than the turn of the millennium, anyway."

"Well, that's good to know. Because it kinda looks like an old person's attic or something," I say, chuckling.

"Smells like it, too," Cat laughs.

"Right?" I say, flipping my left hand upside down and pointing her direction.

"Okay, before you get started, you should know, you may not like everything you find," Colton says, placing his hands on the table and leaning in.

"Mmkay. *Ominous*," I say.

"I just wanted to be up front," he says, tilting his head. "There's a lot down here and, well...whatever you find needs to come to you. Does that make sense?"

"So, is there anything you can actually just *tell* me? Or is this some sort of initiation kind of deal where I need to do it all on my own?" I ask, grabbing the back of a chair and pulling it out.

"A little of both, but first, it's sorta better if you uncover a bit on your own. Because, well, you probably wouldn't believe us if we told you," he says.

My eyebrows tug in. What could they possible say to me that I wouldn't believe? I go to a supernatural school and I'm surrounded daily by people with incredible gifts I could only dream of wielding.

I turn to Cat, who simply nods in agreement.

"All right. Hit me. What should I check out first?" I say, taking a seat.

"Uhm..." Colt says, twisting around and walking over to one of the shelves. He tilts his head to the side while his right pointer finger follows along the spines of the old books.

From here, I have no idea what on earth any of them say. Their etchings are worn and scrolled in a strange kind of typography I've never seen before.

"Ah, here it is," he says, plucking one of the books out and walking it back to the table.

He places the huge book, nearly the size of a scrapbook, on the table and shoves it across the dust to me.

"Start here," he says.

Cat pulls out the chair beside me, then casually drops into it. Her expectant gaze is hard to read.

Pulling the book to me, I run my hand along its worn binding. The brown leather on the front cover is completely blank, but the spine has words along it that have all but rubbed off.

Colt continues to pull books from the shelves, adding to a growing stack in the middle of the table. My eyes widen, but I shake my head and flip open the one he handed me.

Inside the first few brittle pages are handwritten scribblings in the margins. But I finally come to the title page that reads:

Windhaven est. 1786

"Is this some sort of history of Windhaven?" I ask, glancing up.

Cat nods, her face a furry of anticipation.

"Okay," I begin. "Weird place to start."

"Trust me, you'll want to read this. It's important," Colton says, shifting the books aside to take a seat on the table beside me.

"You know there are hundreds of pages here, right? You're not expecting me to read the whole—"

Cat giggles, "No, no. You'll be able to skim it. The important pieces will jump at you. Trust me. It's the way this goes."

Scrunching my face, I narrow my eyes and turn back to the book.

She's not wrong. The very first page pulls me up short as elements inside almost highlight themselves in a glowing light. To the right, in a large picture which as been clearly drawn, is a home that looks oddly familiar. The front façade is older and has slightly different architecture than it does now, but the resemblance is still undeniable.

"Is this my—?"

"Yes," Cat says before I finish.

"Okay..." I say, staring at the black and white image.

A man and woman stand beside the front entry, their faces stoic and blank. The woman's in a light-colored dress, and instantly conjures up images of the woman I saw laying on the entryway floor. In an upstairs bedroom, it almost looks as though children look out of the window.

What would make the artist draw things this way? Why would the children not be drawn with the adults?

I raise my hand, running my pointer finger gingerly over the woman. Could this be the same woman? And if so, am I losing my mind?

"That's your great-great-great, who knows how many actual greats, *grandmother*," Cat whispers with an air of reverence.

"Keep going," Colton urges.

I flit my eyes to him, then back to the book. Turning the page gently, a more modern account, as if cut from a local newspaper, is enclosed in the pages.

THE BLACKWOODS

The first residents of Windhaven, Warren and Abigail Blackwood, began construction on their estate in 1790 and it was completed in 1797. Their home stood as a monument and testament to those who considered venturing out into the wilderness the way they had. The Blackwoods were instrumental in developing the layout of the original town of Windhaven, as well as recruiting similar families for their small community. They had a vision they wanted to fulfill in establishing the small town. With Warren Blackwood's innate ability to commune with the dead and Abigail's gift of healing and regeneration, the couple had no trouble in accomplishing their vision. Unfortunately, Abigail met an untimely death in...

I stop reading and look up, horrified and confused.

Cat leans over and begins to read where I left off, as if she knew exactly what made me stop. "Unfortunately, Abigail Blackwood met an untimely death in 1800, just as the town was beginning to gain more residents and get itself established. She was found dead inside the residence, having fallen from the second-floor landing. Authorities were called in, but no evidence of foul play was found. Her death was ruled a suicide."

I lean back in my chair, my memory flashing to the woman I saw, and the surprise and terror it invoked. Could I have actually seen her?

I glance up, looking both of them in the eye.

Should I tell them?

"Your great-grandmother met an untimely death, which is sorta sad itself. But that's not the part we need you to read. Keep going," Colt says.

Pushing away the surprise, I nod and continue to read out loud, "After the death of Abigail, Warren Blackwood locked himself inside Blackwood Manor, refusing to leave again. Until his dying day in 1838, it is thought he spent his days adding rooms to the estate for all the children he and Abigail would never have. He then spent his evenings trying to conjure her spirit." I stop reading and shake my head. "This is utterly ridiculous."

Colton makes a face. "Keep going."

My eyes narrow and I flip the page back to the photo. The blank stare of a little boy makes me shudder.

"So, if Abigail and Warren didn't have kids...who's this?" I ask pointing to the old photograph.

Cat's eyebrow twitches upward, but she says, "That's your great-great grandpa, or something like that."

"Okay, so Abigail and Warren *did* have kids? I'm so confused," I say, leaning back.

"That's the part you're confused about?" Colt says, cocking his head to the side.

"Well, it said he spent his days adding rooms for...*oh*," I say, realization dawning. "They meant *more* kids. I get it. They wanted a bigger family."

"Well, if the Blackwood legacy died with them, where did you come from?" Colton says, raising a knowing eyebrow.

"Good point," I say, clicking my tongue and mock shooting him with my thumb and pointer finger.

"Your ancestry plays a role into how people in this town, uh...view you and your family, I guess..." Colton says, splaying his hands out in front of him on the table.

"Okay? I don't get that. Why should I be judged by the heritage of my dead ancestors?" I ask, turning the pages.

"It's hard to describe because in some ways, it doesn't make sense to us, either. Keep going," Cat suggests, tapping the book.

There are pages of black and white drawings, or pictures of paintings, along with stories of all of the founding families. My fingers stop when I reach a page that reads: *The Gilberts.*

"Is this your family?" I ask, pointing.

Cat nods, "Yup."

"So our families go way back, huh?" I grin.

"Yeah, actually. Our families were very close. It's why our house is across the pond," Colton shrugs.

"Wow. Okay, now that's kinda cool. I mean, what are the chances we'd become friends? I had no idea," I say, snickering to myself.

"Well, we did," Cat says, grinning sheepishly. "It's part of the reason I reacted the way I did when we first met. Sorry about that, by the way."

"Oh, right. Good point," I say, butting my forehead with the heel of my hand.

I bend in, looking at the family resemblance between their ancestors and the two of them. It's uncanny.

"Wait a minute..." I say, working through the timeframe

and this revelation. "What about, and I don't mean to be a total jerk, but what about slavery? I mean, back then, African Americans weren't really *free* citizens. Right? Your family wasn't owned by mine or anything, were they?"

"No, actually. I mean, yeah, slavery, especially with supernaturals was bad news. But the Blackwoods changed all that for our family," Cat says, smiling.

Colt nods. "Your family was the reason ours was free to live and be a part of the founding of this town. It was practically unheard of anywhere else in the country. Though I gotta say, from the way our mom tells it, the town wasn't real pleased at first. But Warren and Abigail had a...*pull*. No one else could deviate once they were involved," Colt says.

"Cool," I say, leaning back in my seat.

"I know it's a lot to take in," Cat begins.

"No, it's not that. I'm just, things have been so weird since I first got back and now things are starting to kinda make sense in an uber strange sorta way," I mutter. "I mean, if other people know this history, it makes sense they'd be a little dubious with me, I suppose. But they don't have to worry. I don't even believe in ghosts—or whatever the hell else my family was into."

My insides churn and doubt tugs at the back of my mind. I've seen some weird stuff lately—stuff I can't quite explain away just yet—and this is only making it harder.

"Hmmmm..." Colton asks, suddenly serious. He rubs at the space between his thumb and index finger with the opposite hand. "Other than Dominic carving up your car, what else has been weird?"

I meet his expectant gaze. For a moment, I consider telling them about the strange voice and the vision of the woman on the floor.

"Well," I begin, trying to find the right words, "for starters, I think I...*may hav*e... You know what, never mind."

"May have what?" Cat urges, her eyes wide.

"It's stupid," I say, shaking my head.

"You never know. It might not be stupid to us at all," Cat mutters, shrugging her right shoulder. "There's a lot you don't know yet about your past and your family's legacy. It would take a lot to surprise us at this point."

Colton's eyes are a dark pool of concern, but he leans in, placing a hand on mine. "Autumn, you can trust us."

Surprised by the contact, all I can do is stare at the way his hand contrasts my own. Almost as if melding together in some sort of yin and yang, his dark skin is almost mesmerizing. Suddenly, the colors of our skin fade away from my consciousness and, instead, iridescent flames of blue and orange engulf our hands. When I look up, the same flames are mirrored in Cat's eyes.

I tug my hand from his and the flames extinguish.

"I, uh—" I say, blinking back my bewilderment. "You know, I think maybe I should go."

CHAPTER 16

ONE STEP FORWARD, TWO STEPS BACK

Thoughts tumble through my head and I can't shake this uneasy feeling that when I uncover my powers, they're going to be bad. Maybe not bad, per se, but definitely not the kind I was hoping for.

Then again, maybe I really don't have powers at all and this whole thing was a huge mistake. Unfortunately, that would be the biggest let-down of the century, because I feel like I'm finally hitting my stride at Windhaven Academy.

Part of me is desperate to know, and the other is desperate to stay in obliviousness. Unfortunately, the last option isn't a choice. If I don't figure out my powers, I'm sure they're not going to let me stay. They'll have to kick me out and make room for someone with actual gifts.

The one person I wish I could talk to about this is Mom. But she's also a no-go, for a multitude of reasons. Maybe I should think about talking to my dad?

Staring at the ceiling, I let out a sigh.

"What's wrong, beautiful?" Wade says, propping himself up on his left arm.

I switch to a seated position. "Was it that obvious?"

"Maybe a little," he laughs, sitting up, too.

"It's just—I'm starting to get nervous about Windhaven Academy. I don't want to be kicked out for being the powerless kid. At this point, it would be sorta devastating," I say.

"Well, what do you know so far? Has anything unusual presented itself? I mean, more than the other kids at school behaving oddly," he says, shrugging.

I shake my head. "No, not really..." I drift off, thinking back to the bizarre flame that ignited when Colton touched my hand. Was that crossing a line? I mean, I never should have held my hand there so long, but it was like I couldn't help it. What would Wade think?

"Not really? That kinda sounds like a maybe."

My eyes flit to his gorgeous face and I melt inside. "Well, I guess maybe...but it's not really a good thing, if you know what I mean."

Wade lowers his dark eyebrows. "Go on."

I clear my throat, shifting in my seat. "Well, er, I think I may have seen my dead ancestor, Abigail Blackwood, in the main entry of the house."

There's no way I could tell him about Colton's touch. Not yet.

"Really? Well, that's something. Good or not, that could mean you sense the past. Maybe you can see through the veil or, heck, talk with ghosts," he says, excitement tickling at the edge of his tone.

"Oh, don't sound so excited about that prospect. I'm not about to become the ghost whisperer," I laugh.

"Now, see, that's a show I didn't watch," he says, smirking.

"Then how did you know it was a show? Hmmm?"

He raises a knowing eyebrow. "Woman, who do you take me for?"

I pause, then raise my right hand in acceptance. "Fair enough."

"So, what if you can talk to ghosts? I mean, didn't you say that you heard a woman say welcome home?" Wade says, shifting on the bed.

"Oh yeah. I totally forgot about that," I say, my eyes drifting down to the bedspread.

Could that be it? Could I really be able to talk to ghosts?

A shiver races down my spine and goose bumps flash across the backs of my arms.

"We could be on to something here... it would explain why you've never experienced anything unusual at school. Wouldn't it? Well, unless there are ghosts at Windhaven, which wouldn't surprise me."

"Me neither, actually," I say, unable to stay seated. I uncross my legs, standing up beside the bed as I start to pace.

"Okay, so tell me—how do you know it was this Abigail?" He says, scooting to the edge of the bed and reaching for my hands. I take his offering and he pulls me closer to him until I stop right before him.

"Well, I stumbled on some town histories the other day..." I say, tiptoeing to the edge of honesty. "I found a picture in there showing our home when it was built, and the woman in the picture was my super-great grandmother. But when I saw her here, it was strange. I was talking to my dad the other day, at the top of the landing. When I looked over the railing, I swore I saw a woman in a white dress laying on the ground, only she looked funny. Like her body was bent at an odd angle. It freaked me out."

"What did your dad say?" Wade asks, his silver eyes burning into mine.

"Didn't tell him," I say sheepishly. "Is that bad?"

"Well, no, but it might help if you did. Maybe he knows

what's going on. This is his house, after all. And who knows, maybe he knows more about your family legacy than you realize. Have you ever talked to him about it?"

"I haven't, actually. He really hasn't been around as much as I thought he'd be. I did ask him if he'd be here this weekend so he could meet you and he said yes. But here we are..." My words fade out as I shrug.

"Right? You know, I'm starting to get the impression he's avoiding meeting me. Am I being too paranoid?" Wade asks, narrowing his eyes.

I laugh. "I don't think so. He's kind of an introvert. He's probably just giving us space so he doesn't have to face the reality that his twenty-year-old daughter is having sex."

Wade's eyes widen and he quirks an eyebrow. "She is?"

I reach around him, grabbing my pillow and throwing it at him. "You know what I mean."

"Do I?" he says, wrapping his arms around my waist and tugging me to the mattress. "Is that an invitation, then?"

"No invitation necessary, Mr. Hoffman. Unless of course you'd like one. In which case, consider your invitation formally served," I purr, running my fingertips through his dark locks.

"Well, Ms. Blackwood, I may just take you up on this..." he whispers, bending in and letting his lips graze the side of my neck.

The hairs all over my body stand on end again, but this time, for far more enjoyable reasons. However, he stands back up and gently pulls me to my feet.

"What are you—?" I begin, dazed.

"Oh no...we'll get there, trust me. But you deserve more than convenient-whim sex," he says, flashing me a mischievous grin. "I have plans for you, Dru."

Butterflies erupt from deep inside my belly and I blink back my surprise.

He does sexy soooo well.

"So, if not now, when?" I ask, unable to help myself.

"You'll just have to wait and see," he says softly, flashing me his incredible wink.

I let out a sigh intermixed with desire and impatience. "What are we doing then?"

"Let's see if we can't suss out your powers a bit," he says, grabbing my hand and twisting around. He leads me out of my bedroom and down the hallway, back toward the main entrance. "You said you saw your uber-great grandma here...right?"

As we turn the corner, my eyes land on the rug beneath the second-floor landing and I nod.

"Were you doing anything? Touching anything? Maybe it's tactile," he offers.

I shrug. "I was just admiring the light coming through the windows and looked over. There she was, like it had just happened."

"Did she seem like a ghost? You know, like wispy? Or was she solid?"

"Solid, I guess. She didn't look like ghosts in TV shows, anyway," I say, remembering back.

Wade nods. "Okay, that's something. How did she die? Did it say?"

I scrunch my face and take a deep breath. "Yeah, basically she died after falling from there." I point up to the landing above us.

"So, she was showing you her death. In my experience, that's pretty significant," Wade says, casting his gaze over the rug. "What happens if you touch the rug?"

"I don't know, I've never bent down to give it go," I snicker.

Wade eyes me expectantly.

"Oh, fine," I mutter, dropping to my hands and knees. "I feel completely ridic—"

The moment my hands touch the rug, a swirling red and blue iridescent flame consumes both of my hands and radiates up my arms. I shift to a crouched position, pulling my hands from the fabric and stare at them. Other than the color being slightly different, the experience is almost exactly the same as when Colton touched me. The flames continue to travel up my arms until my whole body ignites in them.

Wade rushes to my side, his eyes wide, "Autumn, are you — does it hurt?"

I blink back my surprise, shaking my head. "No, not all."

Then, as quickly as they sprang up, the flames extinguish. Exhaling in a loud puff, I drop onto my backside.

"Well, I have no idea what that was, but it's safe to say, dear Dru, mundane human, you are not."

I lift my gaze, staring at his sideways grin and sparkling eyes. He's so happy about this, but the only thing I can think about is how similar it was to when Colton touched my hand.

With wide eyes, I nod quickly. It's all I can think to do.

Wade drops to a crouch beside me. "You don't seem happy. Why aren't you happy?"

I chew on the side of my cheek and swallow hard.

"What is it? What's wrong?" He says, an air of panic rising in his tone.

"I have something to tell you," I say, patting the spot beside me.

Wade's eyebrows lower and he actually stands instead. Cramming his hands into his pocket, he eyes me suspiciously. "It's something bad, isn't it?" His voice is barely a whisper.

Pushing myself to a stand, I shake my head. "No, I mean, I don't think so. At least, not in the way you're probably thinking."

"Okay..." His silver eyes narrow to slits and his goofy grin has all but evaporated.

"Yesterday, I went to the library with Cat and Colt," I begin, watching his every move.

"All right?" he says, his face guarded.

I clear my throat, casting my gaze to the rug. "We were only researching, but something strange happened when Colton touched my hand. It was weird, and I didn't tell you about it because I wasn't sure how I felt."

"How you felt?" Wade says, his eyes widening.

I take a step back. "No, not like that. I mean, I wasn't sure how I felt when it happened. It was weird." I lick my lower lip, suddenly parched. "Innocent, even. It's just...when we made contact, it was like I was completely mesmerized by his skin—then it burst into flames. Almost identically to how it did just now."

Wade's dark lashes flutter as he takes in the new information. He's utterly silent.

"Say something," I whisper.

"I'm not sure what to say. I—" he shakes his head. "Part of me thinks, 'so what? Some guy touched your hand. It was just your hand.' The other part of me is furious he even had the audacity to do that. Then, there's the other part of me..." his voice trails off.

"The other part of you what?" I ask, walking up to him.

His eyebrows tip up in the middle and his jaw clenches. "The other part wonders why him and not me? Why would you have that reaction with such an innocent touch, but never with—"

"I don't know how it works. I don't even know what it is or why."

Wade takes a deep breath through his nose. "Why did he touch you?"

I take a step away, trying to remember. "I don't know. I think he was trying to console me. Or try to get me to trust them. We were talking about all the weird goings on and they're trying to help me sort out all of the confusion around my family and my powers. They know more than they're telling me and he was just trying to make me feel better."

"Good people don't keep the truth from those they care about."

I flinch, knowing his words are aimed at more than just the Gilbert twins.

"There is nothing going on between Colt and me. You know that, right?" I whisper, pushing back the urge to cry.

"Maybe for you. But what about him?" Wade asks, his face scrunching together like he ate something horrible.

Taking a step toward him, I wrap my arms around his waist. "I don't care what he thinks or whether or not he'd like there to be more. I'm yours, *Angel*. And I'm not going anywhere."

Wade takes a deep breath, relaxing his shoulders as he wraps his arms around me. I sink into his embrace, resting my head against his chest. His heartbeat is loud and fast, but he pulls me in tighter, dropping his chin to the top of my head.

Just when I think things are going to be okay, I hear a voice over my shoulder whisper, "You shouldn't make promises you can't keep."

CHAPTER 17
A TRAIL TO FOLLOW

Wade's cell phone rings and I can tell by the way his back is ramrod straight, it's not good news. Nothing like getting bad news at 5:30 a.m. to set the day off with a note of anxiety.

"Are you going to have to leave?" I say, reaching for Wade's hand as he throws back the covers.

Wade nods, still half asleep. He tugs out a new dusty-blue t-shirt from his backpack and puts it on. His voice is gruff as he whispers, "Yeah, Grandpa's not doing well. I gotta go check on him."

"Do you want me to come with? I could—"

"No, no... Go back to bed," he says, bending down and kissing the top of my head. "No reason for both of us to get up at this ungodly hour. Besides, you have homework, remember?"

"Ugh," I groan, pulling the covers over my head.

Wade chuckles, zipping up his jeans. "You won't figure out how your powers work if you don't test them out. At least you know for sure you can test them here instead of hunting down what's-his-name."

"Not fair," I say, dropping the covers and glaring at him.

He laughs it off as he takes a seat on the bed so he can slide his shoes on.

"Wade..." I begin.

"I'm over it, Autumn. Really. I trust you, and that's what matters. Just don't expect me to like the guy. Okay?"

I sit up, resting my cheek on his shoulder so I can plant a kiss on his neck. "Deal."

He twists around, but there's still a hint of insecurity hiding in the depths of his eyes.

Shifting closer, I plant a kiss on his lips, then reach around, taking his face in my hands. I kiss his cheek, his eyelids, his chin.

His kisses back are gentle, but reserved, and I can't help but worry that he's still taking things with Colton to heart. As he shifts off the bed, his grin doesn't quite reach his eyes.

"Will you be able to come back?" I ask, sliding my legs over the bed's edge.

Wade's eyebrows tip up in the middle and he shakes his head. "I don't think so, Dru. I need to spend some time with him to know if he's getting better or worse. You know? I wish I could—"

I cut him off with a swipe of my hand. "I know. I totally understand."

He nods, more to himself than me, by the looks of it. "Good. Well, I suppose I better..."

"Right," I say, nodding. "Let me walk you out." Standing up, I reach for my pajama bottoms and throw them on.

"You don't have to. Really. You should go back to bed and stay comfortable."

"Mr. Hoffman, I insist." I stare him hard in the eyes and his pupils widen.

"All right, then," he grins, raising his hands in defeat.

We walk the hallway in silence, but when we get to the big front door, I wrap my arms around him.

Without a word, his strong arms encompass my body, and we melt into one another. He places his cheek to the top of my head and pulls me closer. Standing there, I wish I could keep this cocoon around us forever.

"You better let me know how your grandpa is. I hope he's okay," I whisper.

"Me, too." He pulls me in tighter.

"Drive safe, okay?" I whisper into his chest.

"I realized something yesterday," Wade says, his words reverberating through me.

Pulling back, his expression is a difficult mixture to read.

"With all this Colton stuff, your powers, everything with my grandpa and how close to... I realized I don't want to waste time. It's too short. So, here goes. I'm falling for you Dru. And not"—he bites his lower lip—"...not just kinda-sorta. I mean, I love you."

Tears brim in my lids and I can't help but reach out for his face. With my index finger, I trace the lines from the crease of his left eye down to his lips. "Wade, I love you too. I wasn't looking for you, but I know I never want to lose you."

His eyes are wide and he leans into my touch, grabbing hold of my wrist and giving my palm a kiss. Smiling softly, he bends forward until his lips are crushing down on mine. Unlike the reserved kisses in the bedroom, his true passion bleeds through, as he places his hands on either side of my face and presses down hard. My lips buzz from the pressure and intensity of him and when he finally pulls back, I'm left in a state of dizzy bliss; tingling from head to toe.

"I'll see you soon, okay?" he says, kissing my eyebrow.

Without another word, he opens the door and walks out.

Raising my fingertips to my lips, I stand there, watching

as he drives off. I wait until I can no longer see his taillights in the driveway before closing the front door.

Exhaling slowly, I plant my forehead against the ancient wood.

"How did I ever get here?" I whisper out loud. I never knew falling in love could hurt, even when it felt so good.

Taking a deep breath, I turn around to head back to bed. I'm wide awake now, but I need to at least make an attempt at more sleep. Wade and I didn't fall asleep until well past midnight and goodness knows I don't want to figure out how little sleep that actually is.

As I make my way past the grand staircase, some movement to the right catches my eye. I take a step back and have another look.

"Dad? Are you awake?" I call out, my heart suddenly thumping in my chest.

Silence greets me and I take a tentative step up the first couple of stairs.

"Dad?"

At the top of the landing, the bottom of a woman's white dress moves from view, heading down the hallway toward my Dad's wing of the house.

Goose bumps flash across my skin and the hairs on the back of my neck and arms stand on end.

"He—hello?" I call out, clearing my throat midway.

My chest is about to burst as I take another couple of steps upward. Flitting my gaze all over the space, I clutch the railing and race up the rest of the stairs, turning to the right to face the woman.

However, as I reach the top landing, I again catch the bottom of her dress as she turns to the left and heads down the hallway that leads to my dad's room. Without thinking, I race after her. If she's here to do any harm, or hurt my dad...

When I reach the end of the hallway and turn left, she stands outside the door to his bedroom, staring at it. My footsteps slow down as I make my way closer, but my heart rate continues to pick up. The adrenaline coursing through me makes my limbs shake, but I press myself forward despite it.

"Abigail? You are Abigail, aren't you? " I call out. "What do you want?"

The woman turns to look at me, her piercing gaze practically sees straight through me. The moment our eyes lock, there's no doubt in my mind this woman is my ancestor, Abigail Blackwood. Then, without a word, she again faces the door.

I struggle to take in a cleansing breath, but I walk as close to her as I dare. While she's dressed in clothing from a completely different era, she looks as real and corporeal as any other person I've ever seen. Part of me feels totally validated. She can't be a ghost. Aren't ghosts supposed to be transparent or something?

Suddenly, Abigail surges forward, entering my Dad's bedroom without even opening the door.

A tiny squeak escapes my lips and I stumble backward, clasping my hand over my mouth. Before I have the chance to fully process, I race forward, flinging the door back to warn my dad. When I enter his room, however, I pull up short. While his bed is slightly disheveled, he's not in it. With the sheer amount of dust in the room, you'd think no one had been in here for ages.

Abigail stands before an ancient-looking, ornate desk. There are tiny little wooden carvings and small pull-out drawers and slots for papers or mail all over it. Down its legs, there are three deeper drawers on either side.

My insides shake and I can't quite get a grapple around the thought that maybe I was wrong. Maybe ghosts *do* exist.

Getting up enough courage to walk up beside her, I ask, "What is it you want? Why won't you talk to me?"

She turns to me, her solemn face unchanging. Raising her right arm, she points at the desk.

My heart races like I've just run a marathon, but I force myself to take a step closer.

"What about it? It's a desk. I shouldn't even be in—"

Suddenly Abigail raises her hands and the contents of the entire room shake.

I flinch, raising my hands to my face, in case anything goes flying.

"It was you—you broke the vase in my bedroom," I stammer, as things start to make more sense.

Abigail's face pinches tight and her jaw clenches. Again, she points to the desk.

"What? What is it? I'm not going to snoop through my dad's things. That's just—"

Without anyone touching it, a hidden drawer just under the desktop flies open. There are a few papers, bound in some sort of twine, an old-fashioned looking feather quill, and an adorned bronze handle.

My jaw drops open and I take a step closer. "Is that—?"

My mind is wheeling, but from here, it looks like a fit for the missing handle in my bedroom. Why would my dad have it hidden in a drawer?

"Honey?" Dad says from behind me.

I spin around, pushing the drawer in with my hip.

"What are you doing in here?" he asks, surprise and confusion written across his face. He walks over to his bed, eyeing the mess, and returns his gaze to me.

"I was, uh, looking for you. I haven't seen you all weekend and I was getting worried."

"Sorry, sweetie. I had to leave on urgent business," he says, shaking his head. "I should have told you or had James... I'm still not used to checking in with anyone else. It's been years since I had to think about that sort of thing."

I hold a hand out in front of me. "No, I get it. I was just hoping to introduce you to Wade."

Taking a few steps away from the desk, I look over my shoulder. Abigail is gone.

Dad's forehead crinkles. "Oh, right. You mentioned that. Wow. Sorry, Autumn. I must be getting old. Forgetting stuff left, right, and center."

"It's okay. He had to leave, though, so maybe next weekend? His grandpa isn't doing well. So, I thought I'd..." I bite the side of my cheek, trying to think of why I'd want to come to his bedroom to talk to him. "I'd just make sure you weren't avoiding him."

"No, of course not. I'm very excited to meet the new man in your life," Dad says, smiling.

I smile back, trying to make a graceful exit as I inch closer to the door.

"Well, I guess I should..." I start, jabbing a thumb toward the hallway.

"Sure. Did you want me to have James make you some breakfast?"

"No, it's okay. I didn't get much sleep, so I think I'm going to try and go back to bed for a little bit."

"Sounds good, sweetie. Love you," he says, nodding.

"Love you, too," I say absently, walking out of the room and down the hall.

As nice as Dad is, I know there's a reason Abigail waited to show me the door handle when he wasn't in his room. He's obviously hiding it for a reason, and who knows what it is. I don't want to piss him off or make him think I've been snooping in places I shouldn't. If I ask him about the handle, it could put this good thing we have going in jeopardy. The last thing I need is to be contained to certain rooms, like when I was a kid.

But now that I know where the handle is, I have to see what's behind the door. The curiosity will gnaw at me. And as soon as Wade knows we can solve this mystery, he's going to be chomping at the bit to get back here.

There's just one problem. Dad flits around this house like a ghost. Most of the time I don't know where he is. For all I know, he spends the majority of the time in his room.

How on earth am I going to get back in there to get the door handle?

CHAPTER 18

SHADOWS & TATTERED WALLPAPER

Practically tiptoeing, I make my way to my bedroom with my insides twisting into knots.

Abigail is nowhere to be seen, but hopefully that also means I'll have a few uninterrupted hours to do some investigating on my own. Not to mention sort through some of the crazy things happening to me lately.

I *mean, seriously...* What's my dad hiding? And can ghosts really be real? Or am I just seriously sleep deprived?

Glancing over my shoulder, I release a slow breath.

If she was a ghost, why did Abigail seem as alive as anyone else I've met?

I reach my hallway, scanning the space for her, but thankfully, I'm still alone. Taking a deep, cleansing breath, I enter my bedroom and close the door behind me. Without hesitation, I lock it and take a seat on the end of my bed. Instead of heading straight to the hidden doorway, I flop down on my back and stare at the ceiling. I seriously don't remember the last time so much was pressing down on me all at once. And the majority of it doesn't make a bit of sense.

For a moment, I close my eyes, trying to let all the weird stuff wash over me so I can get to the heart of the truth. When I was younger, I hated this space—hated all it represented. But now...

"Quell your fear, Autumn. The truth shall set you free..."

The whisper is breathless and right beside my ear. I bolt upright on the end of the bed, my heart practically ripping itself out of my chest. I scan the room for the source of the voice, but there's nothing. No one but me is in the room, but I know what I heard.

"Abigail?" I call out, backing away from my bed.

My eyes flit to the wall with the hidden door and determination takes over me. I need to find out what's going on and take control. My tongue flashes across my lower lip and I march over to the wall. Pushing my dresser out of the way, I don't even try to do things delicately. The urge to figure *something* out in my crazy, mixed-up world has taken seed in my gut and I start ripping the wallpaper back. The decorative sheets shred, falling to the floor the way leaves tumble from the trees.

When I've managed to peel it all back from the doorway, I take a step back and tilt my head to the side. Surprisingly, the door is tiny in comparison to the other doors in the house, and not at all what I originally expected. Nearly half the height and width, it was practically built for a dwarf—or a kid, I suppose.

My eyebrows tug in and I walk up, sticking my fingertip inside the lip of the hole. Obviously, there's no handle, but it's pretty clear how it should set inside it. Snorting, I take a seat on the floor, staring at my handiwork and the handiwork of whoever built the door. It's ancient-looking with its thick planks of wood. Most of them are warped and in desperate need of a good sanding. Yet the hinges and delicate bronze handle plate are beautiful.

"Why are you here?" I whisper to myself, placing my hands on the floor behind me and leaning back. "Why were you hidden?"

Loud knocking makes me jump and sit upright. It takes me a moment to realize it's actually coming from my bedroom door.

"Honey? I don't mean to disturb you...but are you still awake?" Dad says on the other side.

I suck in a breath and hold absolutely still.

Would he be pissed to see the mess?

"Yeah, I'm awake. But trying to fall back to sleep, though," I call out, deciding I better give him a reason not to find the key and come on in.

"Okay, sweetie. Sorry I bugged you," he says.

"Don't worry about it," I say, pushing up to a kneel as I stare at the back of the door. I silently pray he doesn't try to open it anyway.

Guilt clings to my gut, because I'm sure he had something on his mind, but I need some time to myself with this. Especially since I'm clearly being haunted and I didn't even know it was a possibility, not really, until just now.

After a few quiet moments, I grab an armful of wallpaper and rush over to my small desk. I cram as much as I can of the decorative paper into the tiny wire basket underneath it. It's clearly one of those minuscule trash cans that are only good for crumpled-up paper and tissues. Maybe a broken pencil. It overfills far too quickly as I rush back with another armful.

"Ugh. I'm gonna have to sneak out for a garbage bag," I whisper to myself when it becomes painfully apparent it's not going to all fit.

Dropping to my knees beside the door, I bend down, trying to get my fingertips between the door and the floor to see if I can pry it open without the handle. Unfortunately, whoever took the handle off also made sure to lock the door.

"Figures," I mutter. The only way in is to get the handle from Dad's desk.

There's no chance in hell I'm going to risk that. At least, not yet. I'm also not going to risk leaving this room until I have a better plan. Besides, I want to keep this mystery to myself, even if only for a little while. I'm sure I'll have to bring Dad into it at some point. I can't keep it hidden forever. It wants to be seen.

Standing back up, I glance at the bed, shaking away Abigail's words and the creepy way she could appear completely normal, even though she clearly wasn't. Instead, I walk over to the desk and open my laptop. I click on the Skype icon, my finger hovering over the button to call Wade. He's probably still driving and likely worried about his grandpa. Instead of clicking it and hopping on a call, I sit back in my chair.

How did everything get so confusing?

I run my hand down my face.

"Maybe it's best I don't talk to Wade right now," I mutter, closing the laptop. "He has more important things on his mind."

Instead, I pull my phone from my pocket and text my mom. It's been ages since I connected and I know she'd like to hear from me. Besides, I could use a little Mom encouragement right about now.

Hi, Mom! Thought I'd check in. Are you awake?

After a few moments of staring at my phone, there's no reply. I'm sure she'll be up soon, but she's probably still asleep.

I almost set the phone down, but instead, I text Cat. Typing quickly, I send my first hello in days.

Hey, are you up?

I hold my breath, waiting for an answer. Just as I'm about to put the phone down, an answer pings back.

Not really. You okay?

I bite my lip, realizing I've probably woken her up, too. It's pretty early for a Sunday in Windhaven.

Yeah, sorry. It's okay. Go back to bed.

A second later, my phone rings.

Taking a deep breath, I walk back to my bed and answer her video call. Cat comes into view, only the side of her face evident, since the other half is still buried in her pillow.

"What's up, Autumn? You don't usually text like this," she says, blinking away the dreaminess from her eyes.

I shake my head, pulling my legs into a cross-legged position. "I really don't know where to start."

"Start at the beginning," she offers, propping herself on her elbow.

"I think... I think something strange is going on in my house," I finally spit out.

Her eyes narrow, but she quirks an eyebrow. "Explain. Strange, how?"

My jaw sets and I press my lips tight. "Do you remember the stuff you showed me—at the library. All the stuff with Abigail and Warren?"

"Of course," she nods.

I swallow hard, shifting uncomfortably. "It sounds ludicrous, but I think Abigail is still here."

Cat's head pulls back from her hand and she sits up fully. "Like...she's still alive? Like an immortal?"

I shake my head. "No, I—I don't think so. I think she's something else. A ghost?"

"Why is that a question?"

"Because I didn't believe in ghosts. And she seemed *real*. Like she should be alive. Only, she walked through a door," I say.

Cat's eyes widen. "Really? That's so cool. I mean, I'm sure that was super weird."

"It was—but scary, too. And I don't know what any of this means. I feel like there's so much going on in this house and none of it's making any sense," I say, letting my thoughts tumble out.

"It makes perfect sense, actually," Cat says, one side of her face scrunching apologetically.

"How?"

"Look, I wish we could explain more, I really do. There's magic involved and if we step outside its laws, it won't be good. For any of us. We need to get you back to the library. There's more you need to read. I know the last time freaked you out, but..."

"It wasn't that," I say, shaking my head.

"Well, regardless...with everything that's happening right now, I think the sooner we get back there, the better."

"Why's that?"

Cat exhales loudly. Her eyes flit to the space above her

phone and she looks back to the camera. "Colt's here. He's wondering if he can talk to you, too."

My insides recoil, but I nod. "Sure."

Cat sets the phone on her nightstand so they can both be in view.

"Hey, Autumn," Colt says, tipping his chin upward.

"Hey."

Colt clears his throat and says, "Look, I hope I didn't upset you or anything."

"No, we're good. I just got overwhelmed with all of the history and stuff. Don't worry about it."

He leans back a bit, relief flashing through his features. "Good."

"Cat, you were saying something before Colt came in. What's happening now?" I ask, happy to have some of the awkwardness dissipate between the three of us.

"There are rumors about those missing girls. They believe there's concrete evidence pointing authorities to a magical creature—it's called a Vodník. And it's been here in Windhaven before."

Cat and Colt exchange a significant glance and I can't help but feel agitated by their insider knowledge—whatever it might be.

So much for the truth shall set you free.

"Okay...?" I say, waiting for more details.

"Well, obviously, it wasn't caught. But they thought it was gone. If it's back, that means bad news—*really* bad news for those girls. Vodníks are underwater ghouls that drown humans to collect their souls. Forever."

My eyes widen. "That's horrible. Are you sure?"

Cat nods. "They're pretty rare, but they're not to be trifled with."

Colt shudders. "You should know...the last time—"

"The last time—" Cat says, interrupting, "powerful magic was cast to expel it, but something must have happened to allow it to come back. Maybe too much time had passed since the last time the protection wards were put up. Or maybe something..." Cat pauses to cross her legs. "Look, all I'm saying is, with the pond nearby, we need to be careful until it's caught—or cast out."

"You aren't kidding. That would be horrible. What are people doing to track this thing down, or cast it out?" I ask, my heart racing.

Cat shakes her head. "Dunno. That's all the intel we got. I overheard Mrs. Karlgaard saying something to Ms. Cain Friday afternoon."

"Autumn, I think you'd benefit from a little more history at the library," Colt says, his eyebrows furrowing. "Like Cat was saying, there is powerful magic in place, but we think the way around it is for you to uncover the truth yourself."

"Yeah, I agree," Cat nods. "Let's make a plan to go there tomorrow. I'd say today, if the damn thing were open on a Sunday. Small town, though..."

"Right." I nod. "That's okay. I have homework and stuff."

"Okay, well, let us know if anything else weird happens," Cat says. "Or if you see Abigail again."

"I will. Thanks," I say. "Have a good rest of the day, you two."

Hitting the red button, I end the call and set my phone on the nightstand.

On one hand, I feel better about the two of them and glad the air has been cleared a bit. On the other hand...this thing about the Vodník is a bit creepy.

Could that be what I saw at the edge of our pond the other day?

Flitting my eyes to the little door, I let out a puff of air.

I really should do someth

again with my dresser or sc

bothered.

My entire body feels drainec

into bed and ignore the rest of th

get undressed or anything. Insteac

crawl into bed, pajama bottoms a

practically unheard of. For a few

awake before I finally roll onto my ... I can watch the sky get lighter.

After ten minutes staring out the window, watching the trees blowing in the breeze, I feel the inklings of sleep starting to draw me back in. My eyelids feel heavy and I finally start to sink into my bed, letting the comfortable mattress cradle my body.

Just as I start to nod off, a strange scratching sound enters my consciousness. At first, it doesn't register, not really. But the longer it goes on, the more my brain starts trying to work out where the sound is coming from. The next thing I know, I'm wide awake with my eyes slammed shut. For whatever reason, I'm not strong enough to face whatever's making that sound.

Without a doubt, it's not a natural house sound. Maybe it's gigantic mutant mice...or maybe it's something else. Whatever it is, it's not going to let me go back to sleep.

Gathering the courage to sit up in bed, I continue to keep my eyes shut as I listen for the source of the sound. When I pinpoint the direction, I open my eyes. Swallowing back a scream, I place my fingers over my lips and stare in shock. An eerie, reddish glow emanates from beneath the tiny door, illuminating its edges. I clutch my blankets close to my chest as I try to cram my heart back into my body.

Just when I get brave enough to throw my legs over the

have a closer look, a shadow moves on the
ne door, then disappears.

CHAPTER 19
LEGACIES AND CURSES

Monday classes blur by with a ferocity I've never experienced before. My brain is a whirling mess of questions, and no matter what I do, I can't seem to calm it. After the shadow beneath the hidden door, I don't know what to do. My bravado to check things out has all but vanished because now I have no idea if it's even safe to stay in my room. What if the Vodník is camping out in there? Worse yet, could my dad be protecting a creature that captures souls? And if it is the Vodník, what in the hell am I supposed to do about it?

Before I know it, I find myself following Cat and Colt to the county library to do some more digging. Colton leads the way, back down to the older portion of the library.

"I didn't think you'd ever want to be back here after what happened on Friday," Cat says, plunking her backpack down on the table we vacated the other day.

"Yeah, it was a bit much," I say, entering the space and walking to one of the large tables in the center of the room.

Colton's eyes burn into me and I can't help but feel self-conscious. I run my hand through my hair, trying to tame some of the flaming flyaways.

Taking a deep breath, I drop into a chair. I flit my gaze from Colton to Cat and back again.

"Look, I don't know how this is going to sound, but I gotta get it out there because I feel like I'm going crazy," I begin.

Colton takes a seat at the table, but Cat hovers closer, choosing instead to lean against the table.

"What's going on?" Colt asks, leaning forward.

"Well," I begin, getting back up and to pace, "I honestly don't know where to start."

"Start at the beginning," Cat suggests.

"The beginning..." I laugh. "I'm not even sure where the beginning really is."

"Okay..." she says, throwing an ominous look at Colton.

"It's been a long time since I was here in Windhaven. Like, a really long time, I was seven. Anyway, when I was last here, I hated it. I hated everything about it. I hated my dad. I hated the manor. Everything. It was stifling and boring..." I say, my voice trailing off as my memories swirl. "This time, things are different. It's like my original memories of being here don't make sense. The house is actually kinda cool. My dad's been nothing but awesome, and it's been anything *but* boring."

Both of them watch me expectantly as I look up to meet their gaze. Neither of them say a word; they just wait for me to continue.

I rest my hands on the back of my chair and lean in.

"One of the first few days I was here, I saw—" I say, shaking my head. "I thought I saw a woman sprawled out on the floor, like she had fallen from the second floor landing.

Then you showed me the picture of Abigail and I realized, it was the same woman."

"Is that the first time you saw her?" Cat asks.

I nod. "But I think I may have heard her before then. It's weird though. Whenever she's appeared to me, she's never spoken. But there are times when I don't see her, and I swear I hear a voice speaking to me."

"Cool," Colt says, then he pins his lips tight and leans back in his chair.

I chuckle. "It's sorta cool, when it's not creeping me out. But there's more," I say, shooting them both a significant glance.

Colton crosses his arms.

"Later on, I found something in my room."

"What?" both of them say in unison, their wide eyes and open mouths proving they really are twins.

"A hidden door," I say, chewing on my lower lip. "Well, technically, it was the door's handle plate hidden behind the old wallpaper that drew my attention, but it was a door."

"Okay?" Cat says. "I'm not sure why that's overly significant. I mean, that house is nearly two-hundred years old. I guess I wouldn't be surprised if there were a few covered-up passageways in that house."

"True," I say, nodding. "And until last night, I would have agreed with you. I was actually kinda excited to find it and wanted to go exploring. But the doorknob is missing, so I knew I'd have to wait until I found a way inside. Then yesterday morning, God, I can't believe I'm even saying this..." I say, shaking my head, "Abigail's ghost led me to where the door handle was hidden. It was in my dad's bedroom. He interrupted me before I could grab it, but then..." I shudder away the memory of the light and shadow beneath the door.

"Then?" Colton repeats.

I take a deep breath, blinking rapidly to fight off the urge to chicken out. "Let me back up a bit... Abigail said something to me last night..." I say, tapping my chin. "Before I texted you yesterday."

"What did Abigail say?" Colton asks, his eyebrows furrowed.

"The truth shall set you free," I say, raising my eyebrows knowingly.

"Wait, like what Dominic wrote on your car?" Cat says, leaning forward and snorting.

"No, not like what Dominic wrote. She didn't say it in Latin or anything. It was English," I say, shaking my head.

"Freaky," Cat says, sitting in one of the chairs.

"Right? It gets freakier," I say, widening my eyes.

"You're kidding?" she says.

"Nope. So there I am, trying to sleep after our call, and I realize there's light shining from underneath the hidden door."

"No," Cat says breathlessly.

I nod.

Colton's gaze is stone-cold, but he barely blinks.

"Dead serious. So there I am, staring at the glowing light of the door, and someone, or *something*, freaking moved on the other side," I say, leaning in to whisper.

"Shut up," Cat says, flicking her eyebrows up.

I nod. "I'm worried that—what if it's the Vodník? What if my dad's in league with it? I mean, why else would the door from my room be hidden? And why would Abigail only show me where the doorknob was when my dad wasn't around? What if—"

Colton leans forward, catching Cat's eye, and tipping this head to the side.

"We should try, Cat. We should just tell her," he says.

Surprise floods my being and I pull up short. "Tell me? Tell me what?" I flit my gaze from Colt to Cat and back again. "What in the hell is going on?" I ask, trying to keep the anger swelling in my stomach at bay.

Cat sighs. "I don't know how much of this you'll be able to retain. Like I said, there's heavy magic around your memories, Autumn. I can't even begin to understand why, but I could sense it the minute I realized who you were. You're gonna wanna hear us out before you totally freak. Okay?"

I narrow my eyes, "Shit. I'm right, aren't I? Oh, God—" Despite myself, I take a seat.

She clasps her hands out in front of her and places them on the table. "This town, *Windhaven*, has a secret legacy. Everyone who's lived here for years, the old family bloodlines, we all know about it," she begins. "The academy was built here under its premise..."

"What she's trying to say is...this town, or more specifically, certain families in this town, are cursed," Colton interjects.

"Cursed?" I sputter. "You mean me? *My* family?"

"The Blackwoods, Abigail and Warren, they started something powerful when they moved here. I don't know if it's the energy the town is built on or the magic in your ancestors' blood, but—" Cat trails off, her eyes going distant.

"But after Abigail's death, things went sideways. Warren went from being a prominent member of the town to a recluse. Like the newspaper said before, he started building more and more rooms to the manor. Supposedly adding on to it for all the children they'd never have. Or, at least, that's what everyone says. But we know different..." Colt says.

Cat nods, reaching for my hand. "Our families go back —*way back*—and we know it had nothing to do with the children. When Abigail died, Warren was lost. He didn't want to let her go, so he tried to summon her back. But he didn't have that kind of power. He was what we call a postmortem medium. He could see and talk to the dead, but he couldn't *raise* them. Abigail, on the other hand..."

"Abigail was a necromancer," Colt whispers.

New questions circle my brain like vultures, and I can't seem to pluck one out that's more significant than the others.

Necromancer? Postmortem medium?

The monikers tumble around, not really sticking, but almost making sense with the way things are unfolding.

Am I a postmortem medium, like Warren? Is that why Abigail has latched onto me? What does any of this have to do with the door?

"I'm so confused," I finally say.

Colt stands up, looking at a few spines of the large books nearby. The section he's in is far newer, but it's got the same spine that reads Windhaven History.

"Look, there are things that have happened in the past, and more specifically, the *recent* past, that you need to dig through. If we tell you about it, I'm not sure it will stick. Like Cat said, your mental wards are strong. Someone performed some very powerful spells to keep you from remembering your past. From what we can tell, if we told you straight out, you'd either forget immediately, or it would blow up in our faces."

"Keep me from remembering what? I don't have any holes in my past, Colton. I remember everything perfectly," I say, scrunching my face, but accepting the books.

"Not everything," he says, shaking his head.

"How would you know?" I snicker, crossing my arms over my chest.

"Well, for starters, do you remember Cat and me?" he says, his eyebrows rising into his hairline.

"Uhm, you mean like right now?" I say, tipping my head to the side.

Cat chuckles. "No, dummy. He means when we were kids."

I snicker. "Kids? I never..."

Both of them stare at me expectantly.

"Wait, what?" I sputter, dropping my arms and leaning forward. "We were friends as kids?"

"Autumn, that's just the start. You really need to do some more digging," Colt says, tapping the cover of one of the books. "There's more—a lot more."

"Well, that's all swell," I mutter, trying to calm my insides.

Could I really have known the twins when we were kids? How would I not remember that? Could someone have messed with my mind? And if so...who? *Why*?

"There's one last thing..." Colt says, his voice trailing off as he watches me expectantly.

I shrug, unable to be surprised anymore. "Okay? What?"

"You need to be careful—*really* careful about who you let into your circle. Not everyone will have your best interests in mind," he says. "There can be people who you let in who shouldn't be anywhere near you."

"Well, isn't that true for just about everyone?" I say, quirking an eyebrow.

Cat nods, glancing back to Colt. "Girl's got a point."

"True," he says softly, "but I have it on good authority you need to be careful about someone you've already let in."

I stand up, backing away from the table. "Good authority? *Whose* authority?"

"One of the psychics on campus. It doesn't matter who—" he says, shaking his head.

"Of course it matters," I sputter. "Why would a psychic care about who I spend time with? Is this someone I know? And if they had something important to say, and this seems pretty damn important, why didn't they say who exactly I need to watch out for?"

Colton shifts his gaze from me to Cat and back again. He scrunches up his features and whispers, "He did."

My mouth pops open. "Alright then, spill it. Who am I supposed to steer clear of?" I say, anger building in my gut. Whoever this person is, they should have come to me, not talk behind my back with the Gilbert twins.

"You won't like it—"

"I don't care. Spill," I demand, trying hard to hold back the fury.

"Wade," Colt says, his voice low and reserved. "They told me you need to be very careful around Wade."

CHAPTER 20
BROKEN LOYALTIES

Could Wade be hiding something from me? Would he do that?

I pace at the foot of my bed, eyeing my phone on the nightstand as if it's going to be able to give me the answers.

This is ridiculous. Just ask him, Autumn.

Sighing to myself, I drop onto the bed and reach for my phone.

Without giving time to talk myself out of it, I dial his number.

Wade grins as he answers the video call. "Hey, beautiful. I was just thinking of you."

Guilt coils through my insides, and I suddenly feel traitorous for entertaining any ideas Wade might not have my best interests in mind.

It must show on my face because he asks, "Everything okay?"

I set my phone on the stand. "Can I ask you something?"

Wade's silver eyes widen, and he takes a seat. "Anything. You know that."

I clear my throat, trying to decide on the best way to put things into words.

"What is it, Autumn? You're worrying me," he says, his skin crinkling in the space between his eyebrows.

"I'm not quite sure how to put this, so I'm just going to lay it out there. Are you—do you have any nefarious plans going on that involve me?" I say, scrunching my face.

I sound utterly ridiculous.

Wade blinks wildly, shaking his head. "What?" he snorts. "Is this a joke? Did I miss a punchline? Tell me this is a show reference I just happened to miss."

I pull my legs up, crossing them in front of me. Sighing, I shake my head. "It's not. I wish it were. Believe me, it sounds stupid to ask. It's just—"

"Who's filling your head with such nonsense?" Wade says, a hint of anger flashing through his silver eyes.

I wish I'd thought of an answer to this question before it presented itself.

"It was that Colt guy, wasn't it?" Wade says, taking the leap.

I flinch.

"Shit, it was," he says, dropping the phone on whatever flat surface it was up on. I'm suddenly staring at the ceiling of the room.

The silence that floods the space is deafening until a loud thud breaks the stillness.

"Wade, I need to talk to you about this. Please, come back," I call out, hoping he's still in the room.

A few moments later, Wade picks the phone up and props it against something. His face is a blank slate, completely guarded, but he cradles his right hand in his left.

"Is that blood? Did you—?" My mouth drops open and I lean forward, grabbing the phone. "Did you punch the wall?"

Wade's jaw clenches.

"Look, it doesn't matter that he's the one who told me. He's not the one who originally said it. He was just passing on the information," I say, trying to reason with him.

His distant eyes flicker a bit, but he doesn't say anything at first.

"Wade..."

"And who is this mysterious *other* person?" he says through clenched teeth.

"Well, I don't know who specifically, but they're one of the psychics on campus."

Wade snickers. "Convenient, don't you think?"

"Maybe? Regardless, he warned me to be careful. That's all," I say softly. "I just need to know if that's true."

"What do you think?" Wade says, his dark eyebrows blocking out anything but his black pupils.

"Of course I want to believe he's wrong. I just—why would he say that?"

"You know why, Autumn," Wade retorts. "He has a thing for you."

"Not the other guy. And even if that were true about Colton, we've never..."

Wade's eyes open wide. "Never what?"

"No, nothing about Colt. It's just...*you've* never told me what kind of supernatural powers you have, or are going to have. You're always so interested in discovering my powers, but we've never really talked about yours."

Wade shrugs. "That's because there's nothing to tell. My powers, if I actually do have any, none of it will reveal itself until certain events are triggered, and who knows? Maybe I'll never get the chance to be supernatural. My family skips generations sometimes. I might get powers, I might not.

Why do you think I'm so interested in helping you uncover yours?"

I sigh. "I'm sorry, it's just..."

"Look, I get it. People are filling your head with nonsense and it's easy to let that infiltrate your mind. I was worried about that before you left. Especially if I'm not there to defend myself. I wish you knew you could trust me, but I guess I'm not that lucky."

"Wade, that's not fair..."

"I gotta go. Grandpa's not doing well today. We'll talk about this later," Wade says, glancing over his shoulder.

"I didn't mean—"

"Doesn't matter. It's not life or death. This is. So, I guess I'll talk to you later, Autumn."

With that, the call ends and I'm left staring at my phone's background picture of the two of us in happier times. Clicking off my phone, I flop backward onto the bed.

Am I ruining a good thing here by entertaining what Colt said? Wade has been nothing but supportive and sweet. He's damn-near perfect and I'm questioning him? God, I'm so stupid.

"Hey, sweetie. Are you okay?" Dad says from the open doorway.

I sit up, fighting back the urge to cry. "I'm—everything's fine."

"Yeah, you look the spitting image of fine. I hope you don't think I was spying. I was coming to see if you wanted anything for supper. But I kinda overheard some of that..." he says, wincing slightly. "May I come in?"

"It's your house," I say, splaying my arm out in offering.

"But it's your space now, and I respect that," he says taking a step inside.

"Well, thanks," I mutter.

"Wanna tell me what's going on?" Dad asks, stopping in the middle of the room and eyeing me expectantly.

I sigh. "Everything's just...getting so *confusing*."

"Welcome to the land of the living, sweet girl," Dad chuckles.

I raise my gaze to him and nod. "Yeah, I suppose. It's just —on one hand, I have Wade. Dad, I really wish you'd meet him. He's amazing and I know you'll love him as much as I do," I bite my lip to keep it from quivering. Taking another cleansing breath, I continue. "On the other hand, I have these friends...they're helping me to make sense of some things. But Wade thinks Colt is—"

"Your friends are the Gilbert twins?" Dad interjects.

I nod. "Yeah."

His eyebrows tug downward and his jaw sets. His lack of words is deafening.

"Something wrong?" I finally say to break the silence.

Shaking his head, he walks over to my desk. My eyes flit to the dresser, which is haphazardly hiding the hidden door. My pulse races as I flit through my options.

I stand up, walking over to the door to the hallway and lean against it, hoping to draw his eyes away from the dresser.

"Not wrong so much..." he says, looking over his shoulder at me. "It's just, you should be cautious with them."

"Cautious? How?"

"It's hard to explain, but their family and ours have a long history," he says, taking a step away from the desk and toward me.

"They told me that. They've been helping me understand the history of Windhaven a bit better."

Dad's eyebrows fly upward, and he takes another step forward. "They have? What else have they been doing?"

My mouth goes dry at the sudden interrogation and I'm

acutely aware of the fact that everyone in my life has their own secrets—my dad being one of them. I'm not entirely certain how much information I want to divulge until I piece out which ones I can trust.

"N-nothing. Mostly, they've been helping me with my studies. They're good people," I stammer.

Dad watches me closely, but his head tips in acknowledgement.

"Dad, do you have any powers?" I ask. It's never seemed like a good time to ask him, but it's obvious any supernatural abilities I may have stem from his side of the family.

His blue eyes sparkle, and he runs a hand through his strawberry-blond hair. "If you count being able to move around this house like a ninja, then sure—"

"Not what I meant," I say, shaking my head.

Dad chuckles. "I know. Well, I have always gotten feelings—vibrations of energies. Sometimes they'd make sense and other times, not so much. I always wished I had a more powerful ability."

I bite the inside of my cheek. "What do you know about Abigail and Warren?"

Again, surprise flashes across Dad's face. "That's a pretty specific question. Where did you learn about them?"

I fiddle with the doorknob, gazing at the floor. "We were at the library. I wanted to learn more about our family history and the town. Plus..."—I pause, trying to decide what to tell him—"I think I've been seeing Abigail."

Surprisingly, Dad smiles. "I thought you might."

"You did?" I say, practically squeaking.

Dad's face scrunches and he says, "Yeah, that day on the landing, I could sense her energy, but I didn't want her to upset you in case you felt things the same way I do. But it seemed like there was more with you. I was hoping you'd trust me enough to open up. I hate prying."

Guilt rushes through me and I suddenly feel so stupid for even thinking my dad was hiding things, like the Vodník or the little door.

"It's been a long time since someone in our family could see the dead. But you, you've always been..."

"Does Mom know? About you and the Blackwood family? Is this why she hates all things to do with supernatural beings?" I ask, unable to help myself.

Dad scratches at the sides of his forehead. "No, your mom's distain stems from other places. She wasn't always that way."

I snicker. "You're kidding me. For as long as I can remember, she's hated anything and everything to do with powers and the people who have them. She practically flipped her lid when I first got my acceptance letter to the Windhaven Academy."

"I can imagine," he chuckles.

"You don't...do you know how I got the acceptance letter? Because I never applied," I say, shaking my head. "I mean, don't get me wrong, I'm glad. But it was surprising, to say the least."

Dad clears his throat. "There has always been a fund here for you when you went to college. Whether or not you attended Windhaven Academy. But I may have...set a few things into motion."

I look up into his sheepish gaze.

"Dad, it was you? You sent them my application?" I gape.

"Something like that," he says. "I hope you don't mind. It's just—"

"No, it's fine. I just wish I would have known about all of this family stuff earlier. I feel like I'm at a total loss about everything. Hell, Cat and Colt know more about my family than I do. It feels weird."

"I can imagine. But there was good reason to keep you sheltered, Autumn. You must always remember that your mother and I did what we thought was best for you," he says, his voice barely a whisper.

"How? By separating and leaving me completely in the dark? Do you know how many times I wished I had supernatural abilities and Mom made me feel like a complete freak for even wishing it?"

Dad's face drains of color. "That was never... I'm sure your mother was doing what she thought was best for you."

I snicker, balling my hands into fists. It seems like everyone around me keeps doing *what's best for me*, but not a single one of them wants to do the one thing that really matters.

Dad stares at me with wide eyes but doesn't say anything.

"Tell the truth, Dad. Why is it so damn hard to just be honest with me?" I say, walking out the door and into the hallway. I don't know where I'm going or why, and at this point, I kind of hope Dad sees the hidden door. Maybe then we'll have an honest conversation about that, too.

My anger isn't really for Dad. It's aimed at no one in particular and everyone at the same time. It's like every single person in my life has an agenda, and I can't fully trust a single one of them.

I guess I'll just have to take matters into my own hands.

CHAPTER 21
REMNANTS

It's taken three days of diligently watching and waiting for Dad to be out of the house. As it turns out, it's harder to keep track of him than I'd expected.

Standing outside his bedroom door, I take a deep breath and reach for the handle. Without hesitation, I push it open. I know exactly where I need to go and what I need. The sooner I get it, the sooner I can get out of his room and back to my own.

I walk to the small desk and reach for the drawer handle to pull it open. But to my horror, the handle isn't there.

My heart leaps into my throat, and I stare at the empty space, completely dumbfounded.

What do I do now?

Stumbling backward, I make for the doorway. I'll need to regroup or...

Suddenly, there's movement to my left and Abigail has returned. Her white-laced arm points to a nightstand on the far side of the room. Without hesitation, I leap the bed and pull open the drawer. Shuffling papers and trinkets out of the way, I find the handle has been shoved to the back.

"Thanks," I say, looking over my shoulder, but Abigail is gone.

I shove the drawer closed and race out of the room, closing the door behind me. Just in case, I shove the handle under my shirt and beeline toward my bedroom. Luckily, getting to my bedroom is far less exciting. When I'm safely inside, I close my bedroom door and lock it.

My eyes flit to the dresser. My apprehension about going beyond the doorway alone has all but vanished. It's been replaced by a determination to take control of something that's all my own.

"Now or never," I whisper under my breath.

Walking to the dresser, I place the handle on top and give the whole thing a shove to the right. Adrenaline rushes through my veins, but I grab the handle and place it in the small hole until it clicks into place.

I take a step back, viewing the doorway in its entirety for the first time. There is something so familiar about it, but I can't figure out why.

Trembling, I reach for the door handle, knowing without a doubt this act could change things. I've always been one to love a good mystery, but this is different. The air is charged with energy and anticipation and I don't know if that's a good thing.

As my hand touches the cold metal, I bite my lip.

Should I really be doing this alone? Probably not.

Despite myself, I twist hard and pull the door open before I can talk myself out of it.

Frigid air rushes up at me, encircling me in its chilling embrace. I shudder away the imagery of cold, bony fingers and suck in a deep, cleansing breath. Grabbing my cell phone out of my pocket, I flip on the flashlight and exhale.

"All right, Autumn, time to see what you're made of," I

whisper, straightening my shoulders. "Nothing to worry about. There's nothing down there in the dark that wasn't already there in the light."

I leave the door open behind me, just in case, and start my descent.

The wooden steps creak and groan as they release years of dormancy. Dust scatters into the air, fluttering about in the low rays of sunlight coming in through the small beveled-glass window. It cascades in sideways before the autumn night snuffs it out entirely.

With every creaking step, my heart slams against my chest, but I push myself forward anyway, forcing myself through the fear so I can come out on the other side. There are answers in here. There have to be.

Reaching the bottom of the rickety stairs, my feet hit the combination of stone and sand in what appears to be a small sub-basement room. I raise my phone, shining as much light around the space as the LED will allow, which isn't much.

I curse myself for not bringing a proper flashlight.

The only sound in this tomb-like environment is my own shallow breathing, and I stop—deliberately taking a full inhalation to calm my nerves.

Following the space to the right, the sub-basement is fairly small—no larger than a twenty-by-twenty-square-foot room built out of stones and clay mortar. The air is musty, with a hint of something herbal lingering behind. There are no windows in the tiny room, but dim light still permeates the space from the stairwell, as well as from the two large pillar candles resting in the middle of a tiny table that looks like it's meant for a little girl's tea party.

The flames flicker ominously, making me both curious and apprehensive.

Narrowing my eyes, I don't dare take another step closer.

Casting my gaze around the dimly lit space, I'm acutely aware candles don't burn forever. So, somehow, someone was able to get down here before I got the door handle in place. I shine the light into all four corners of the room, under the stairs, and even under the table, but there is literally nothing else in here. No doors, no passageways, nothing except the one way in and out.

Was the shadow beneath the door real?

Shuddering away the trepidation rising up my spine, I take a step closer to the little table. It's about the size of a small coffee table, and the large white candles reside on either end. In the center is a bundle of sage, lavender, and rosemary, a large pentacle, and a framed photograph...

Of me.

Snatching the frame from the table, I shine the light from my phone onto the photo and gawk at it.

The photo is weathered, like it's been exposed to the air and elements for years, and based on the age I am in the photo, it very well could have been. I can't be more than seven or eight years old. Basically, the same age I was the last time I was here in Windhaven.

Sitting on a small bench with an enormous willow tree behind me, my smile is broad and authentic, albeit slightly off.

There's just one problem. I don't recognize any of it. When was this photo even taken?

Rubbing my thumb across the dusty bottom of the frame, I kneel down next to the candles to get a better look.

Something isn't right. I'm wearing clothes I've never worn before and something about my smile doesn't feel right. Like I was sleepy that day, or maybe had a cold.

Shuddering away the completely new level of the creeps, I swallow hard.

I really shouldn't be down here alone...

"Yes, you should..." a voice echoes off the stone walls, answering the thought in my head.

Stumbling backward, I toss the photo onto the table. It clatters loudly as the corner catches the tabletop, cracking the glass upon impact.

I spin around, searching for the source of the voice, but the goose bumps flashing across my skin already tell me I'm not dealing with someone corporeal. Standing beside the base of the stairs, Abigail takes form as if manifesting herself from the dusty floor. Her green eyes are piercing, as they stare right through me.

"The truth *shall* set you free," Abigail's voice beckons.

Filling my lungs with as much air as possible, I watch her as she moves to the center of the room. Suddenly, the flames from the candles on the small table expand outward, and the entire lower level is filled with the warm glow of flames flickering.

The table in the center of the room disappears and in its place is a large pentacle drawn on the dirt floor with...*white sand? Salt?* From here, I'm not sure which. Along the outer edge of the circle are large platforms, perhaps repurposed tree trunks, each with a mixture of candles in varying sizes and shapes.

Outside the circle, Abigail is dressed slightly differently, her gown is no longer white, but instead covered in a dark royal-blue floral pattern. She hovers over a lump of fabric, bound in the shape of a small human body, in the corner of the room, just beneath the stairs. Standing beside it is a young girl no more than thirteen or fourteen.

"I could only muster but a bit of salt, darling," Warren's words ring out across time and space as he enters the space from the stairwell.

He passes her a large bowl, and she nods at him.

"This will do," she announces. "Thank you, my love."

Taking the salt to the pentacle, she begins to walk around the circumference in a counterclockwise motion. She pinches the salt between her fingers, muttering something under her breath as she adds it to the outer circle. Warren stands to the side, watching her intensely. His eyes take in all that she does, as if calculating all of her movements.

When Abigail has walked the circle three times, she kneels down at her starting point and sets the bowl aside. Next, she removes a small vial from her waist and pops open the small cork. Her words continue in fervent fashion, but from here I still can't make out what they mean. After a moment or two, she tips the contents of the vial into the center of the pentacle, right in the main pentagon at its core.

The sweet stench of blood wafts to my nostrils and I shudder away the images it conjures. Whose blood was it? Why was that even necessary? And who's hidden beneath the sheet? As the blood spreads out, the pentacle itself begins to light up a bright, brilliant white until it has cast out any darkness trying to hide in the corners of the room.

Turning to Warren, Abigail raises her left hand toward him, and as if receiving a silent command, he saunters to her in three big strides. Holding out his hand, he garnishes a small blade, barely six inches long from hilt to tip.

"Thank you," she whispers, taking it from him.

Warren tips his head, but rather than returning to where he began, he stays by her side.

"She is very much afflicted and time is of the essence. She's beginning to fade," he whispers.

Nodding, Abigail's words begin again, a little louder this time, but I only catch snippets...

"Death ... offering ... breath ... remnants ..."

Clutching the small dagger in her right hand, she places the blade in her left palm and pulls it through, slicing her own flesh open. Thrusting her arm out so it hovers over the pentacle, the blood rushes from her grasp, falling into the mixture puddled on the floor. Her fresh blood mixes with the old, spiraling together in a strange dance as it cyclones upward from the center of the pentagon.

Warren steps back, his face open wide in awe. Abigail, on the other hand is stoic; holding her ground, refusing to lower her arm until every last drop of blood has fallen from her hand. When the stream has ceased, she points the dagger at the cyclone of blood. As she does so, the blood reacts, stretching toward the tip of it until it almost touches the blade.

Flicking her wrist, she directs the blade to point toward the body in the corner. Instantly, the blood rushes out of the circle past the two of them and embeds itself into the huddled mass on the floor. The blood stains the white fabric, soaking into it until it's nothing more than a crimson heap.

Under her breath, Abigail continues her uttering until it gets almost loud enough to hear fully.

"Death, taker of life ... accept my offering. Bone ... breath ... Recover ... her remnants—and return her ..."

When not even a drop is left inside the pentacle, energy begins to pulsate from the corner where the body lies. At first, it's subtle, just a gentle push and pull, but it intensifies. Growing until the entire sub-basement room throbs with its potency.

Then, something moves from beneath the sheet.

Without thinking, I open my mouth and squelch a scream.

The young girl is gone.

Everything abruptly switches. I'm no longer watching

Warren and Abigail. Instead, I'm back in the here and now, staring at the small table in the center of the room. Beyond, standing in the space the body was once located, Abigail's ghost looks up at me.

"I don't understand. What in the hell is all of this? What are you showing me?" I say, shaking my head.

At first, Abigail doesn't move. The candle flames from the table reflect in her green eyes as she moves toward me at an unearthly speed.

"It is your birthright to wield the power I displaced. You must understand from where it is you come from in order to understand where you are beckoned to," she says in a soft Colonial accent. "You must break this curse."

"Okay," I say, blinking wildly.

"It has been but centuries that I have been bound here, unable to escape. I am going to avail of your assistance. You are the only one who can release me from this binding."

I snicker.

"And on that note," I say, turning on my heel.

I've seen plenty of horror movies, and let me tell you, they never end well when a ghost wants to be set free. Especially after what I just witnessed.

What does she want? A new body or something?

I'm terrified to find out.

CHAPTER 22

CAREFUL WHAT YOU WISH FOR

The following morning, I put out my feelers, trying to find Dominic. After last night's chat with Abigail, it's more important than ever to find out why he carved *veritas vos liberabit* on my car. It's the exact phrase Abigail used and I'm sure it's no coincidence. I need to understand more about my situation and what Abigail wants. Preferably without having to have another chat with her, because that was creepy as fuck.

Besides, the whole thing is on my mind anyway, since I had to drop my car off at the body shop to be repainted and I won't have it back for days. Instead, I'm at the mercy of other people, which mostly means riding with Cat and Colt.

It's difficult, though, because there's only a handful of people who I trust that have a clue about what's going on at my house, or with my family legacy. Wade...and Cat and Colt. But this whole thing with adding Dominic into the mix makes me feel weird. Like the twins are secretly judging me about talking with him, but I don't know why. The one thing I do know is, he's the one who kicked all of this off, and Abigail's apparition continues to reinforce his sentiment.

Unfortunately, no one has seen hide nor hair of him lately.

Not good.

Alas, the day drags on with little to break up the monotony of learning the basics of magic. Not even lunch seems to take away the weird edge of jittery energy I feel. By the time the last class of the day rolls around, I'm so ready for the day to be over and to just get on with things.

"I'm so sorry, Autumn, I won't be able to walk you to Grimoire Crafting today. I have to go chat with Mr. Magnuson about the missing girls. Evidently, he thinks I'm showing signs of being able to hone in on the life force energy of others. Something about how the element of fire is more powerful than just burning stuff down. Apparently, it's pretty rare, so he wants me to give it a try to see if I can get a read on the girls," Cat says, shooting me a look of apology.

"Really? That's amazing, Cat," I say, trying not to let the surprise flush my face.

She shrugs.

"Well," I say, brushing my hand out in front of me, "don't worry about me. That's *way* more important. I'm pretty sure I can find my way at this point."

"All right, well, gotta go. See ya after school," she says, walking backward down the hall.

"You got it."

A broad, goofy grin spreads across her ebony cheeks and despite the admonishment of the Gilberts from my dad, I can't help but smile back.

"Go. You're gonna be late," I say, shooing her with my hands.

Cat holds up both hands, "Going—*yeesh*."

Sighing to myself, I drop my backpack from my shoulder and dig around. After much longer than expected, I pull out the crumpled-up piece of paper formerly known as my map.

Staring at the tattered layout of the school, I orient myself and finally figure out which way I need to go. It's amazing how little you really take in when someone else leads the way for you.

"See? You got this, Autumn. Easy peasy," I say aloud as I start moving. As I make my way, the twists and turns look familiar and I can't help but feel a sense of satisfaction for having maneuvered this journey on my own.

With my head buried in the piece of paper, I take the final turn toward my last class of the day and accidentally slam into the back of a guy standing still in the middle of the walkway.

"Oh, jeez. I'm so sorry. I didn't see you," I begin.

It takes me a moment to recognize the white-blond hair and broad shoulders.

"Dominic," I say, my mouth dropping open.

He grins slowly. "Hey, there. I hear you've been looking for me. I figured we'd bump into each other at some point."

I roll my eyes. "Yeah, I have, actually," I mutter, dropping the map and sighing.

"What can I help you with?" he asks, his grin sliding into more of a smirk.

"Dominic," I begin, "weird stuff has been happening to me lately and I think you might know something about it."

Slowly, he cocks a blond eyebrow.

"I mean, you were the first one telling me I need to seek out the truth. And I'll tell you, after the weeks I've had, I could really use some truth," I continue.

He watches me for a moment, his face flipping through a couple of conflicting expressions. "Here's the thing... I don't know if you're ready for the entire truth just yet."

I snort. "I'm so sick of the runaround I keep getting. I'm not some small kid who needs to be coddled. I've seen shit, okay? I *know* things. I wish you'd just be straight with me."

"Fine, you're a damn necromancer," he spits.

My eyes pop open wide and I can't help but snicker. "What? First of all, how would you know that?"

"Because I do. You come from a long line of witches with that legacy," he says.

"That's absurd," I say, narrowing my eyes. Without a doubt, I now know I have Warren's ability to see the dead. But necromancy? It's not possible to have both...is it?

He takes a step back, running his hand through his white-blond hair. "I see things, too. Things that don't always make sense. Sometimes I can move things without touching them. I technically don't know how it's manifesting in you, but I figure, if I had to lay money on it, you're more like Abigail..."

It's my turn to take a step back. My mind instantly recalls my last interaction with her. "Abigail?"

"Yeah, she's your—"

"I know who she is," I say, goose bumps flashing up and down my back and arms. "She was my uber great-grandmother."

His mouth slides into a silent 'o' and he blinks away his surprise. "Yeah."

"So, you're psychic or telekinetic? That's your ability? Can you read minds?" I say, leaning against the windowsill.

"Er, something like that," he nods. "It's one of the reasons I knew who you were without talking with you."

"So, what am I thinking about now?" I ask, blinking expectantly. I need to know if he's just playing with me or if he's actually telling the truth.

He tilts his head to the side. "Other than I'm apparently full of shit?"

"Yeah, I guess. What else?" I chuckle.

"Okay, when I mentioned Abigail, your mind flitted for a moment to a vision of her. Not an old black and white photo, but an in-color, moving image of her. You've seen her, haven't you?" he says, his intense blue eyes burning into mine.

"I—maybe?" I say, confusion settling around me like a fog.

"Did you know necromancers can't typically see the dead they're trying to resurrect? They need a postmortem medium to guide them. Warren was—"

"I know. Supposedly he could see ghosts," I whisper, dropping my gaze to the floor.

"Right."

"So, if I can see Abigail, wouldn't that mean I am not a necromancer?" I say, shaking my head. "I have Warren's gifts, not—"

"Look, I'm just gonna lay it out there. Abigail has come to me, too." Before I can interject, he raises a hand to stop me. "Not...not in the same way as she comes to you, but in dreams, visions. She's the one who wanted me to give you the nudge. She senses your presence and power. Whether or not you think you have the ability doesn't matter. She thinks you *do*. If that's the case, it would make you one of the most powerful necromancers this godforsaken town has ever known. Maybe the world. She has big plans for you," he whispers.

I snort, unable to squash the rising panic from the night before. I swear, I will not let her take over my body, if that's what she thinks she wants.

"Big plans?" I squeal. "What in the hell does that mean?"

"I don't know. I'm just the messenger," he says, shrugging.

"Shit," I mutter. I can't wrap my brain around any of this.

"Look, I know it's a lot," Dominic says, taking a step forward. "But you should know..."

I raise my hand, backing away. "I need a little time to think. Th-thanks, Dominic."

Turning on my heel, I leave the hallway and keep walking. I don't even go toward my next class. Instead, my feet carry me instinctively and I don't even look at my map once. Before I know it, I'm out the front door and walking through the parking lot.

Could I really have both powers? And if so, how could I be the last to know?

I tug my jacket in tighter and cram my hands into my pockets. In practically a daze, my feet carry me to the library, and as I walk up the stone steps, I've never been so happy to see the familiar building.

My fingertips sting from the brisk autumn wind and my nose won't stop running.

Warm air greets me as I open the door and step inside. Keeping my head down and avoiding eye contact with the librarian, I meander the shelves and pretend to peruse a bit before heading down to the basement archives room. I don't know why, it feels like the kind of place that should require a permit or something, and I certainly don't feel like I have the credentials all on my own.

My footsteps echo louder in my mind than I'm sure they do in reality, but I ignore the panic arising and push myself onward. When no one races after me, telling me I'm not allowed down here, I release a slow, relieved exhalation.

"It's not like you're robbing the place, Autumn. Get a grip," I mutter, pulling out my phone. As I sit there, staring at the screen, a text pops in from Cat.

`Heard what happened in the hall. You okay?`

Breathing a sigh of relief, I sit down on the nearest chair.

`Yeah. Decided to go to the library. Needed some space.`

After a few seconds, she texts back.

`Good idea. Settle in. We'll be there in a bit.`

Without texting back, I set the phone on the table. My eyes flit to the large bookshelves that extend from floor to ceiling. The stack of books Colton had taken down for me before still rest in the middle of the table—clearly not an urgent project for the librarian to put away.

I grab the one the twins showed me before and flip to the page with my house. Despite having some blueprints of the original home, there's nothing about hidden rooms.

Setting that book aside, but still splayed open, I reach for another one. The next book is on local Windhaven hauntings and ghost sightings.

Cocking my head to the side, I slide it in closer and open the book.

At first, it reads like a philosophical textbook on the physics of ghosts and their existence. How postmortem mediums can see and sense them...and how the practice was first recognized. Just as my eyes begin to glaze over with the scientific evidence, I get to the meat of the book.

While no one has had access to the Blackwood Estate for a number of years, it continues to be the most talked about haunted locale in Windhaven. In the 1940s, two teenagers trespassing on the property were sent into mental health treatment after reportedly tangling with the spirits inside the building. When mundane ghost hunters were called to the scene, they were turned away by family who had reclaimed the property after the incident. However, there are oral histories of ghosts, apparitions, and spectral beings at the estate dating all the way back to the mid-1800s.

Without even reading the rest of the accounts, I already know why the sightings would date back as far as they claim. Not only because the town would have been only a few decades old, but it was also shortly after Abigail died. With each story, my anxiety actually starts to dissipate.

The next book is on local lore and history. As it turns out, people from all over the country come to Windhaven because of the vortexes and magical energies, and have done for almost a century. It's weird to think, because right now in the fall, it appears to be a wasteland. Not some sort of magical vacation destination.

I sit back in my chair and soften my gaze.

How could I possibly be one of the most powerful necromancers in the area, when I feel anything but powerful?

Flipping open the next book, I stare down at a set of old newspaper clippings spanning from super old—up until about a decade ago, by the looks of it.

I skim various clippings about stranger-than-normal goings-on in this town, supernatural news coming out of the academy, and I'm about to close the book when a picture catches my eye. It's the scenery more than anything, because it's almost the same view I was just enjoying a few days ago from my bedroom window.

POSSIBLE DROWNING AT BLACKWOOD MANOR

WINDHAVEN—October 10th, 2009

Authorities were called out to the residence of Mr. Lyle Blackwood after an urgent 911 call was made from someone inside the home claiming a seven-year old girl had fallen into the pond on the property.

No body was recovered at the scene, though divers were sent in and the pond was later dredged.

Mr. Blackwood was at the home, and reportedly retrieving lifejackets from the family boathouse when she went missing. Based on evidence collected, he is not a suspect at this time. The investigation is ongoing.

Surprised, I sit back, staring into the sea of books and shelves in front of me.

I never drowned. I never died or went missing. What on earth is going on here?

Could I have a...*twin sister?*

My memory of the girl in the photograph resurfaces. She looked like I did, but slightly different. And I know for a fact I never had clothing like whatever she was wearing.

Would my parents have hidden a sister from me? Is that why they separated when I was so young?

Raking my fingertips over my forehead, I turn the page to the next set of stories.

BLACKWOOD PLEADS FOR LEADS

WINDHAVEN—October 20th, 2009

It has been ten days since the disappearance of Mr. Lyle Blackwood's seven-year-old daughter. The mystery upon her disappearance and who made the 911 call the day of her disappearance continues to swirl. While the 911 call from the home was that of a woman's voice, new evidence was uncovered that Mrs. Blackwood was visiting family in Mistwood Point at the time of the incident.

Mr. Blackwood is urging anyone with any information to contact him directly or speak with the authorities.

I scrunch my face, trying to make sense of what I'm reading.

Someone called from the house, but Dad was out in the boathouse... How is that possible?

Continuing, I search the next page.

NEW EVIDENCE EMERGES ON MISSING BLACKWOOD GIRL

WINDHAVEN—October 23rd, 2009

New evidence suggests a possible supernatural explanation for missing Blackwood girl. Windhaven Academy experts were brought in to survey the scene of the Blackwood pond and energetic psychics found traces of a possible Vodník attack. After thirteen days missing, positive outcomes in the case are not looking good.

Mr. and Mrs. Blackwood are appealing to any and all supernatural beings and witches to aid them in the search and to find their daughter and bring the Vodník to justice.

I cover my mouth with my hand, unable to move my eyes from the word: *Vodník*.

Trembling, I flip the page to one last entry.

MISSING BLACKWOOD GIRL FOUND, WET & CONFUSED

WINDHAVEN—October 31st, 2009

> Authorities were called out to Blackwood Manor after Lyle Blackwood's missing daughter was found on the property's dock, soaking-wet and confused. The frigid October air had nearly frozen the water to her frail body, but she is in otherwise good health. She is being treated at Windhaven General Hospital for hypothermia.
>
> She has no recollection of her missing time, nor any details on the Vodník. A public search is ongoing to capture the creature.

My heart feels like it's about to burst from my chest, and I can't seem to settle it down. The twins had mentioned this had happened before—*the missing girls, the Vodník*—but everyone failed to mention the one it happened to looked like *me*.

CHAPTER 23

SURPRISE

Cat and Colt pick me up at the library, and for some reason, I can't seem to shake the intense feeling that I'm on the precipice of something big—monumental, even. I have the overwhelming urge to call my Mom, but I know she'll tell me I'm nuts. Or worse...want me to come back to Mistwood because I don't belong here.

"Do I have a twin sister?" I blurt out, unable to restrain myself any longer.

"What? Why would you think that?" Cat asks, chancing a quick glance over to me before turning her gaze back to the road.

"Well, I found something weird. Like, something that's unusual even for *my* world." I snicker. "I found this picture, and it's got a girl who looks like me, but I swear it's *not* me. She's wearing clothes I don't remember, and something is, I don't know, off about her smile."

Colt clears his throat and leans back in his seat.

"Oh, turn here," I say, pointing to our driveway.

"Yeah, I know," she chuckles, tapping her blinker and turning right.

"Where did you find the picture?" Colt asks.

I weigh my options on just how much I want to tell them. Ultimately, though, I realize that I can't do this alone.

As Cat comes to a stop in the front circle of our driveway, I unbuckle my seatbelt and twist around. "You know, it might be easier to show you both. Come on."

The three of us exit the vehicle and head up to the front door. As I reach for the doorknob, Cat leans in, whispering something in Colt's ear, but I can't make it out. All I catch is, "should we?"

Pulling my eyebrows in, I shake my head and swing the door open.

"Dad, I'm home," I call out. "I have the Gilberts with me if you'd like to stop and say hello."

Cat and Colt take their shoes off at the door just as dad descends the stairs.

He feigns a smile that I'm sure looks genuine to Cat and Colt but looks forced to me.

"Nice to have you home, but I have errands to run, sweetie," he says, refusing to acknowledge Cat and Colt as he continues through to the kitchen.

I shuffle awkwardly, hoping the twins don't take offense. I make a mental note to dig more into the frigid air around the Gilberts.

"Okay, well, I guess we should keep going," I mutter, trying to change the subject.

Cat and Colt exchange an odd look.

"So, there's more than the picture I need to show you," I start, "but please, don't tell anyone else. At least, not until I figure out what the hell it all means. Deal?"

The twins both nod, but neither of them say a word.

Nodding to myself, I tilt my head. "All right, follow me."

As we walk down the hallway toward my room, Cat's eyes are everywhere. The walls, ceilings, floors.

"This place, it hasn't... I mean, it's amazing," she whispers.

"Right? It's like living in a museum sometimes, though," I say, opening my bedroom door.

Colt is the first to step inside as I hold the door open for them. Cat follows afterward, tipping her head in thanks.

I drop my backpack on the floor beside my desk, and step into the middle of the room.

"All right, so I really need your help in sorting all of this out. There's been a lot of weird coming at me and after the conversation with Dominic, and the stuff I read at the library, I don't know what to believe anymore. But this—*this* has really freaked me out," I say, walking over to my dresser and giving it a shove.

The twins gasp audibly, as I twist the handle to the hidden door. When I turn to look back to Colt and Cat, both of them carry the same expression—eyes wide and mouth dropped open.

"How? Was that always here?" Cat says, not removing her eyes from the doorway.

I shake my head. "No, it was hidden behind wallpaper. Then, when I uncovered it, the door handle was missing. But..." My voice trails off as I try to figure out how to explain it just showed up.

"But?" Colt urges.

"But then one day, I was led to it."

"What?" Cat mutters, her eyebrows flying up to her hairline.

"Come on, I'll show you the rest and you can decide for yourself if I'm nuts or what," I say, bending down and entering the stairwell.

Soft light filters through the little window, but we only

have another hour or so before it really gets dark. Pulling out my cell phone for more light, I shudder away the draft and lead the way.

Their footsteps behind me echo down the staircase as we creak our way to the bottom. A gnawing sense of guilt washes over me because Wade would be so upset that he wasn't the first I brought down here. He was with me when I found the doorway, after all.

"Whoa, this is creepy," Cat whispers.

As we turn the corner at the bottom of the stairs, she pulls up short and gawks.

"Did you light those?" Colt asks, ever the pragmatic one. He raises his hand and points to the candles on the little table.

I shake my head.

His dark eyebrows tug in and he takes a step closer to inspect them. "This is an altar," he says, running his fingertips over the pentacle.

"I figured," I say.

Cat steps forward, picking up the frame. "Is this...this is the one you were talking about, right?"

I nod.

Cat passes it to Colton without saying a word. He holds onto it, his expression as stoic as a statue.

"You have to understand..." Colt says, setting the frame back down on the altar, "our families have been here a long time. All of us—the Gilberts and the Blackwoods, not to mention Dom's family, we have a certain *history*."

"I get that. But what about this?" I say, shaking my head and opening my arms wide to suggest the whole space.

Cat steps forward. "Who do you think left this behind? What are your guesses?"

I flit my gaze to her and shrug. "How should I know?"

"You should, because I'm pretty sure... Ugh, I'm pretty sure it was you," she says, her eyes refusing to stray from mine.

I snort indignantly, "What?"

"This was your bedroom before, right?" she offers. "Upstairs?"

"Yeah, but so what?" I say, clearly not following her.

"And you also said you found the doorway—and that you're seeing ghosts," she whispers, looking at me from under her eyebrows.

It still sound so ludicrous when it's said out loud.

"Yes, I've seen Abigail," I nod, wishing she'd just spit out what she's getting at. "She's not super happy about being dead."

Colt inhales sharply, and they share another significant glance.

"And...I take it you found out more in the library today," she continues.

I roll my eyes, circling my right hand in the air to urge her to hurry up.

"What Cat's trying to say is, we think it's time to tell you more about the Blackwood curse," Colton says, his eyes suddenly dark and serious. "At least, what we know of it. Maybe this time it will stick."

My heart races. This isn't the first time a family curse has been brought up. Walking away from them, I blow out a puff of air and run my hands over my face. I take a beat before twisting back around. I first look at Cat, then Colt. Splaying my arms out, I tilt my head to the side. "Okay, let's do this. I'm ready."

"Maybe we should go upstairs so you have a place to sit down?" Colton suggests.

I shake my head. "I'm a big girl. And I've waited long enough. So spit it out."

"You know the Vodník? The last time this happened, a girl went missing," Cat begins. She glances down, fiddling with the bracelet around her wrist. "A *Blackwood* girl."

My heart races as my mind flips back to those pages at the library. This is it. This is exactly information I was looking for...

"*You* were the missing Blackwood girl, Autumn. You don't have a long-lost sister or a twin, okay. We believe—well, we think the Vodník took you and somehow, you managed to get away," Colt whispers.

"Okay, now I know you've lost your ever-loving minds," I say, shaking my head and backing away. "If I were kidnapped and escaped, I'd remember. I'd remember something as monumental as that."

"Your bloodline has a long history of pissing off the wrong supernatural beings—angels, demons, maybe even gods. But your ancestry is so powerful. Think about it. You see Abigail, you connect with spirits like they're real people, maybe you even call them to you and don't even realize... Whether you know it or not, you have the power of resurrection and spirit summoning. It's your birthright. But you don't know how to harness it because..." Cat's voice trails off.

"Because your mom took you away from us," Colton finishes for her.

I try to make sense of what they're saying. Part of me wants to tell them they're absolutely mad. The other part of me, a deeper, more innate part—is scared that they might be right.

"She what?" I finally whisper, narrowing my gaze.

"After your...*accident*, she wanted to protect you. Who

knows what was really going on in her mind? No one really knows except maybe your dad. The point is, you should have had the tools you needed long before now so you could understand the powers you really possess. We were all in the process of training together before, but you don't even remember," Cat says, her voice trailing off. "You were learning how to summon spirits, while Colton and I were learning to manage our elemental magic. We've seen what you could do firsthand—"

Blinking wildly, I back away. "This doesn't make any sense."

"What do you remember from the last time you were here?" Colt asks.

"I dunno. Mostly that I was stuck in here and couldn't do anything. I was bored to tears and I hated it. Hated my dad. Hated everything. It was a relief to finally go away," I say, shrugging.

"What if I can give you an alternative history on what happened?" Colt whispers, stepping closer and placing his hands alongside my upper arms.

His hands are warm and the contact sparks the same orange and blue flames, igniting them along my triceps. I stare down at them mesmerized by the swirling vortex.

"Dru—you did it. Are you down here?" a voice calls out from the top of the stairs.

My eyes widen and my heart suddenly feels far too big for my chest as it thumps awkwardly.

Only one person in the whole world calls me *Dru*.

"Wade?" I sputter, twisting away from Colt and Cat and racing to the bottom of the stairs.

Wade's signature leather jacket, dark hair, and silver eyes come into view as he crouches in the doorway.

"Hey," he says, his eyebrows tugging in, "is it as creepy as I imagine? Can I join you?"

I cast a gaze over my shoulder, widening my eyes and mouthing to Cat and Colton to *stay put.*

Racing up the stairs, I crouch to get out into my room.

"I was—" I stumble for words, "w-what are you doing here?"

His silver-gray eyes lock with me and he grins. "I couldn't leave things the way they were after our last conversation. I scheduled an alternate PCA to come in so I could leave a day early. I wanted to surprise you."

"Ha—well, you definitely accomplished that," I snicker, trying to get my nerves under control.

"God, you look... I've missed you," he says, his eyebrows tipping up in the middle as he pulls me in close. His heady scent of sandalwood and soap draw me in and the strange sense of safety only he brings wraps around me like a blanket.

"I've missed you, too," I whisper, melting into him. For a moment, I almost forget about Cat and Colton in the sub-basement. After all the confusion and crazy, I'm so glad to have him here. He brings things back into focus, as well a sense of stability and normalcy.

"I saw another SUV parked in the driveway. Is your dad finally here so I can meet him?" Wade asks.

Behind me, someone clears their throat and I lift my head off Wade's chest to stare into Colt's wide eyes.

"Oh, I didn't realize you had anyone else down there with you," Wade says, suddenly serious as he glances from Cat to Colt. His eyes rest a beat longer with Colton and he straightens his shoulders. "I'm Wade, Autumn's boyfriend."

My insides constrict at the heavy layer of testosterone that's managed to seep into the space around us.

Colt's lips press tight, but he recovers quickly, nodding to himself. Shoving his hands in his pockets, he constricts back into himself, becoming the guy I met the first day of school and no longer the self-assured guy I was beginning to see.

Breaking away from Wade, I sweep my arm out. "Wade, this is Cat, er, *Caitlyn*, and her brother, Colton."

Wade thrusts out a hand to Cat, who shakes it quickly. Her smile is authentic, but she shifts back awkwardly as soon as Wade releases her hand.

When he does the same to Colton, the best he gets is a glance at his outstretched limb. Wade arches an eyebrow, but as Colt meets my wide eyes, he sighs, nods, and extends his hand anyway.

"I've heard a lot about you both. I'm glad I finally get the chance to meet you," Wade says. His natural, good-natured aura is more closed off than I've ever seen it before, but I can tell he's trying hard not to be completely uptight.

"Yeah, same," Cat agrees, nodding. She glances from Wade to Colt. "You know, Autumn, we really appreciate you showing us the...basement. But we really should get going."

"Agreed," Colt says, heading for the door.

"Thanks for the ride, guys—and the insights," I say, trying to sound more centered than I feel.

"No problem. We can talk more about everything later," Cat says, shooting me a look of apology.

I tip my head in agreement. "Good."

Cat rushes after Colt and, after a few moments, Wade turns to me. "So, that was Colt, huh?"

I wince. "I don't know what you think was going on. It was a weird day and I—"

"You don't have to explain, Autumn. I get it. I'm not always...*here*," he says, taking a step back.

Exhaling loudly, I walk up to him, sliding my left hand inside his. "Wade Hoffman, you are *always* here." I place our joined hands over my heart.

His silver eyes take me in, watching me for a beat. "I hope so."

I can see his faith in me cracking, no matter how unfounded, and it sends waves of panic coursing through my body. If I'm not careful, I could lose the one person in the whole world who's been nothing but honest with me.

CHAPTER 24
FORBIDDEN

Turning back to the little doorway quickly, I sweep my hand out. I need to find a way to set things right as quickly as possible.

"Do you want to see?" I say, trying to sound upbeat and not like I'm a traitorous bitch for not waiting for him to go inside.

Wade pauses for a second before his coolness melts a bit. "God, yes. I thought you'd never ask."

I chuckle, urging him to go first. He shoots me a sideways glance but bends down and descends the steps. Sighing in relief, I follow after him.

"Wow, this is—" he begins as we hit the lower level.

"Freaky, right?"

"Well, I was gonna say ridiculously awesome, but sure, freaky works, too," he says, turning to me. His eyes twinkle with amusement. "So, where'd you find the doorknob?"

Reaching up, I fiddle with the bottom of my earlobe. "I was—well, Abigail showed me."

Wade's eyebrows rise to his hairline. "Does that mean we were right? You're a postmortem medium?"

I bite my lip, still confused and reeling from the concept that ghosts are real and that maybe I really can see them.

"Looks like it," I say, nodding and walking the circumference of the small altar.

Wade takes a step forward, reaching for the photo frame. "Is this you?"

"I guess," I shrug.

Setting it back down on the altar, he turns to me. "You don't know?"

"Not exactly," I say, scrunching my face. "There's a lot I need to fill you in on. Maybe we should go somewhere to get a bite to eat and I can tell you all about it. I'm starving."

Wade looks longingly at the rest of the space, but nods. "Sure."

Without another word, we make our way up the dusty wooden stairs to my bedroom. I close the door and push the dresser in front of it.

"Just in case..." I say, squinting my eyes at Wade.

"In case of what? Something tries to come up or someone else tries to go down?" he laughs, scratching at his temple.

"Both," I mutter, making a face. "I still haven't talked to my dad about it yet. There just hasn't been a good time."

"Ah," he says, following me out into the hallway.

"I will, though. *Don't worry*," I say, shaking my head.

"I'm not worried."

"Sure you aren't. I know that tone, Angel." We reach the front door and I grab my purse from the entryway table. We can tell him together later, if you want. He still has to meet you anyway. You can save the day and bring it up," I say.

"No chance. You're not pawning off your adulting responsibilities onto me," he laughs, opening the door.

"Fine," I mumble, "be that way. Psh." Smiling back at him,

I make my way down the stairs and climb into the passenger seat of Wade's Impala.

Wade closes the front door, follows me to his car, and gets in.

"Still no sign of Blue, huh?" Wade asks, pulling out of the driveway's loop.

I shake my head. "Not yet. Probably Monday." I shoot him a sideways glance and reach for his hand. "That's why Cat and Colton were here, you know. They dropped me off after school."

Wade bristles at the sound of Colt's name, but he nods.

An awkward silence falls over us and the next few minutes pass like molasses. I reach over to the radio and click it on. Classical music blasts through the speakers and I fumble to turn it down.

Wade chuckles.

"Wow, you sure like your classical music," I say, groping at my chest to calm my racing heart.

"I was actually listening to music through the Aux cable. I didn't set the station," he says, picking up the lead that's dangling from the dashboard.

"Oh sure, that makes more sense," I chuckle. "So, what were you listening to at such ear-shattering decibel levels?"

"Walking on Cars," he laughs.

"Walking on wha?"

"Cars," he repeats. "They're an Irish band. Fantastic music."

"And here I thought for sure you'd be cranking something like Marshmallow or Breaking Benjamin," I say, smiling broadly.

"Oh boy. Ye lack musical taste," he says, smiling.

The town lights come into view and our banter time with

the radio is going to come to an abrupt end. Hopefully, I can continue to keep things on the lighter side.

"The burger place over there is really good," I say, turning my head. We lock eyes for a moment, and his gaze takes me in, practically reducing me to soul level in a matter of seconds.

"Okay," he whispers, returning his eyes to the road.

I clear my throat. "I want you to know, I'm glad you're here. I know things kinda got off on a weird foot."

"I'm glad to be here, too," he says, smiling back.

He turns left, entering the Bourbon Room's small parking lot. It's a busy night—the majority of cars are parked along the road.

"My dad says this place has the best burgers he's ever had. Evidently, that means something," I say, tipping my chin toward the building's façade as we exit the small parking lot in lieu of parking on the street. "I haven't had the chance to try it yet."

"Well, if it's that highly esteemed, how could we pass this old folk's home up?" Wade says. His tone is more playful and I can tell he's starting to settle in.

"Right? See, I said the same thing when we first drove by it. It looks like someplace where the people inside should be sitting around big round tables playing poker and drinking bourbon—talking about the good ol' cowboy's code or something."

"Right?" he snickers.

"Ready?" I say, reaching for the door handle.

As I turn to look over my shoulder, Wade has already left the vehicle and has walked around to my side to finish opening my door.

"Whoa, that was...*fast*," I mutter, taking his outstretched hand.

"My lady," he says, with a flourish of his hand.

I shake my head, but I can't help but smile.

"You're ridiculous, you know that, right?" I laugh.

"Ridiculous, perhaps. But a gentleman, nonetheless." He quirks an eyebrow, placing my right hand on his left forearm and locking arms with me.

I tip my head in acknowledgment and let him lead the way to the door. As the gentleman he is, he steps out in front, opening the door and ushering me inside with the sweep of his hand.

"Thank you, kind sir," I say, shaking my head at the absurdity of our exchanges. Sometimes I really do wonder if we'd ever find another person who gets the insanely weird things that light us up.

Thankfully, the atmosphere between us has softened and more of our original, playful banter is returning. It makes my heart sing and my body swoon. It's not that I've forgotten, but it's a nice reminder to know just how much I really do love him.

When we walk in, it's no surprise when the place is packed. There are people bellied up to the bar, while others are playing pool in the other side room, and more yet are eating dinner at tables scattered throughout the restaurant.

"Just the two of you? Would you like a table or a booth?" a tall, blond server asks. She shifts to the side to allow us to view the room better.

I stand on my tiptoes, eyeing the small, open table toward the back windows. It's barely big enough for one person, but at least it has a lake view.

"Can we have that one?" I say, pointing.

"You got it. Follow me," she says, grabbing two menus and making her way through the crowd.

Both Wade and I follow after her and when we reach the

table, again, Wade positions himself so he can pull out my chair for me.

A slow smile burns across my face and I lean in when he's taken his seat. "You know, I can pull out the chair myself."

He raises his eyebrows in a knowing fashion. "I happen to be *well* aware. However, if there's one thing that's rubbed off on me from being with my grandpa, it's that we need more chivalry in this world. So, why not be the change? You know?"

The server's smile broadens, and she says, "Awww, aren't you two cute? Would you like anything to drink to get you started?"

She passes the menus to us and pulls out a tablet computer from a pouch on the front of her outfit.

"I'll have a cherry Coke," I say without even glancing at the menu.

"Same." Wade nods.

"Okey-dokey. Be back in a second to take your order," she says, tapping the screen and walking away.

I take his hands in mine and lean back in. They're freezing, so I rub them, trying to warm them up with some sort of friction. When I look up, Wade is watching me with a goofy grin.

I clear my throat. "So, is your grandpa one of those cute old guys who used to treat your grandma like a queen?" Images of an old couple doing everything together flashed through my mind.

"Yeah, they were really kinda sweet when she was still alive. The two of them used to take turns, too. Grandma would make cookies and be sure Grandpa got the first pick. Or make cups of coffee throughout the day for him, even though she didn't touch the stuff. I don't know, it's all kinda sweet and it gives me a goal to aspire to reach. You know?"

I nod, placing my chin on top of my left fist. "Sounds like they've left an impression on you."

"Yeah, I guess they have. After my parents... They were always sweet, really. They tried to tame me and make me stay with them, but I just had too much of a rebellious streak, I guess. But what about you, though? You said you had more you wanted to talk about?" he says, turning the menu over.

My eyebrows tug in and all the events of this past week play over in my mind. As much as I really do trust Wade, I feel like I need to protect him, too. He has so much to deal with because of his grandpa...

"Well, it's been a crazy week, as you probably guessed. I've been busy trying to keep up with school and figure out my powers. Plus, I'm still getting used to Dad...and evidently, *Abigail*," I say.

"So, start there..." Wade says, glancing up. "You said she showed you where the doorknob was?"

I glance down at my menu and nod. "Yeah."

"So what happened?"

"I don't know, really. She's been trying to guide me to it for a while, but for some reason, only when my dad isn't around. I wasn't able to get to it right away. Yesterday was the first time I went downstairs."

Our server comes back and places our Cokes in front of us. Absently, I pull mine close and take a sip.

"Are we ready?" she asks, pulling her tablet out again.

Blinking hard, I realize I haven't even taken in anything from the menu.

"Uhm..." I say, pulling it close again and staring at it blankly.

"Can you give us a couple more minutes?" Wade suggests, shooting a smile at the server.

"Sure thing. If it helps, our mushroom and Swiss burger

basket is the special tonight," she says, starting to walk away. "I can personally attest to its deliciousness."

"Oh, I'll go with that," I nod, handing her the menu. "But can I have onion rings with ranch dressing?"

She takes the menu and nods. "Yep, we can do that for ya, honey. How about you?"

Wade tips his head in return. "I will have the same. But fries for me, please."

The server's fingers tap across the screen and when she's done, she smiles, grabs Wade's menu, and walks off.

"So, tell me about tonight. What was going on when I broke up the party?" Wade says, watching me with the kind of intensity that makes me squirm in my seat like a kid who was caught stealing.

"There was no party..." I mutter, taking another sip. "I was feeling really overwhelmed with everything I'd found. I needed someone to talk to..."

"You know you could have called me? You could have Facetimed me and brought me in the basement with you," he says. A slow grin slides across his features—an easy, lopsided smile that almost reaches his eyes. But not quite.

I glance down at the table and stretch my hands out across the void between us. He takes the hint, reaching forward himself, and taking my hands in his.

Sighing, I say, "I should have, I'm sorry. It's just—I thought you had so much to deal with already. I didn't want to put more on your plate."

"You never have to worry about that. Seriously. Whatever you need, I'm here for you. I know it didn't seem like it last time we talked. I'm sorry I blew you off the other day. I didn't mean to make light of what your friends were telling you. If someone had told me that I need to be cautious of you, I'd need a moment, too."

I shake my head, staring at the tabletop. "It was stupid. Wade, I know you've been nothing but honest with me. I didn't mean to turn everything into such a cluster."

"How about this?" Wade says, placing a crooked index finger under my chin and making me look up. "No more secrets from now on. And no more lies through omission, either. Even if it's under the guise of protecting the other. Deal?" he says, his eyebrows tipping up in the middle.

"Deal," I whisper.

"We have an accord." Bending forward, he places his lips against mine, sending shockwaves right down to my toes.

"I've missed you," I blurt out, dreamily.

"I've missed you, too," he whispers, grabbing my right hand and rubbing the back of it with his thumb.

"No, I mean, I *really* have. You have no idea how strange it is to realize you can see and hear ghosts," I say, my voice trailing off. "Especially when you didn't believe ghosts even existed."

"I can imagine," Wade says, nodding.

"There's something new that's come up and I'm trying to decide if there's any truth to it. Maybe you can—"

"Hey, Autumn," a voice calls out.

I glance over, blinking hard as Dominic leans forward and tips his head in my direction. He's seated at a booth a couple of rows over, grinning in his cocky, irritating way.

"Uh, hey, Dominic," I say, nodding back in acknowledgment.

Wade's face falters and his smile fades.

"Wade, this is Dominic. He's...ah, I go to school with him," I say.

Wade tips his chin up and manages a half-hearted smile.

I grimace, returning my gaze to Wade.

Dominic clears his throat, sliding out of his booth, and

walking over to us. "And, are you going to introduce me to..." Dominic raises his eyebrows and sweeps a hand out to suggest Wade.

Shaking my head, I mumble, "Yeah, of course. Sorry. This is my boyfriend, Wade."

Wade's expression lifts and he sits up a bit straighter.

"Oh, I see," Dominic says, leaning toward us and outstretching his hand. "Well, nice to meet you, Wade."

"Likewise," Wade nods, eyeing Dominic over.

"Annnywaaaay," I say, drawing the word out longer than normal. "Where were we?"

"I believe we were saying how much you missed me?" Wade says, his voice a bit louder than it was a few moments before.

"Oh, that's right," I say, nodding. I was actually about to tell him about the crazy notion that I could be more like Abigail and it could mean bad news if she wants me to break some sort of curse, but with Dominic hanging around, that's a conversation that will have to wait. I don't need Dominic interjecting and making things worse by spouting off any of his necromancer nonsense.

"Hey, Autumn," Dominic interrupts. "Since we're all here having supper, why don't we join forces and share a table?"

I shake my head, "No, I don't think that's a good—"

Dominic pulls out one of the extra chairs from a table behind us and takes a seat.

My insides recoil at the discomfort sprouting around us. "Dominic, we're on a date."

Our server walks up with a platter in her hand and surveys the scene. "Everything okay here?" she asks, passing our burgers to us.

"Uh..." I begin.

"No, actually. This gentleman is bothering us. Is it possible to get another table?" Wade asks.

The server nods, "Of course. Sit wherever you'd like."

Standing up, Wade grabs his plate and drink and tips his head to a table across the room, "Let's go sit over there. That okay?"

Swallowing hard, I nod and grab my things. The waitress steps back, typing something into her tablet—probably our new table arrangement.

As we turn away, Dominic's chair screeches across the wooden floor. He drops the façade of being a 'nice guy' and his face contorts into something else—anger, disdain? He sidesteps around, standing directly in Wade's way.

"You shouldn't be here," Dominic sputters, standing toe to toe with Wade. While their heights match up almost equally, it's like a battle between light and dark as Dominic's white hair practically glows in the lighting of the restaurant, while Wade's black hair and leather jacket vibrate with a level of mystery and darkness I've never really noticed.

"And why is that, exactly?" Wade asks, setting down his plate and drink at the nearest table. The people sitting there scoot over, with surprise and apprehension painted on their faces. Wade's hands drop to his side as they ball into fists.

Dominic juts out his chin. "You know exactly why. You've sensed it from the moment you met her, you just didn't want to admit it. It's written clear as day in your aura."

"And how the hell would you know jack about what I sense?" Wade says through clenched teeth.

"I know what you are and she shouldn't be anywhere near *your kind*." Dominic's gaze flits for the briefest of moments from Wade to me—and hidden in their depths is something I've never seen before... Panic? Desperation? Both?

My jaw slacks open. "What in the hell is going on here?"

CHAPTER 25

WHEN THE DEAD RISE

Wade backs up, his mouth agape. No words escape his lips. Instead, he shifts his gaze between Dominic and me.

Rounding on Dominic, it's my turn to step into his space. "What in the hell are you talking about?"

"Ask him," Dom says, tipping his chin toward Wade.

Wade shakes his head, confusion and alarm clear across his features. "I have no idea where he's going with any—"

"Cut the shit, Wade. I can hear your damn thoughts. I get impressions all the time. You need to be honest with her about what you are," Dom spits, shooting me a sideways glance.

"Guys, you're gonna have to take this outside," the waitress says, coming over to us and pointing at the door.

Turning on my heel, I bound straight out the door and into the parking lot. When I twist back around, both Dominic and Wade are right behind me.

"I have no idea what this asshat is talking about," Wade says.

"Dude, she's a *necromancer*, man," Dominic says, his face hardening.

I roll my eyes.

Wade takes a step back, clearly shaken. "No, she's a..."

For whatever reason, being a necromancer means something to Wade, but I don't know why. He swallows hard, trying to recover from the impact that blow had on him.

"That's not true, is it?" Wade asks, turning to me.

Suddenly, his phone blares from his pocket.

Blinking wildly, he takes another step back and pulls it out. After staring at the screen for a moment, what color he had left fades from his face and his gaze drops to the ground. "Shit, I need to take this."

Walking away from us, I stare at his back in surprise.

"What the hell could possibly be more important than the conversation we were having?" Dominic scoffs. "He seriously needs to reassess his *priorities*." But as soon as the last word is spoken, a spark of sympathy flickers in his eyes. "Oh," Dom whispers.

Wade hangs up the phone, shoving it into his pocket. He doesn't turn around at first, but instead drops his chin to his chest.

"Wade? Is everything—" I begin.

Wade turns around, tears brimming in his eyes. "My grandpa was just taken by ambulance to the hospital. He's aspirating and they're not sure if..." his voice chokes out.

"Oh my god, Wade, I'm so sorry... Go, go to him," I say.

"Yeah, I need to get you back home," Wade says, his eyes glazing over.

Dominic steps forward, his demeanor a complete turnaround from a moment before. "Look, man, I can take her. It's on the way to my house anyway."

Wade's jaw sets, but he nods. In any other circumstance,

he would have put up a hell of a fight, but I can see just how much this has caught him off guard.

Taking a step toward me, Wade places his hands on either side of my arms. "Autumn, I promise, we'll talk about all of this. Everything. But this...it takes priority right this moment."

As much as I wish I had more answers, I also know how much his grandpa means to him.

"Of course it does. Go. Don't worry about me."

"I'll call you as soon as I know something," he whispers, bending in and kissing me on the cheek.

I reach up, pulling his face to mine so I can kiss him properly. My skin burns at the point of contact and I can't help but feel like whatever is going on, it's about to tear apart everything.

Wade pulls away, grabbing hold of my hands. "I love you, Dru. I really do."

With that, he makes his way to his car and hops inside. He casts a quick, distant wave and speeds off.

"God, I hope he's safe to drive," I whisper under my breath.

"He'll be fine," Dominic says with more confidence than I feel.

I take a deep breath and turn on him. "You have some explaining to do."

Dominic snickers. "It's not my secret to tell. As much as I would love to wipe the smug look off that guy's face, he has to be the one to tell you."

I roll my eyes. "Not more of this bullshit. Come on, Dominic. I thought we were past all of this."

"Let's just say his presence could have dangerous consequences. That's as much as I can tell you," he says, crossing his arms.

"So helpful," I mutter.

The door to the Bourbon Room opens and four patrons walk out, their voices jumbling together in hushed, hurried tones.

"I can't believe they found a body. We're gonna need to hurry," one of them says.

"Is it one of the new kids?" another says.

"They aren't sure. They're trying to ID the body now, but it's a girl, that's all I know."

Unable to help myself, I reach out and grab the closest woman by the arm. "I'm sorry...did you say they found a body? What did you mean by new kids?"

"Two more kids are missing—a boy and a girl. It's horrible, just horrible..." she mutters, turning back to continue on with her group.

My mouth drops open and I cover it with my hands. The Vodník is still at work and here I am, thinking I have problems. I'm so petty.

"Look, let's get you home, Autumn. If there's one place where you can get answers, it's there." Dominic walks out into the street, making his way to a bright red Honda Civic.

Without a word, I slide into the passenger seat and buckle up. I clench my jaw and turn to look out the window. If I was stolen by the Vodník before, I should be helping... If I remembered more, maybe I could have done something to stop all of this.

"There's nothing you could have done," Dom says, reading my thoughts.

"You don't know that," I mutter.

We drive in silence until we reach the end of my driveway and I point to its entrance.

"Yeah, I know," Dominic mutters.

When I throw him a quirked eyebrow, he shrugs. "It's a

small town, Autumn. Besides, I just live down the road, too. A couple miles past Cat and Colt."

"Oh, well I didn't know," I say, returning my gaze to the trees.

When he pulls up to the house, he stops to take a closer look at the weeping angel statue. "Interesting choice of decor."

"Yeah, I thought it was interesting, too," I say, nodding. "Well, thanks for the ride, Dominic."

I kick open the door, not wanting to be in his presence any longer than I have to. He's been nothing but a pain in the ass since I met him and trying to get more information out of him is pretty futile.

Hopping out of the driver's side, Dominic places his forearms on the roof of the car. "Hey, Autumn, if it matters, talk to your dad. I think he'll have more answers if you ask him directly. He knows more than you think he does."

Narrowing my gaze, I say, "Okay..."

"Just my two cents' worth. Anyway, catch ya later," he says, getting back into the car and driving off.

I stand there for a moment, watching his Civic fade into the distance. When the car disappears completely, my focus shifts from the driveway to the angel.

What's really going on with Wade? Even if I was a necromancer, why would that matter? Or does it have to do with something else? Something tied to Wade instead of me? Dominic said *your kind...*

Could Wade be the Vodník?

The thought filters in without restraint and it makes my insides recoil. The disappearances have only happened when he's in town... Could that be it?

I turn to the door and head inside. Panic wells inside me and I need more answers.

"Dad? Dad, are you home?" I call out, trying to pull back the edge of panic permeating my voice.

A few strained moments later, Dad appears at the top of the stairs. "Hi, sweetie. Did you go out for a bit?"

I scratch at my temple and take a step around the large table in the middle of the entry. "Yeah."

"Everything okay?" he asks, walking down the stairs to meet me.

"No, not really. I have to ask you a serious question. I don't know who else to turn to," I blurt out.

"Okay, that seems ominous," he says, his blue eyes surveying me critically.

"Do you—" I begin, standing up straighter and pulling my shoulders back. "I mean, did you know there was a hidden door in my bedroom?"

Dad's eyes widen and his mouth opens and closes, but no words come out.

"Because I think you do. I think you were hiding a door handle that opens it, and Abigail brought me to it. I think there's something big going on with this house, or with me —*us*. I need to know what it is..." I say, my words coming out in a jumbled mess.

For a moment, Dad puts his hands in prayer position and brings his hands to his lips. "Autumn, you may be treading in waters you don't want to be entering," he warns.

"Really? How about let's talk about the month I was missing when I was a kid... What was that all about? Why don't I remember it? Why have you never told me about it?" I say, anger and indignation rising to the surface. "What happened to me?"

Dad takes a step back, clearly shaken. "I thought things would be clearer by now. I was waiting for your mind to... Look, I didn't want to upset you."

"Upset me? You don't think finding out by reading a newspaper article would be a bit upsetting? At first I thought—" I blink, looking away. "At first I thought there must have been another kid—someone who looked like me. Or the newspaper was confused. But...it was me."

"You were in a fragile state. You needed to be kept calm—"

"Calm? Really? That's what you're going with? Everyone in this damn town knows more about me, and our family history, than I do. Why is that?" I yell, my voice rising with my anger.

"Sweetie—"

"Don't call me that. Not now," I say, raising my hands and backing away.

"Autumn, I had to..." his voice trails off and I stare at him in disbelief.

"You had to...*what?*" I urge.

He takes a deep breath before standing up and taking my hands in his. "You were lost to us. I was only gone a moment —just a quick second to get your lifejacket from the boathouse..."

I narrow my eyes, waiting for him to continue.

"When I came back, you were gone. I couldn't find you anywhere. I called you. I did everything in my power to locate you, but I knew... I just *knew* something horrible had happened. I felt it."

My stomach lurches and I take a step back.

"The police were called," he says, his eyes pleading with mine. "There was an investigation, they searched everywhere, but no one found you—or your body. We suspected a water demon, a Vodník, as having been involved. But we were never a hundred percent sure. Then, one day, well past the point of giving up hope, I found you. You were in that resurrection chamber, the basement room of yours, but didn't quite look yourself. You were pale and wet, and your clothes were tattered. I realized you hadn't come from inside the house. You'd somehow managed to come from the catacombs beyond."

"What on earth are you talking about?" I demand.

"Our home is built on catacombs—they hold the remains of our ancestors as far back as our history in America reaches. It's a sacred place. One you knew well because we had been working on your powers when you were younger, testing your abilities and what you could do." His gaze shifts to the floor. "There are only a few ways you can get to it... None of which are easily accessible."

I narrow my eyes and run my hands through my hair. "None of this makes sense. The newspaper says I was found wet and near the pond? On the dock or something..."

"You were soaked—that was true. But I had to think fast. As much as we like to believe people have accepted supernatural abilities, I knew with something like this, there'd be...*questions*. Questions I didn't want to answer at that time. I needed to understand more about what happened to you and why. I made the pond bit up for the police, hoping it would be enough that you were returned from the water, since they suspected the demon."

"What about the small table with my picture? Why was the door covered up?" I say.

"These are all good questions, but—"

"Dad, I need answers," I say through gritted teeth.

"The table has been there since the day I found you. I didn't dare touch it, just in case..."

"In case of *what*?"

"In case the spell was only temporary," he whispers. "That's why I hid the doorway. In case the candles needed to stay lit. I don't know what I'd do if I lost you again through my recklessness..." Tears well in his eyes and for a moment, all color drains completely from his face.

"Lose me?" I say, stepping toward him. "You say that like you mean something other than me going missing..."

His eyebrows knit together, and his lips tug downward.

"Dad?"

"You *drowned*, Autumn," he whispers.

My mouth pops open. "That's ridiculous."

"The doctors all said your body was showing signs of decomposition and trauma through drowning...but they couldn't make head nor tail over why you were up and walking around. You were recovering quickly, but we couldn't get out of you what had happened. It's like you had no memory of any of it. Your mother and I thought maybe... perhaps this was a way out. You didn't have to follow in the footsteps of the rest of the Blackwoods. Your mother felt it was the right thing to do—to take you out of this world and embed you in her mundane one. I agreed..." Again, his gaze falls to the floor. "But I knew one day you'd be drawn back."

"How could you possibly know that? I didn't even know."

"Eventually, our legacy catches up to everyone. It was just a little earlier with you," he whispers.

"What's that supposed to mean?" I say, shaking my head. This entire conversation is swimming around my head, simultaneously making zero sense, and resonating at soul level.

Dad's eyes lock with mine, and he tilts his head to the side slightly. "Autumn, that day...when you returned to us... I don't know how, but I'm convinced you *resurrected yourself*."

CHAPTER 26

SHOWTIME

A frantic knocking practically makes me jump out of my skin and interrupts me from the insane revelation my dad just dropped. My mind is reeling, but together, we make our way to the front door.

As I open it, there stands Dominic, his eyes and hair wild in the failing sunlight.

"Dominic, why did you come back?" I ask. "Now isn't really a good—"

"Autumn, *please*," he pleads, groping for my hand and pulling me up short, "you have to come with me. Something... *something's* happened."

"Come on, Dominic," I groan, rolling my eyes. "I'm not in the mood for more games. I've just had a bomb dropped on me. I really need to talk with my dad about—"

"It's Cat," he says, his voice quivering. Until this very moment, I didn't think Dominic cared about anyone beyond himself, but it's clear something has shaken him to the core.

My insides contort by the simple look upon his face. Anguish, desperation, and fear radiate from his very atoms.

"What's happened?" I ask, a strange calm settling over me, despite my heart thumping heavily in the silence.

He swallows hard and frowns as he shifts his gaze from me to my dad and back again. "She was just—we need you. *She* needs you."

I blink furiously, my thoughts tumbling through my brain at warp speed.

"What's happened?" I demand again.

He looks over my shoulder at my dad hovering just behind me. "There was a car accident. Colt's fine, but Cat...she—"

"No..." I say, backing away and shaking my head.

"She needs a damn *necromancer*, Autumn," Dominic sputters.

My body betrays me as I fight off the urge to puke. Continuing to back away, I turn to my dad. "I don't have the kind of power or expertise for something like this. I—I'm just a post-mortem medium..."

Even as I say the words, I know they aren't true. Somewhere buried deep inside me is an innate memory of being something much, much more. But whether or not I can bring anything back to life is another story.

"Autumn, I can't," Dad says matter-of-factly.

I whirl on him. "I can't let her die."

His eyebrows tip up in the middle, but his lips tug downward. "If I could, I would. But I can't. I've never had that ability, sweetie. And if I tried—well, let's just say, it wouldn't end well. Witches without the power of necromancy bring back *horrible things*. And that's if they're lucky."

"And what about me? I don't know if I have this power. If I try, and I don't—" I fight off the urge to be sick. What would happen if I tried to bring Cat back and they're wrong? "What would I be bringing back?"

"A revenant," Dad whispers.

"What?" I say, narrowing my gaze.

"A zombie," Dominic says, scrunching his face.

"Swell... That's just...*awesome*," I say, panic threatening to blind me out of this entire situation.

"Look, Autumn, we're all willing to take this risk. Without you, Cat is going to die. We need a necromancer fast or we'll lose her. Her soul is only tethered to her body for a short time—" Dominic says, urging me toward the door.

My hands fly to my hair and I take a step back. "Shit," I mutter, shaking my head.

"She's gone, Autumn, but she doesn't have to be. We gotta go, now," he demands, holding a hand out for me to take.

"I don't know how to do anything. I'm not the person you think I am. I'm just a girl—"

"A girl with immense power she has yet to understand. Trust me. I know it sucks and it's horrible timing to test your powers this way, but I wouldn't be here if we had another option," Dom says, tilting his head to the side and glancing down at his outstretched hand.

"Dammit," I spit, throwing a glance over my shoulder. He's right. Dealing with *zombie* Cat is better than dealing with *dead* Cat.

"Go," Dad says, tipping his head toward the vehicle in the drive.

"This isn't finished. We need to talk about this," I say.

"I'll be here," Dad agrees.

Racing behind Dominic, I fling open the passenger door and get back in. Before I even reach for the buckle, Dominic is in the driver's seat and puts the car into drive. Pebbles and loose stones from the driveway kick up as we speed off.

Twisting around in my seat, I turn to face Dom. "Explain what happened to Cat. *Now*."

His jaw clenches. "I honestly don't know everything. Those two are hard to read because of their bond. But I got a desperate call from Colton—something about a car accident. He wanted my help, but I'm not a damn necromancer and he knows that."

"He knows that? I didn't know you all were friends. I got the distinct impression they don't like you..." I say, trying to ignore the screaming in the back of my head.

"We were best friends as kids—all four of us," Dominic mutters. "But you don't remember, do you?"

"No, I—" I shake my head, refusing to take on more information that might blow my mind right now. "So, Colt doesn't know you're bringing me?"

"Not yet, no. He's trying to find someone else—some other way. I'm sure he doesn't want to pull you into it," Dominic says.

"This whole thing is insane," I say, shaking my head.

"Yeah, I know," he says, taking a curve at a speed that borders dangerous for us as well.

"You might want to slow down a little bit," I warn.

Dominic shakes his head. "We don't have time. They're on the other side of town. Besides, I'd see an accident for us in the works before it ever came to pass."

I suck in a breath, trying to ease the panic rising in my throat. I don't know what the hell I'm doing. If Cat's already dead...can I even help? Just because they think I'm a necromancer, it doesn't mean I really am. Am I prepared to try and possibly risk bringing Cat back as a revenant?

If only I had known more earlier, or if I had been raised here with my dad instead of going to Mistwood Point with my mom. I could have been practicing or testing so much earlier. I could have been prepared for this.

Clearing my throat, I sit up a bit straighter.

"If it fails, and she comes back wrong...what do we have to do?" I say, needing to know the worst-case scenario.

"Then we have to kill her again," Dominic says, shooting me a sideways glance.

My mouth drops open and I nod. "Super."

"You won't have to be the one to do it, so don't worry about that part. Just focus on making this work."

"How am I gonna know what to do?" I whisper, fighting back the urge to cry in sheer panic.

Dominic sighs, cutting the tension in the car. "I don't know, Autumn. I'm telepathic and telekinetic, remember? I'm hoping... I don't know what I'm hoping. I guess I just hope instinct kicks in or something."

"What in the hell were they doing all the way out here?" I say, narrowing my eyes as the trees get even more dense. "They live near me—"

"Us," Dominic says, "They live by us."

"Oh, right..."

"I don't know. There could be a hundred reasons. There are trails out here, places to hike. Colton likes to practice working on his ability away from town."

I turn to look at Dominic, confused. "Why would he have to practice so far out?"

"He's an elemental witch, like Cat. But rather than fire, he can manipulate the element of earth. Bending it and moving it. There's only so much you can do on your own property, I guess," he says.

"Oh, I didn't know," I whisper, realizing just how little I've paid attention to the supernatural abilities of those around me. I've been so wrapped up in myself and my own little world.

We hit a straightaway and Dominic floors it. Trees, scenery, and mailboxes fly by and I squeeze my eyelids shut.

Please make it in one piece... I mentally repeat in a mantra, despite what Dominic said about seeing into the future.

"Shit, there they are," Dominic mutters. "Showtime, Autumn."

My eyes pop open and up ahead Cat's vehicle is turned on its side, halfway in the ditch. Beside it, Colton waves his arms in a wide, sweeping motion.

Time slows down as Dom's car comes to a screeching halt beside Colton. Vehicle parts and personal items are strewn across the road and without even having to check for Cat—the presence of death lingers in the air. It vibrates through the trees with an intensity all its own.

Dominic kicks his car door open and I do the same.

"What's she doing here?" Colt says, jabbing a finger my direction.

"You know damn well why," Dominic says, pushing past him. "Where is she?"

Colton points a trembling finger toward the ditch.

Rushing past them both, I slide down the leaf-infested ditch to Cat's body. Within seconds, both men are practically on top of me.

"Back up and let me have some space," I command, kneeling down and taking my place beside Cat. Everyone does as they're asked, except for Colton who stays right by Cat's side and refuses to let go of her left hand.

There is so much blood; it's everywhere. Her shirt, her face, her hair, her jeans—the ground. It's all over the leaves and grass in a large circumference around her body. Beside us, a yellow-orange ball of light hovers, as if needing to witness what comes next.

"Don't let me go," Cat's voice echoes over the wind.

Suddenly, I realize this orb is different—it's not a ghost,

not like Abigail. It's a disembodied soul looking for a place of its own.

Cat's soul is no longer inside her body.

Shuddering away my own rising panic, I close my eyes, and place my palms along Cat's abdomen.

I breathe and focus on the energy rolling off the scene in waves. At first, nothing happens.

I adjust the way I'm kneeling so I can hover over her.

For some reason, I intuitively know if I can get the right placement, through my hands, *I can sense her.* I should be able to tell if I can do anything to bring her back.

Tuning out the surroundings and the terror of those around me, a strange sensation washes over me. It's like being submerged in water or floating away from everything tying me to the earth.

"Do something," Dominic urges. "This isn't time for a reiki session, for crying out loud."

I flash him a glare and he backs up with his hands raised.

Beside me, tears begin to stream down Colt's dark cheeks.

I close my eyes, summoning my will so it can force her spirit back into her body. The act feels like orchestrating atoms, as if one-by-one, I could pull her back into her body. But as they begin to reconvene, they must be missing something, because rather than congealing, they continue onward as they disperse again.

"It's not working," Dominic warns.

"I see that," I spit, eyeing Cat's orange orb of light as it races back and forth between me and Colton.

"What do we do?" Colt asks, kneeling down by her head and clutching her hand to his chest.

"I don't know. I've never done this before," I say, closing my eyes to hold back the tears threatening to emerge.

Suddenly, movement in the tree line draws my attention

and out steps a man, dressed from head to toe in dark, tattered, soaking-wet clothes. His face is a muddy mess and his movements are slow, like he's drunk or just woke up from a nap.

"Look, man...now's not a good time," Dominic says, stepping between us and the man.

The newcomer peers around Dominic, evidently unfazed by the scene. In fact, he grins, like he's amused by it.

My insides scream. We don't have time for this. Cat needs action, *now*.

"Guys, we need to go. Forget the guy. We need to get Cat somewhere safe to..."

Colton stands up, leaving Cat's hand for the first time. With this single action, the man lunges at Dominic, throwing him out of the way as if he were a rag doll. Colt freezes, refusing to take another step toward him. The man tries to do the same to Colt, but the ground rises up, putting a barrier between the two of them. The man howls in pain as his right arm hits the shifted earth.

It's the first time I've seen Colton use his powers, and he does so with surprising ease. A wave of jealousy rolls through me that I'm the last one to learn how to use my own gifts properly. It doesn't last long, as the man takes another swipe at Colton, clearly trying to make his way to us.

Colton summons the trees; branches and roots flow out of the woods, groping for the man. One makes contact with his left arm, yanking him into the air and sending him flying backward into a tree trunk. He hits it with a thud, but immediately gets up and races forward.

The speed is so fast, it's hard to even keep an eye on it. He slams into Colt, tossing him the opposite direction of Dominic. A smug smirk slides across his dirty lips and he makes his way to me and Cat, as if somehow, we're the prize he was searching for.

Stopping inches from Cat's orb, he raises his nose to the air and sticks out his tongue. "I can taste her...can you taste her?" he asks, his words tumbling out in a slow lilt. "She will be lovely for my collection. Never have I had a Gemini twin before."

My eyes widen and I fight the urge to scramble backward and abandon Cat's body. It's not like I have any powers that match this creature's. Worse yet, there's a deep sense of familiarity bubbling up to the surface. Memories from the day of the Witching Stick, the morning right before the girls disappeared, I saw this man by my pond.

But more than that, I remember his smile... It's the same one he used to lure me into the lake when I was a kid.

CHAPTER 27

I CAN'T DO THIS ALONE

Before I can fully process, Dominic tackles the Vodník. Both land in the ditch with a hard thump. Despite the blows from Dominic's fists, the Vodník seems completely unfazed as he waits patiently with a smirk on his face.

"I'm not gonna tire out, you piece of shit," Dom says, possibly reading his mind.

"We'll see," the Vodník laughs. "Human will is so easily worn down."

Dom raises a fist again and pummels the creature over the bridge of its nose, splitting it apart and sending blood splattering to the ground.

Again, it laughs.

Tree branches from the old oaks behind them wrap around Dom's arms, lifting him off the Vodník. At the same time, rock slabs from deep in the earth push their way up, entrapping the hands and feet of the creature.

In the opposite direction, Colt's dark face is scrunched in concentration as he clenches his fists at his side. The rocks bear down, crushing the creature's extremities.

Colton's eye sockets glow a blinding sky blue as the power he wields builds. Suddenly, he opens his fists. The small gesture expels all moisture from the creature's body into the air. It doesn't linger, either. Instead, it merges with the rest of the atmosphere. Water, blood...instantly, its skin shrivels and eyeballs obliterate.

Colton stands there, his glowing orb eyes refusing to leave the creature as it struggles to take its final breath. With a sneer, Colton crumples his hands back into a fist and the Vodník is reduced to nothing more than a pile of dust.

Dropping to his knees, Colt hunches over, groping at the grass. Dominic tumbles from the tree's clutches and rushes over to him.

"Are you— Holy shit, man. That was awesome," he says, a high level of admiration in his tone.

Colt looks up, his eyes now back to their dark brown. "I didn't even know I could do that. Instinct just...took over."

"Well, whatever your instincts, I do not wanna be on your bad side," Dominic says, helping Colt to his feet.

In the center of the pile of Vodník ash is a clear, ornate glass container, no bigger than a shot glass.

"What is that?" Colt says, taking a step closer and picking it up. He rotates it in the light, peering into the contents. Colors swirl within in, spiraling around the edge, as if looking for a way out.

The tiny object emits an insane amount of energy and it makes my skin crawl. Overwhelmed by the intensity, I say, "Smash it."

Colton doesn't even think twice. He throws it to the ground and stomps down hard. The glass shatters into thousands of tiny shards and unearthly screams floods out, materializing into bright orbs of light in various colors. Some are white, blue, green, yellow... but only Cat is the bright orange.

Each of the new orbs circle around each other, as if totally directionless.

My mouth drops open. "It's where he trapped his souls."

"How do you know?" Dominic says, taking a step closer to the broken glass.

"Can't you see them?" I say.

"See what?" he mutters, taking a step back, his eyes scanning the space around us.

Before I have the chance to open my mouth again, a large black cloud billows open like a tear in reality. As it gets bigger and wider, a man in a meticulously press pinstripe suit steps out. The moment his feet crunch on the leaves in the ditch, the smoky portal collapses in on itself.

His timeworn face bears years of experience, and his dark hair and incredibly light-blue eyes flash around the space. It's clear nothing about the scene surprises him. Instead, he quirks a dark eyebrow and raises his arms out wide. One by one the tiny orbs of light gravitate to him like magnets being called to their source.

When he has them all collected, he turns to Cat's orange light. A wave of acknowledgement rolls through me and I shake my head. "No, not that one. You can't have that one," I tell him, concentrating hard and refusing to release it from my vicinity.

The man's eyes lock with mine and a shiver rolls through my entire being. There's something so familiar about his eyes, yet I can't completely put my finger on why.

With a graceful movement, he walks closer to me, his gaze never leaving mine. Bending down, he leans in close to my ear and whispers, "I will be back, necromancer. Time is not on your side."

As I turn to look him in the face, he's gone—billowing away in a cloud of dark black smoke.

Blinking away my surprise, I return my gaze to Cat's limp body. The color in Cat's cheeks has faded and she's taken on an ashen-gray complexion.

I can't do this alone...

Suddenly, the answer becomes painfully clear. I know what I need to do—and where we need to do it. My eyes pop open and I stare at Dominic and Colt.

"We need to get Cat back to my house. Help me get her in the car," I say, relying on my own instincts the way Colton had.

"She doesn't—" Colt begins.

Dominic shakes his head. "Autumn's right. We need to trust her."

"You asked me to do this and I'm telling you what we need to do," I say to Colton, determination settling in.

"But how do you know?" Colt cries. "What if the time it takes to get to your place makes it impossible to return her to me?"

"There isn't time to discuss this. Quick, help me get her up," I say, trying to grab hold of her legs.

Colt and Dominic spring into action, each taking a shoulder and hoisting her body up. Carefully, they place her across the back seat of Dominic's car. He doesn't even say anything about the blood soaking into the upholstery.

Taking a step back, I reach for the passenger door and hop inside. Dominic races to the driver's seat and Colt slides in back, placing his sister's head in his lap. He runs his fingertips over her forehead and tears begin to slide from his cheeks.

"We're gonna fix this," I say, looking over my shoulder at him.

Without a word, or even looking up, he nods.

Dominic speeds away from the scene so fast, smoke kicks up from the tires.

I keep my focus on Cat's orb, which seems to be straying further and further from her body. As minutes pass by, her essence continues to disperse—like snowflakes beginning to drift from the density of its cloud.

"Almost there," Dom says, twisting down the last road that brings us to my house.

Closing my eyes, I try to reach out to Cat's essence with my thoughts.

Stay with us, Cat. Hang on... We're almost ready... I'm getting us help...

Dominic practically drifts into my driveway, skidding to a stop on the cobblestones next to the front door. Before the vehicle is even turned off, Dom is out the door. He grabs hold of Cat's feet and starts to gently pull her from Colton's lap. Colt scoots with her, helping to maneuver her body out of the back seat until Dominic has enough leverage to grab hold of her. The two of them manage to balance her body and I race toward the front door, kicking it open wide to give them space.

As we enter the main hallway, Abigail's ghost joins us, as if already sensing my impending request.

I'm going to need all the help I can get.

"Come with me. We need to get her downstairs," I declare, practically running the hallway down to my bedroom. Despite having closed it earlier, the little doorway to the basement is flung wide open in acceptance of its offering.

Abigail is ready for us.

"This way," I say, pointing to the stairwell.

Dominic and Colt carry her quickly; their footsteps assured and careful at the same time.

When we reach the bottom, I slide the small altar to the side of the room and drop to my knees.

Quickly, I scrawl the same pentacle I saw on the floor from the vision of Warren and Abigail. Flames ignite around the space, not attached to anything, but available as a source of energy and offering their own enchantment. They burn brightly, as if sensing the presence of magic, and maybe that's truly all it is.

"Set her down over there for a minute," I say, pointing to the spot under the stairs where the body was kept in the memory, or vision, Abigail offered to me.

The two of them do as I say.

"Colton, I need you to go to my kitchen and grab the salt. Find as much as you can and bring it back here—go!"

Without question, he turns on his heel, racing back up the stairs.

"Dominic, I need you to gather some of Cat's blood. I don't need much."

His eyes widen, but he nods. "Be right back. I'll grab something from your room to hold it in."

Not waiting for a response, Dominic takes off running.

My eyes flit to Cat's body in the corner, then to Abigail. She doesn't say anything, but nods in acknowledgement.

A moment later, both Colton and Dominic race down the stairs, each of them carrying their items. Dominic has a jewelry bowl in his hands and Colt has two cylindrical containers of salt.

"Is this enough?" Colton's face is pale with worry as he hands them to me.

"Yeah, this should work. Take a deep breath. Can you do that for me?" I ask, keeping my eyes trained on him.

He attempts an inhalation, but it's jagged and labored.

"She needs you to stay grounded. You're her tether—" I

say, tapping into knowledge beyond my expertise. "In order for this to work, you need to remain calm and centered."

Abigail remains by my side, a silent support. I know somehow, perhaps through our genetic link, perhaps through our shared magical connection, she's giving me knowledge I wouldn't have had otherwise.

"I can't lose her, Autumn," Colt says, tears brimming in his eyes and his lower lip quivering. "She's my twin."

"We're not losing anyone," I tell him, eyeing the fading orange orb with uncertainty.

Turning to Dominic, I whisper, "Fill the container with Cat's blood. Hurry."

Turning back to the pentacle I'd drawn in the sandy floor, I begin to outline it again, but this time in a thin layer of salt. Once the pentagram portion is finished, I walk the outside of the circle and enclose it with the salt. As the circle is completed, the room quakes, sending out a signal to us all —*this is no joke*. We are in a sacred space now.

Dominic rushes back, thrusting a shaking hand out to me. The sides of the jewelry bowl are now soaked in Cat's blood, but it holds a small pool. Taking it from him, I inhale sharply, and try to center myself. Staying calm needs to take precedence right now.

Abigail raises a finger, pointing to the center of the pentacle. "It is paramount you begin with her offering. It opens the gateway between what is, what was, and what will be," she whispers.

Nodding to myself, I pour the deep burgundy liquid from its container onto the floor below. It pools in the center pentagon portion, spreading out to its borders.

Abigail reaches for my shoulder and as her hand comes into contact with me, she begins her incantation. It's quiet at first, but her words start to grow with each repetition until I can hear them all and follow along.

"Death, taker of life, power of gods and givers, accept my offering. Bone, blood, breath, flesh. Recover Caitlyn's soul—her *remnants*—and return her to me," I begin to chant.

I start to walk the circle, counterclockwise, just as I witnessed Abigail do in the vision.

"Now you must deliver your offering, that of your own blood," she says.

Wide eyed, I look up at her. I'd forgotten this part.

Glancing around the room, I practically screech, "A knife. I need a knife."

Without a moment's hesitation, Dominic reaches into his jeans and garnishes a small pocket knife.

"Will this work?" he asks, throwing it to me.

I nod. "It will have to."

Switching it open, I run the blade through one of the fires along the stone wall, cleansing it. I don't know if it's the years watching Buffy, or my own innate guidance telling me to do so, but every fiber of my being hums in anticipation of what comes next. My body knows, my *blood* knows.

Taking a deep breath, I close the palm of my hand around the knife and run the blade across my skin. The sharp pain and tug of skin makes my breath hitch, but I hold my hand out, allowing my blood to drip into the center of the pentacle, mixing with Cat's.

As it makes contact, the mixture begins to slosh and swirl, lighting it with an eerie whitish glow. I take a step back, tossing the knife to the ground. I expect the blood to rise in a vortex in the same way it had for Abigail. Instead, it continues to encircle itself, as if in some sort of a holding pattern.

"This one is different. You need more energy," Abigail offers, splaying her hands out wide to suggest all of us.

"I need everyone. Quick, hold hands," I command.

We each take a place along the outer edge of the pentacle and one by one, reach out to clasp hands. As we close the small triadic loop, the room again pulsates in a wave of energy, and I start the chant again. Eventually, the rest of them follow suit.

"Death, taker of life, power of gods and givers, accept my offering. Bone, blood, breath, flesh. Recover Caitlyn's soul—her remnants—and return her to us..." we say in unison over and over again. The energy rises and vibrates at a higher pitch, but still nothing happens to the blood in the center—nor to Cat's body.

Looking over my shoulder at Abigail, I cry out, "Why isn't it working?"

CHAPTER 28

GEMINI BLOOD

"Of that, I am not certain. This should have been more than ample energy for her resurrection," Abigail whispers, backing away from me.

Turning from her, I look into everyone's eyes, trying to think of what else could be needed. When my gaze rests on Colt's frightened features, it suddenly dawns on me—he's her tether. I even said it in the beginning. But more than that, the Vodník said something about them being twins...

Gemini twins?

That has to mean something. She's bound to him by blood.

"Colton, we need your blood, too," I declare, reaching for the knife and tossing it over to him. "Being twins makes you special. She needs your offering to make this work."

Without hesitation, he flicks open the knife and holds out his left palm. My blood still clings to the blade, but he doesn't stop to try to cleanse it. Instead, he positions the sharp edge into the center of his palm.

He digs the edge of the blade into his skin. Pulling it through the center of his hand, the blood pools crimson in the middle. With a deep breath, he tips his hand over to allow the blood to flow into the spiraling mixture below. The second it comes into contact with the rest, the vortex begins to rise. The orange orb merges with this, causing the vortex to glow of its own accord in a bright blue and orange light.

In the corner, Cat's body erupts in an eerie, almost otherworldly glow, as a wispy white and peach-colored energy encircles back and forth around her, like some sort of energetic cocoon.

"Good. This is good. Now, it is of critical importance that you should use your athame to direct her raised life force back into her body," Abigail says, pointing to the knife still clutched in Colton's hand.

Nodding, I turn to him. "Colt, the knife." I flip my hand over, flicking my fingertips with my request.

He places the knife in my outstretched palm, and I point it toward the vortex of blood and light. Under my breath, I whisper, "Please, please work."

The blood heeds my command, reaching to the tip of the knife until it almost comes into contact with the steel. Flicking my wrist, I aim the vortex of blood and light toward Cat's body on the floor beneath the stairs.

It rushes forth, shooting through the open space between Colt and me, and straight at Cat's body. Unlike the vision Abigail showed me, where the body was covered in a white sheet, Cat's mangled vessel rests on the floor unhindered. The blood vortex enters her slightly agape mouth and instantly the wispy white and peach veil of energy transforms into a cocoon of blood red.

The three of us stand slack-jawed as we take in the scene unfolding before us.

"Oh my god," Dominic whispers, taking a step backward. "This is so friggin' awesome."

"Let's just hope it works," I mutter, refusing to look away.

The crimson glowing cocoon that is Cat's body continues to radiate until the entire room shifts to a blinding orange light. Then, just as abruptly as it began, it pulls back like an explosion in reverse, as the energy and light pulls entirely into her body. Like a candle snuffed out, the light disappears.

"Is anything happening?" Colt asks, craning around to get a better view. "Is she..."

I shake my head, turning to Abigail. "I don't know?"

Abigail doesn't say a word; instead, she simply holds up a finger.

"Give it time," Dad offers, entering the basement from the final step. He was so quiet, I didn't even realize he had arrived.

The space falls eerily silent; the only sound permeating the stillness is our ragged breaths as we practically hold them in.

"It doesn't look like—" Colton begins.

Suddenly, Cat's chest begins to rise and fall. Then, cracking and pops reverberate off the stone walls, as if her broken bones are mending themselves. Her right arm angles itself backward, then twists around, until she places her hand on her torso.

"Holy shit," Dominic mutters under his breath. "It's like watching a horror movie, but in real life."

"Let's hope that's not how this ends," I say, unable to look away from the scene.

Please don't be a zombie, or a revenant...whatever.

Sputtering out blood and bile, Cat rolls over, clutching at the dirt on the floor.

Colton races for his sister. "Thank you, thank you, Autumn, you have no idea..." his words trail off as he drops to his knees and takes Cat in his arms. Despite the bloody mess, he clutches her tightly, rocking back and forth.

My own desperate grief washes away, replaced instead by relief—*and joy*.

I did it.

We—did it. Cat's alive.

Abigail catches my eye, a slow smile spreading across her lips. She nods as if reading my mind.

Leaving the circle, I stand behind Colton and Cat for a few moments, allowing the two of them some time. Dominic also hangs back, his eyes wide, but there's more to it than that, I think. He knew I could do this, and it was his way of proving it to me, too.

"How are you feeling?" I ask, finally kneeling down beside Cat.

"I—" Cat begins, then clears her throat.

"Don't talk if it hurts, it's okay. We're here," Colt offers. "You need some time to heal."

She swallows hard, nodding to him. Closing her eyes, she leans into his chest.

Colton's eyes flit to me. "Autumn, how does this work? Will she need the hospital?"

I shrug. "I don't honestly know." I turn to Dad, hoping he'll have some answers.

"She'll need rest. Lots and lots of rest," he says, raising his eyebrows knowingly.

The look on his face prompts my mind to flash back to my childhood memories of this place. Being locked in my room... Suddenly, it all makes sense. It wasn't to keep me from going anywhere. It was so I could heal.

Cat swallows hard, eyeing each of us. She finally manages to say, "Why are we here? What...*happened*?"

"Do you remember anything, Cat?" Dominic asks, finally

risking to edge nearer.

Cat shakes her head. "Not really. I remember—" her eyes go distant as she tries to recall, "—I remember driving out to the trails, but..."

"Something ran out in front of us. Do you remember?" Colt whispers.

Cat shakes her head. "No, I don't."

"It doesn't matter," he says, shaking his head and pulling her close again. "I'm so glad you're back. I thought I'd lost you..."

Cat closes her eyes again, allowing her head to rise and fall with the inhalations of her twin brother.

"You did good," Dad says, walking up behind me.

Taking a deep breath, I stand up to give the twins some space.

"I didn't know I had that in me..." I whisper, walking to the other side of the room.

"There's so much in our history, Autumn. Our legacy has always been shrouded by secrets, but I didn't want to inundate you. Not as a child, and certainly not when I'd just gotten you back to the manor. But it's time that you learn everything..." he says, his voice trailing off. "You know, when you returned to us, all your mother and I wanted in the whole world was for you to have a normal life after everything. More than anything, that's what I wanted for you, because I know what kind of toll this gift can take."

I glance up.

"We can talk more about it later... But just know that I'm very proud of you, Autumn," he says, smiling awkwardly. It's pretty clear giving compliments isn't his strong suit.

"Thanks," I whisper.

"Her parents will need to know about what's transpired here. They'll all need to contact the Academy to lean on their magical support while she heals," Dad says. "Make sure she doesn't exert herself or try to get up. Her body won't be ready for that."

"Okay. I'll make sure it gets done," I say.

"Good. I'll give you all some space. If you need me, I'll be around the house," Dad says, leaving my side to make his way upstairs.

Standing back, I breathe a sigh of relief and take in the scene. Abigail is no longer with us, apparently having better things to do with her ghostly time. The pentacle in the center of the room is already starting to fade into the sandy floor from the back and forth motion of our footsteps. Even the magic keeping the flames lit is beginning to dwindle as the light in the space dims.

"We might want to think about getting everyone upstairs," I say, turning to the twins. "Cat needs to rest, and we'll have to have a word with your parents. They'll need to know."

Colton's face drops, but he nods. "That'll be a fun conversation."

"But a necessary one," I say, walking over to them.

"I suppose you're right," Colt says, gingerly pulling away from Cat as he stands up. "Autumn, you're amazing. I hope you weren't offended that I didn't call you. I mean, I just—I know you weren't really sure about all of this and I needed help fast."

"Of course not. I'm just glad it all worked out."

"That makes two of us. Thank you again," he says, pulling me into his embrace. A masculine, earthy scent permeates my senses and suddenly, the energy between us shifts, like an electrical current suddenly switched on.

Just like before, strange blue and orange flames lick at my arms where his touch lingers, and the hairs on the back of my neck rise. I pull back, peering into the depths of his dark-brown eyes as anxiety unfurls in my gut.

His eyes take on more seriousness as wrinkles in his forehead emerge. Racing his tongue over his lips, Colton's eyes fall to my mouth, and he inhales sharply. As if moving in super speed toward me, his mouth suddenly bears down on mine, taking my breath away.

When my brain catches up, I push him back, cutting off the kiss. I take a step back, covering my lips with my hands.

"I—I'm so sorry, Autumn. I shouldn't have..." Colton says breathlessly.

I shake my head, turning away from him. "No, you really shouldn't have."

Sucking in a jagged breath, I shake away the tendrils of panic welling inside me. Wade was right.

The elation from Cat's resurrection begins to dissipate and all I can think about is what happens now?

How do I deal with Colton going forward? And worst yet, how am I going to explain everything to Wade?

As if on cue, my cell phone rings in my pocket, making me jump. Fumbling for it, I pull it out, and stare at Wade's face smiling back at me. My heartbeat thumps loudly in my ears and debate on whether or not to answer it.

I'm a big girl. I can do hard things.

I straighten my shoulders and tap the button. "Hey, handsome. I was just—"

"Autumn, can you come to Mistwood?" Wade's voice is gruff, and I can tell instantly something is wrong.

Stepping away from everyone, I swap the phone to my other ear. "Of course. What's happened? Is your grandpa—?"

There's a long pause and just before I pull the phone back to see if he's still on the line, he whispers, "He just died. I don't really want to be alone right now."

CHAPTER 29
CIRCLE BACK AROUND

Funeral homes give me the creeps.

"Have I mentioned how much I appreciate you being here, Autumn?" Wade asks, taking a seat in the front row of the chapel.

I smile softly, sitting beside him and resting my hand on his knee. "I wouldn't be anywhere else."

His lips curve, but the smile doesn't really make it to his eyes. Through all of the arrangements and conversations about his grandpa's life, Wade's never broken down. He's been very matter-of-fact, despite the grief that's so evident in his aura. I wish he'd open up more, even if it was just with me.

My eyes flit to the urn in the middle of the table in front of us. "Is there anything else I can do?"

"Come with me to the cemetery, I suppose," he says, clasping his hands in his lap.

"Are you sure you don't want an actual service? I mean, we could put this off and let his friends and your family—"

Wade chuckles, shaking his head. "The funeral director

keeps asking me that. All of his friends are long gone and I'm all that's left of our family. So…"

"There's no real point. I get it," I say, squeezing his knee. "Well, when you're ready, I'm with you."

"Thank you. Do you mind if we wait here for a few minutes?"

"Of course not." I lean into him and rest my head on his shoulder.

We sit in silence for the longest time, only listening to the sound of the clock ticking on the wall. It's almost like a metronome, keeping the pulse of life for those still living.

The funeral director quietly walks up to Wade and kneels down next to him in the aisle. "I do not want to rush you, Mr. Hoffman, but light is starting to dwindle. If you'd like to bring your grandfather to the columbarium, we really should be heading out in the next fifteen minutes."

Wade's dark eyebrows tug in, but he nods. "We can go now. I guess I wasn't paying attention to the time."

The funeral director tips his head, standing back up, and making room for the two of us to leave the chapel. Wade breaks from the aisle, walking up to the urn and collecting one of the large floral arrangements of blooming lilies. Clutching it to his chest, he makes his way back to me.

As we walk out, the funeral director heads back to the table and gently lifts the urn. Wade pauses in the doorway, waiting for him to catch up.

"Would you like to take the hearse or ride on your own?" the funeral director asks as he reaches us.

Wade swallows hard, shaking his head. "No, I think we'll drive, if that's okay."

"Of course. Whatever you are most comfortable with. I'll meet you there," he says, tipping his head and walking by.

"Come on. I'll drive," I say, interlocking my right arm in his left.

He nods. "Thanks, Dru. I appreciate that."

Together, we walk out of the Mistwood Point Funeral Home and out into the crisp fall air. It still smells like the death of summer, but the chill of winter lingers in the air. Snow is on its way.

Without speaking, we walk over to Big Blue and get inside. Wade holds the vase in his lap and the entire car fills with the pungent odor of lilies. We wait for the hearse to leave its garage and I flip on my headlights and follow. The two-minute drive to the cemetery takes ten minutes thanks to the snail's pace of the hearse and its memorial procession. The silence in our vehicle is a heavy weight. A final good-bye is pressing upon us and, I know all too well, I'm not terribly good with good-byes. Mine, or anyone else's.

By the time we pull into the cemetery, the funeral director is already opening the small columbarium container.

"So, this is it," Wade whispers.

"Guess so," I nod.

Leaning back in his seat, Wade takes a quick look around the cemetery. "This is where we first met."

A smile spreads across my lips. "It certainly is."

"Interesting how we both keep getting drawn to the dead," he says, reaching for the door handle.

"Yeah," I nod, opening my car door.

Guilt pangs through my insides and I promise myself for the hundredth time that when this is all over, I'm going to tell him about Cat's resurrection—and *Colton's kiss*. Neither of them seemed overly important in light of all of this.

As we get out of the truck, I walk over to him, adjusting his tie again before sliding my hand in his. He adjusts the vase of flowers, holding out to the side to give me some room.

"Would you like to do the honors?" the funeral director asks, holding out the urn.

Wade's eyes widen and he shakes his head. "No thanks. I'm... I'm okay."

Nodding, the funeral director places the urn inside its new home and bows his head in silence. We do the same, sending a final wish for a peaceful afterlife. The peacefulness of it makes me wonder, now more than ever, what happens when we die. Is it simply the end? Or is there something beautiful on the other side?

A pang of guilt tugs at the back of my mind. What if I stopped Cat from going someplace beautiful?

After a moment or two, the funeral director closes the container and places a hand on Wade's shoulder. "Your grandfather was a lucky man to have had you in his life."

"Thanks," Wade croaks out, dropping his gaze to the ground.

"I'll be in touch, Mr. Hoffman. Have a good night," he says softly before turning to me. "You as well, Ms. Blackwood."

"Thank you," I say, tipping my head.

When the hearse has left the premises, Wade steps up to the columbarium and sets down the vase of flowers. Without a word, we take a seat on the granite bench near the memorial wall.

"Well, I guess my time in Mistwood Point is officially coming to a close," Wade says, swallowing hard.

"Have you decided what you want to do?" I ask, looking over my shoulder at him.

"I don't know. I need to close out his estate. Something about probate, whatever that is. But I'll have to get things in line for next year. I suppose I'll need to find an apartment in town. You don't happen to know of any good places in Windhaven?" he says, turning to me.

I shake my head. "Not when it comes to renting. But..."

Wade quirks an eyebrow.

I smile. "What if you just come to live at the manor? I mean, there's plenty of rooms and it's not like you wouldn't just be at the house anyway."

Wade snickers quietly. "And who's to say you wouldn't be spending all your time at my new pad?"

I narrow my gaze and shrug. "Mmmm...rented bachelor pad or enormous, historical manor. Tough choice. I see your point."

"Bachelor pad. Psh," Wade says. "I'm pretty sure I'm spoken for, but I'll give you the manor versus apartment debate. Are you sure your dad won't mind?"

I grin. "Of course not. Then it's settled. When you're ready, you move in with me and my dad."

"How could I pass up staying at Blackwood Manor? I mean, if for no other reason, it contains the most beautiful woman in the world," Wade says, taking me into his arms. "I'll certainly have to thank your dad...as soon as we can get him to stay put long enough for me to meet him."

I laugh. "Well, living in the same house, it will be kind of hard to avoid each other. Don't you think?"

"Very true," Wade says. "It will be nice to leave Mistwood Point behind."

"I can imagine."

Wade shifts on the bench slightly, his gaze falling on the flowers. "Do you—would you mind if I have a moment alone, Autumn?"

Looking up, sadness and anxiety linger in his silver eyes. "Of course. Take as much time as you need. I'll just... wander a bit. I have some old friends I'd like to visit."

I pull back from him and stand up. It's been a while since I wandered this graveyard...and after all that's gone on, I could certainly use a little bit of its stillness.

Bending in, I kiss the top of his head and make my way toward the older graves. They look totally different in the semi-daylight, but still have an air of mystery and romance to them. In fact, as the sun sets low behind the trees, the air of mystery is heightened.

Brushing my hands along the older tombstones and statues, I can't help but wonder how we lost our desire to honor the dead with more than a flat slab of rock. We used to take more care—put more effort into honoring the love we shared for a lost friend or family member.

I edge my way to the place where I first met Wade and take a seat. Charlotte's grave looks the same—aged and worn, but still beautiful in its etching.

"Well, Charlotte, we meet again," I say. "A lot has changed since the last time I was here."

A single red rose sits beside the tombstone, perhaps left by family or someone like me who admires the past. I study the markings and small ornate sculptures along the outer edge of her headstone. She must have been a prominent woman in the town to have such a beautifully crafted piece.

When I was last here, I had no idea I had powers. No idea I could resurrect the dead or see them. I just...felt called to be near them. That was all.

I suppose it's why I wanted to be a forensic scientist, too. Death is a part of me. It's engrained into who and what I am.

Death is my gift. Or is it life?

Perhaps it's a fine line to tread.

Even though I'm convinced I did the right thing with Cat, I have this innate urge to bury the gift of resurrection.

Because really, who should ever have the power to decide who lives and who dies? Who should have the right to play God and alter the fate of another?

What if I altered the future by saving her?

My gaze falls to the rose. It reminds me of the first time Wade was at Blackwood Manor and the vase of roses shattered to the floor. Wade and I had been on the verge of taking things to the next level that day.

Sighing to myself, I place my fingers on my lips. I don't know how to tell Wade about Colton's kiss, but I know it'll have to be done soon or he'll think I was keeping it from him. Which I suppose I have been. But not for my sake—*for his*.

My eyes flit to the headstone again and I read its inscription: *May the Angel of Death Lead Thee into Paradise.*

I truly hope on the other side is paradise. Knowing that would make it easier to let go. Picking up the rose, I spin it between my thumb and index finger. As I do so, a tiny red thread drops to the ground. Curious, I pick it up. It's no longer than two or three inches, but the center is frayed and looks like it could snap in two at a moment's notice.

I know the feeling.

I set the rose and string down, letting them rest beside the headstone.

"Good talk," I say, patting Charlotte's grave as I stand back up.

The sunlight is nearly gone, and only bright-red tendrils slip through tiny cracks between tree trunks. Making my way back to the columbarium, I continue to take in the names of people around me, wondering what their lives were like and how long it's been since anyone visited them.

As I make my way into the newer part of the cemetery, I'm pulled up short when I realize Wade isn't where I left him

—and he isn't alone. Yards away from the columbarium, he stands with his back to me. His arms are out wide, flailing about in the air, as if he's passionately describing something.

I edge closer, trying to see if I can get within earshot. As I do, I notice the man he's talking to isn't a stranger. He's the man who billowed out of the black smoke and collected the souls at the site of Cat and Colton's accident.

"What the—?" I say, narrowing my gaze and creeping closer. I stop a few meters back, shrouding myself behind a large oak tree.

"It is forbidden, Wade. You know the consequences if you —" the other man says.

Wade counters. "I don't care what you say. I'm not like you. It could be a full lifetime from now before I ever have to—"

"The duration of your human existence doesn't matter. The fact is, she breaks the laws balancing life and death. Her kind is in direct opposition to what it is we've been put here to do. You know this," the man says.

My eyes widen and I take a step back.

Are they talking about me?

"You don't know that. She can see the dead, that's true. But she might not be a necromancer," Wade retorts.

"Has she not told you of her friend, then?"

"I—what are you talking about?" Wade says, clearly flustered by the question.

I bite down on my lip and curse myself for not having been honest sooner.

"We are done here. Talk to her and see for yourself," the man says. "Then, end this charade. This forbidden relationship will only end badly. Should the Moirai catch wind..."

"They won't," Wade says, taking a step forward.

"You don't know that. If they do, hers will not be the only thread they cut loose." Before Wade can say anything in response, the man vanishes into his billow of black smoke.

CHAPTER 30

SINNER

Straightening my shoulders, I move around the large oak tree and make my way over to Wade as nonchalantly as possible. Before I jump to any conclusions, I'm going to need to hear what he has to say. Besides, I'm acutely aware he's not the only one who's been keeping secrets still.

"Hey, who was that?" I ask as I reach him.

Wade spins around, eyes wide. All the color has drained from his face and it takes him a moment to recover. "I, uh—that was no one. Just some guy who was looking for the caretaker."

I narrow my gaze and tilt my head. "Really? It sorta looked like you knew each other."

Wade clears his throat, walking back to the columbarium. "Er, yeah. I think I've seen him around town before."

Following behind him, my heart clenches at the lie. Maybe if I come clean, he'll feel open enough to do it, too.

"So, I have something to tell you..." I say.

Wade runs his hand along the backside of his neck and turns to look at me. "Okay, what is it?"

"The other day, when you called me about your grandpa... something happened." I search his eyes, hoping to see some glint of emotion, maybe guilt, for having just lied. But all that's reflected back at me is curiosity. I look down at my shoes and clear my throat. "I, uh—I think I've finally gotten a good grip on my powers."

Wade's eyes widen and he takes a step closer. "That's *fantastic*, Autumn. Why didn't you tell me sooner? This would have been good news..."

I shake my head. "Not exactly. I guess I can say I'd rather I didn't have to practice the way I did."

"What do you mean?" he says, narrowing his gaze and taking a seat on the granite bench. He pats the spot beside him and I sit down.

"Well, Colton and Cat were in an accident...something ran out in front of them. They swerved to miss and..." I turn to face the columbarium and my words drift off.

"And?" he presses.

I press my palms together and slide them between my knees. "Cat died."

"What?" Wade says, indignantly. "And you didn't tell me? This whole time you were here when—"

I wave a hand. "She's fine."

"Jesus Christ—say that part first, would you?" he says, clutching at his chest and walking away. I follow behind him, reaching for his arm and spinning him around.

"There's more to it, though," I whisper, biting on the side of my cheek. "I'm the one who brought her back."

Wade's inhale is sharp and I see the recognition in his eyes. Recognition he was hoping wasn't true. "Like, you gave her CPR?"

I press my lips tight and raise an eyebrow. "You know that's not what I meant."

Wade shakes his head. "But you...you can see the ghosts. Abigail—"

I shrug. "I know. For some reason, I can do both. I don't understand how it all works. I just know Cat's alive because of what I did."

Wade's hands fly to his head and he rakes his fingertips through his hair. "This is—*bad*. Really bad."

"Bad? I thought you were excited for me to figure out my powers," I say, trying to coax him along.

His eyes flit back to me and he nods. "You're right. It is. Totally. I just mean..." His eyebrows tug in and the lines across his jaw tighten. "How horrible for Cat. And you. That must have been terrifying."

I stare at him, shocked that when faced with the truth, he still isn't willing to open up fully to me.

My heart clenches and my gaze falls to the ground. Leaves billow past in colors of brown, gold, and red, and I can't help but wish things were as simple as their lifespans. Leaves bud, grow, and eventually wither and die. They fall to the ground without holding on to what once was. Instead, they just...let go.

Nodding, I finally say, "Yeah, it was pretty bad. I can't say I'm in any hurry to use that power again. You know?"

Taking a deep breath, I return my gaze to him. If he can keep secrets of his own, maybe I should keep a few of my own. Like Colton's kiss...

Wade steps forward, wrapping his arms around me. Melting into his embrace I close my eyes.

"If there's anything I can do, let me know," he whispers, stroking my hair.

"There's nothing to do. Cat will heal..." I say. "She is healing. In fact, everyone's surprised at how fast she's getting better."

Wade doesn't say anything at first and when I look up, his facial expression is contorted with worry.

"What is it? What's wrong?" I say.

Wade shakes his head and forces a smile. "It's nothing."

"Are you sure, because it kinda seems like something."

"I'm just—worried for you is all. Necromancy is a big deal. It's not a power that's easy to shoulder," he says.

"I don't have to do it alone. I have you," I say, watching his every movement.

Holding still at first, he finally nods. "You do," he whispers.

"Then that's all that matters. Come on, let's go for a drive. We've been trapped in this town for the past few days. I think we need some time away from all of this. Let's go back to Windhaven for the night. I'm sure the estate stuff can wait until another day," I say, dropping my arms so I can slide a hand into his.

"I like the sound of that," he says, trying to force his lips into a smile.

"Good, because you don't get a choice," I say, turning on my heel and leading the way back to Blue.

We both climb into our seats, but Wade stares at the columbarium in silence.

"Do you need more time?" I ask, my hand poised on the keys in the ignition.

He shakes his head. "No, I'm good. There's nothing left for me here."

My heart breaks a little for him, knowing that whatever is going on must be tearing him up inside. I just wish he'd let me in...

Slipping the car into drive, I pull out of the cemetery and out onto the road. I turn on some music and lower the windows to allow the scent of fall to wash away the lily fragrance still lingering in the cab of my vehicle.

We drive in silence, each of us wrapped up in our own thoughts and worries. If there's one thing I've learned in all of this, it's that we should hold tight to those we love...not push them further away. You never know when your time together could be cut short.

The farther north we drive, many of the trees still hold tight to their leaves. It's like a resurrection in and of itself. The bright reds, yellows, and oranges all mix together in a blazing array of life's final breath.

Rather than going straight to Blackwood Manor, I find myself driving the country roads in admiration of the changing season. There won't be much time left before the leaves are gone completely and snow will blanket the ground. Wade doesn't seem to mind as we drive the winding and twisty roads, hand in hand.

However, before long, I'm well out of my comfort zone for knowing how to get back home and the sun's light has completely faded from view. I pull over to the side of the road.

"Everything okay?" Wade asks, speaking for the first time in a while.

I nod. "Yeah, just got myself a little lost. I was too busy admiring the leaves. Just need to get a little digital direction."

Dropping Wade's hand, I pick up my phone, and press the Maps app, so I can follow the GPS home. How people ever found their way when all they had was a paper map, I'll never know.

Wade smiles and pats my leg.

Within seconds, the application pinpoints my location, and the fastest route home. Luckily, we're not too far out. Only another twenty minutes or so. As I shift into drive and look out over the road, I see a woman walking along the side. Partway on the road, partway on the shoulder, she moves with a strange sort of limp. Her outfit is odd—a mixture of old and new. She's in jeans, but her coat flows behind her like some sort of grayish hooded cloak.

Sweeping my gaze up and down the street, there doesn't appear to be any houses nearby.

"Where did she come from?" I say to Wade, as I tip my chin toward her.

"Who?" he says, looking around. When his gaze lands on her, he quirks an eyebrow. "She going to a renaissance festival or something?"

I shrug. "Your guess is a good as mine."

My eyebrows tug in and I drive forward slowly. As I come up next to her, there's something strange, an energy rolling off her in waves. It doesn't feel right at all.

"Can you feel that?" I whisper, shooting a look at Wade.

"The creep-me-out vibe?" he asks, returning my gaze.

I nod.

"Yup, getting that one loud and clear. Maybe we should just keep going."

"Do you think she's okay?"

"She seems like she knows where she's going. But I'm not sure we really want to stick around," Wade says, raising his eyebrows and shivering.

I shrug, realizing he's probably right. But I need to at least check on her. Rolling down the window, I call out, "Excuse me. Are you okay? Do you need a ride?"

Wade's wide eyes turn on me.

"What?" I say, sheepishly.

The woman continues to walk, not even giving me a glance over her shoulder.

"Hello?" I repeat.

I continue to troll along, following the woman for a moment, until she comes to an abrupt halt. Goose bumps flash up and down my forearms as I realize where we are. We're at the location of Cat and Colt's accident.

My headlights cast a warm glow on the pavement, but I know what the dark stain is that the woman is staring at. Cat's blood is still evident, but it has turned a darker color, no longer the vibrant red it was days ago. Small fragments of their SUV are still scattered about, but for the most part, whoever came out to clean up the mess did a good job.

I turn to Wade, unsure if I should tell him where we ended up.

The woman stands in the middle of it all, her head down, hood up, and feet in the exact location the SUV had landed.

Taking a deep breath, I put the vehicle in park and reach for the door handle.

Wade grabs hold of my right hand, pulling me back into my seat. "Do *not* go out there."

I take a deep breath. "It'll be fine. I need to know if she's okay. I don't know why, but this is something I have to do."

"Then I'm coming with you," Wade says, kicking open his door and exiting before I can. I open my door and follow after him.

"Excuse me, can you hear us?" he calls out. "Are you all right?"

The woman doesn't acknowledge him at all. Walking up to her, I reach out to turn her around, but my hand goes completely through her wrist and I nearly stumble over. Wade catches me and pulls me back.

As the woman turns around, a haunting remnant of Cat locks eyes with me. Where her dark brown eyes should be, there's nothing but a strange white haze.

Stumbling away, I cover my mouth to hold back the

scream of surprise. Cat should be at home and in bed. Not here—not where I found her. And not a *ghost*.

Instantly, the specter is in my face. Her wide, white gaze pleads with mine. "Sinner," she shrieks.

Then, she vanishes before our eyes.

To Be Continued in Book 2: Soul Legacy.

Start Reading Now!

DID YOU LIKE *SECRET LEGACY?*

If so, sing your praises, my friend. No, you don't have to put on a jester's hat or do a TikTok video (though, that would be cool).

All ya gotta do is leave a review.

Thanks for reading! <3

SOUL LEGACY: BOOK 2 SNEAK PEEK (CHAPTER 1)

LOOSE ENDS

After everything we've been through, why this?

"You can't be serious, Wade. Everything is almost done here at Mistwood Point and you'll be free to move to Windhaven. We have more than enough room at my dad's house. Why on earth would you want to get an apartment?" I say, combing my fingers through my hair.

Wade sets down the cardboard box, letting it teeter precariously on top of a small stack of others just like it. "I know you don't get it, and to be honest, it's hard to explain. I guess after everything that's gone on, I just don't think I'm comfortable with that. It's not you, not at all. This whole thing with my grandpa, going through all of his belongings and life history—it hit me harder than I expected, and I just need some space alone to think."

My heart skips a beat, practically plummeting into my stomach.

Alone.

Not a good sign.

Taking a deep breath, I pinch the bridge of my nose. This is also about the conversation with the man at the cemetery last fall. I know it is.

"Wade, is there anything you want to tell me? Anything that's been on your mind since...I don't know, your grandpa's funeral?" I ask, once again trying to open the door that will allow him to be honest with me.

His silver eyes widen, and he blinks back surprise. Holding very still for a moment, his gaze turns downward and his jaw clenches. "I—not really. I mean, I know I've been a bit off. It's just...losing everyone who's related to you, it kind of cuts a hole, you know? I need to make sure I'm in a good place for us."

I nod, trying to ignore the sinking feeling. "I get that."

There's a ring of truth to his words, but I can sense there's so much more in the undercurrents of his thoughts. Why won't he open up to me?

I narrow my gaze, watching his movements.

He fidgets with the lid of the box, refusing to look back up at me. "Besides, after taking care of everything here, the last thing I want to do is bring you down before the new semester starts. Getting some independence again will help me get grounded, literally."

"I understand wanting space and independence, and I'm trying to be supportive of whatever you need. It's just—there's plenty of space at the manor. Take a whole wing, if you want. I don't mind," I say, standing up and walking over to him. I place my hand on his upper arm, hoping he'll hold me close.

He twists around, wrapping his arms around me. "It's not that simple, Autumn. I wish I could explain it in a way that makes sense for you, but it doesn't even fully make sense to me. You'll have to just trust me. This is for the best."

"It doesn't feel like it..." I whisper, blinking back tears.

"Hey, don't be sad. This isn't goodbye. Not at all. I'm moving closer, remember?" he says, tipping my chin up to look at him.

I nod. "I know."

His lips curve upward as he traces my eyebrow with his pointer finger. "This will work out really well, you'll see."

He places his chin on the top of my head and we stand in the middle of his grandpa's living room, both of us refusing to make a move. There are so many unanswered questions and feelings of upheaval.

I know I'm going to have to ask him outright about what I saw at the graveyard, but I need to build up the courage first. It's been weeks, and neither one of us have brought it up. I had hoped by now he would have opened up to me on his own time. Instead, I've had to go into research mode, trying to figure out who the man was. Of course, with absolutely no luck whatsoever.

"Wade, I need to ask you something..." I begin.

His gaze lifts to mine, but the moment is broken by a knock on the door. He holds up a finger. "Hold that thought, okay?"

I exhale, letting my shoulders relax.

Wade shoots me an apologetic look and walks to the front door.

"Can I help you?" he asks, standing in the doorway with one hand resting on the frame.

I crane my head, trying to get a better view. A short man with a dark comb-over and navy-blue suit stands in the doorway. It's not the man from the graveyard, but his appearance screams "official business."

"Mr. Hoffman, good. I was hoping you'd be here. I've been trying to get in touch, but you're a difficult man to get ahold of," the man says, pulling his briefcase forward and clutching it to his chest. "We have a date for the official reading of the will."

Wade nods, sweeping his right arm out to allow the man inside.

The man tips his head and steps into the entry, then walks to the living room. When he sees me, he smiles and says, "Ma'am."

"Please, it's Autumn," I say, holding my hand out.

He takes my hand, giving it a good shake. "David Moore. Mr. Hoffman's estate attorney."

"Nice to meet you," I say, shooting him a genuine smile.

Wade steps around Mr. Moore and cleans off the small coffee table in the middle of the room.

Taking the hint, the lawyer drops his briefcase and clicks it open. Inside is a large manilla envelope, which he pulls out, and then snaps the case shut.

"Here are the details. The closing for the house is set for the first Friday of January, and we will go over the reading of the will two weeks from then. All of the location details are in the envelope, as well as the information we've received from your grandfather and you. I'd like for you to review it to make sure there's nothing we're missing," he says, handing Wade the packet.

Wade clears his throat, swallowing hard. He takes the envelope and drops his arm to his side without even looking at it.

"Okay," he mumbles.

Mr. Moore's lips press tightly, and he attempts a smile. "I truly am sorry for your loss, Wade. Your grandfather was a good man. I thoroughly enjoyed our talks through the years. He was very fond of you."

"Yeah," Wade says, biting on the inside of his cheek.

The awkward silence fills the space between them, and I step forward. "Is there anything else he needs to take care of? Or is that all?"

Mr. Moore takes a step back and shakes his head. "No, that's all for today. I just needed to make sure in person that Mr. Hoffman was aware of these final details. Thank you both for allowing me to take the time. Have a nice night." He pats Wade on the shoulder and turns back the way they came in. Wade doesn't move a muscle. Instead, his forehead is scrunched in thought.

"Here, I'll show you out," I say, stepping around them both and leading the way.

I open the door and smile as Mr. Moore steps out onto the front steps. He nods but continues on his way. When he's gotten into his black Lexus, I close the door and turn back to Wade.

"Everything okay?" I say, entering the living room. Wade hasn't moved from where I left him.

He flings the packet onto the coffee table and nods.

"You knew this was coming, right? I mean, isn't this what you wanted?" I ask. "To finally have it all come to a close?"

"Yeah, it is. It's just...strange, you know?" he says, trying to smooth out the pained expression that's taken over his features.

I nod. "I can imagine. But this is good. It means the end is near and you'll be able to move on with your own journey. You've done a lot these past few weeks. I've been impressed by how you've known exactly what to do. I mean, if it were me, I'd still be fumbling."

"I had to learn quickly, I guess. Grandpa was pretty specific on what he wanted. It made it easier," he says.

"So...what's on your mind, then?" I say, walking around so I can be in his direct line of sight.

His pupils dilate and he attempts a smile. "I'm just a little worried to find out how it all is going to look, you know?"

"Why?"

"Grandpa had a lot of additional help these past few months and any inheritance I get is supposed to cover my tuition at Windhaven Academy. But I know end-of-life help doesn't come cheap and the county will want to recoup the cost. So..."

"You're worried you won't be able to swing it?" I say, finishing his thought.

He nods, screwing up his lips.

"That, I totally get. There's no way I would have been able to pay for Windhaven Academy, either. But surely with the sale of the house and everything, the funds will cover most of it, right?"

Wade shrugs. "Maybe? I mean, I sure hope so. If not, I have no idea what I'm gonna do."

Walking over to him, I wrap my arms around his waist. "If it comes to that, we'll figure it out."

He chuckles softly. "You don't owe me anything, Dru. You need to worry about you. This semester is going to be amazing for you. Especially now that you know more about your powers."

My lips curve upward at his pet name for me. Maybe he's coming back around?

"It's not about owing anything. It's about taking care of each other. That's what we do, right?" I say, giving him a squeeze. "Besides, it's going to be incredible having you at the academy. I'll be able to show you all of the cool places and I'm excited to see what kind of abilities you might possess. It's almost like our roles have reversed."

Wade places his hands on my upper arms, pulling back from me. "I wouldn't get your hopes up. There's a good chance my gifts won't manifest at all."

I snicker. "What are you talking about?"

Shaking his head, he takes a step back. "Sometimes they skip generations."

"Well, wouldn't you want to know for sure before going to Windhaven Academy? I mean, why work on developing powers you don't know if you even have?"

"You tell me? What was the allure?" he says, raising his eyebrows.

I take a step back and nod. "Point taken."

"Look, my family's gifts often lie dormant until triggered. I don't know when, or if, they will come. But what I do know is that I need to learn more about how to manage them if they're triggered. I can't do that anywhere else. It's not like I have any family members left to ask," he says, frowning.

"Good point," I whisper, considering his words. "Wade... this might not be the best time to ask, but I need to know something. It's been on my mind for a while."

He runs a hand through his hair and takes a seat on the arm of the sofa. "What is it?"

I swallow hard, wringing my hands in front of my body as I search for the right words. "Look, I probably should have brought this up sooner, it's just..."

"Spit it out, woman. The suspense is killing me," he says, concern painting his tone.

"The day we buried your grandpa, I saw you talking with someone," I say, beginning to pace.

"Right, the guy looking for the caretaker?" Wade says, nodding.

I stop pacing and turn to him. Pinching my face tight, I say, "Mmmm... It kinda seemed like you two knew each other."

His eyes narrow and he tilts his head. "Autumn, I don't know what to tell you."

I double-take, stumbling backward. "I swear I heard him arguing with you."

Wade stands up, his eyebrows tugging in, but he doesn't respond.

"I've seen him before," I say. "He spoke to me when I was at Cat's accident."

"How do you know it was the same guy? I mean, there are lots of—"

"He billowed in from some sort of portal and...took the souls from the Vodník's jar. He's not just a person, he's something else, but I don't know what. When he left after the conversation with you, he vanished the same way. I know it was the same guy," I say, jutting out my chin.

"Okay? People get around, especially travelers, if that's what he was. So, what did he say to you?" Wade asks, his face still stoic.

"He told me he'd be back. And that I can only meddle for so long..."

For the first time, his face flickers. "Well, that seems ominous. Did he tell you why? Or who he was?"

"No, but he knew I was a necromancer before I did. I mean, before I ever used my powers to save Cat," I say. I watch his mannerisms closely, but Wade remains an unreadable statue. My shoulders drop and my eyebrows tug in.

Why is he lying to me? What on earth is he hiding?

Continue reading ***Soul Legacy: Book 2***!

A NOTE FROM THE AUTHOR

Thanks so much for reading ***Secret Legacy***, Book 1 in the *Windhaven Witches* series.

This series continues with *Soul Legacy - available now!*

Join my Patreon to read my books as they're being written, get exclusive merch, and get more news and book-related nerdery from me.

Thanks for being here!
xo Carissa

ALSO BY CARISSA ANDREWS

Accidental Alpha

Midlife Wolf Bite

Midlife Wolf Pack

Midlife Wolf Mate

Midlife Wolf Bond

Midlife Wolf Reign

The Diana Hawthorne Series

The Final Five (prequel)

Oracle

Amends

Immortals

Ruins

The Pendomus Chronicles

Trajectory (prequel)

Pendomus

Polarities

Revolutions

Stand Alone Titles

Awakening

Merciless

ABOUT THE AUTHOR

Carissa Andrews

Sci-fi/Fantasy is my pen of choice.

Carissa Andrews is an award-winning and international best-selling indie author from central Minnesota. Her books range from paranormal and urban fantasy to science fiction dystopia. Her plans for right now include the continuation of her acclaimed *Diana Hawthorne Supernatural Mysteries* and a new series called *Accidental Alpha*. As a publishing powerhouse, she keeps sane by chilling with her husband, five kids, and their adorable husky, Aztec.

For a free ebook and to find out what Carissa's up to, head over to her website and sign up for her newsletter:

www.carissaandrews.com

patreon.com/carissaandrews

amazon.com/author/carissaandrews

bookbub.com/authors/carissa-andrews

goodreads.com/Carissa_Andrews

Made in the USA
Monee, IL
12 October 2023

44443800R00180